CHAPTER ONE

"She's got the same illustrations on her stomach."

DS Rupert Bridge was careful not to get too close. The forensics officers had made more allowances than they usually did, but Bridge knew better than to push his luck too far.

"We don't know what they mean though, do we?" DC Harry Moore said.

"Unfortunately, not. We'd better get out of here before Webber loses patience with us."

They went outside into the street. It was late November and even though it had only just gone six, the sun had said its goodbyes for the day a couple of hours ago.

"Do you think Smith is going to come back?" DC Moore said.

"God knows," Bridge said. "The *Preacher* thing really knocked him for a six."

"Have you spoken to him recently?"

"Last thing I heard was he was trying to put a band together, and it wasn't going too well. He's not the easiest bloke to work with and I can't imagine what it must be like to be in a band with him."

"The DI is here," DC Moore nodded in his direction.

DI Smyth wasn't alone. DS Whitton was walking alongside him.

"What do we have?" he asked.

"Webber, Billie and Pete are still inside," Bridge said. "But it looks like a carbon copy of the other one. No obvious injuries apart from the bruises on her neck."

"She was strangled?" Whitton said.

"It looks like it. And she has the same drawings on her stomach."

"What do we know about her?" DI Smyth said.

"Her name is Sharon Atlee," DC Moore said. "And that's about all we know. Her housemate came home from the pub and found her in her room."

"Any sign of a struggle in there?" DI Smyth said.

"We were only allowed in for a quick peek, sir," DC Moore said. "Webber should have more for us when he's finished."

"Where's the housemate now?" Whitton said.

"Next door," Bridge said.

"We'll speak to her in due course," DI Smyth said. "I don't suppose any of these places have CCTV?"

"Most of the houses on the street are student digs," Bridge said. "And I didn't see any cameras on any of them."

"OK," DI Smyth said. "We won't know much until Forensics have finished. In the meantime, I want an extensive door-to-door carried out. It's dark now but someone might have seen something earlier."

"I'll get some uniforms onto it," DC Moore said.

"Do you think this is the start of something?" Bridge said.

"I sincerely hope not," DI Smyth said.

"The drawings on their stomachs suggest it's the same killer," Whitton said.

"We don't know what they mean yet," DI Smyth said. "And we're rather short-handed at the moment, what with Smith's extended leave of absence. Is there any news on that front?"

"You know Smith, sir," Whitton said. "He doesn't do anything he doesn't want to do."

"Well, I hope he gets whatever he needs to get out of his system soon."

"I'm sure he will. The rock 'n roll lifestyle isn't going as well as he thought. He's already auditioned for half a dozen bands and all of them have shown him the door after a few rehearsals. He'll be back."

"I sincerely hope so," DI Smyth said. "And the sooner the better."

Billie Jones emerged from the house and Bridge's eyes lit up.

"That is the woman I'm going to grow old with."

"God help the poor girl," DI Smyth said.

Billie walked over to them.

"It's the same killer as the one in Heworth."

"How sure are you?" DI Smyth said.

"Positive," Billie said. "There are far too many similarities, and unless we have a copycat on our hands, it's definitely the same perpetrator."

"It's too soon for a copycat to crop up," Whitton said. "Rebecca Stone was only killed two days ago."

"The marks on her stomach are still puzzling," Billie said. "They're exactly the same as the ones we found on Rebecca."

"The spike and the two flying saucer things," Bridge said.

"Enclosed by a circle," Billie said. "Drawn by what looks like a red marker pen."

"Did anything else in there give you any idea about a possible motive?" DI Smyth said.

"She had a load of legal textbooks on the desk in her room," Billie said. "It looks like she was studying law. Rebecca was a law student too."

"We'll be able to get that confirmed when we speak to the housemate," DI Smyth said.

"That's about all I can tell you right now. I'd better get back in."

Bridge watched her go. "God, I never get tired of that arse."

"You really need to stop saying things like that," Whitton said. "It's really not right in this day and age."

"Nonsense," Bridge said. "The world has gone soft when a bloke can't say exactly what's on his mind anymore, especially when his girlfriend has a seriously exceptional backside."

"Webber and the team are still going to be some time inside the house," DI Smyth said. "In the meantime, Whitton you and Bridge can go and see what the housemate can tell you."

The screech of a vehicle's brakes caused them all to look in the direction of the din. Two headlights on brights blinded them for a moment and then they were switched off. The car had come to a halt so close to the outer cordon that the front end was touching the police tape.

"Someone's in a hurry," Bridge stated the obvious.

The door of the car opened, and a man got out. He looked left and right, and his eyes found the group of detectives further up the street. He ducked below the tape and made his way towards them, ignoring the protests of the uniformed officer behind the cordon.

"Who is in charge here?" he asked nobody in particular.

"I'm going to have to ask you to step back behind the tape, sir," DI Smyth said. "This is a crime scene."

He explained who he was.

"I'm well aware that it's a fucking crime scene," the man said. "The victim is my fucking girlfriend."

"I'm very sorry, sir," DI Smyth said. "But you really need to stay back."

"I have no intention of doing that. In fact, I'm going to stay right here until you can assure me that the person who did that to Sharon is banged up where he belongs."

"We will find out who did this," DI Smyth said.

"You're not listening to me, are you?"

"I'm going to ask you once more. Either you stand back, or I'll have to arrest you."

"Arrest me? That's the fucking joke of the century. You should be arresting the bastard who killed Sharon. I know exactly who did this to her, and I want him banged up where he belongs."

CHAPTER TWO

Smith placed the guitar back on its stand and looked at it like it was a sworn enemy.

"You and me used to be friends."

He turned his back on the Fender Stratocaster and went through to the kitchen to get a beer. He needed something stronger after the disaster that was the latest band rehearsal, but beer was all he had in the house, and he couldn't be bothered to go out to get a bottle of Jack Daniels'.

He was starting to wonder if his dream of playing the guitar in a band was destined to remain just that – a dream that wasn't supposed to come true. He got a beer out of the fridge and opened the back door. He was surprised when the dogs made it outside before him. Theakston and Fred were clearly desperate to get out. Smith lit a cigarette and watched them. He smiled when he saw Theakston race to the end of the garden with Fred in tow. There was still life in the aged Bull Terrier yet, and the gruesome Pug couldn't keep up.

Smith took a swig of beer and gazed skyward. The stars were visible tonight for the first time in days but that meant the temperatures had plummeted to close to freezing. Smith didn't feel the cold like he used to, and he much preferred the clear sky to the drizzle that seemed to linger for weeks on end at this time of year in York.

His thoughts turned to the phone call Whitton had received shortly before she headed out into the unknown. Once upon a time, it would have been Smith who would answer the phone to get the news that something terrible had happened and once upon a time it was his entire life. He would relish the thought of the start of a new investigation, and it would consume him to the point of obsession. Then everything changed. He didn't know the exact point at which something shifted inside him – it wasn't one of those wake up in the morning to find everything is different moments, it was a number of things that built up until the decision he eventually made was the only logical one to make.

It had concerned him at first. In the first week the self-inflicted limbo he'd landed himself in was uncomfortable and he wondered if he'd made a terrible mistake, but halfway through the second week he started to settle into something that resembled normality. He found he began to enjoy the school runs and the trips to the shops and he started to find peace in the mundane things that normal people did.

The only thorn in this newfound bed of roses was the band practices. It soon became abundantly clear that he wasn't cut out to be in a band. He was just not a team player, and he reckoned that was probably something of a hindrance in a band environment.

Smith was debating whether to smoke another cigarette when the sound of his phone ringing in the kitchen caught his attention. It was a ringtone he'd assigned to someone at work, but he didn't think the person who was calling him wanted to discuss anything work related. He went back inside and closed the back door. The dogs would survive another fifteen minutes in the garden.

The sound of *The Boys are Back in Town* made Smith smile. The *Thin Lizzy* classic had always been one of his favourites. He answered the call before the voicemail kicked in.

"Evening, boss," he said. "Are you missing me?"

"Not likely," DCI Chalmers said. "I'm not interrupting anything, am I?"

"Nothing at all," Smith said.

"I was worried I might have caught you in the middle of doing the laundry. Or perhaps you've taken up knitting."

"Is there something you want?" Smith said.

"Just a friendly chat."

"The answer is no," Smith said.

"I wasn't aware that I'd asked you anything."

"I'm not interested," Smith said.

"I have no idea what you're talking about."

"Cut the crap. I know you too well. The day I come back to work is the day I slow dance with the Super, so you can stop wasting your time."

"Superintendent Smyth happens to be a very good dancer," Chalmers said.

"Will there be anything else?" Smith said.

The line went quiet for a while and Smith wondered if Chalmers had hung up.

"Are you still there?"

"Still here," Chalmers said. "Mrs Chalmers was trying to get me to ask if you'll still be going to the Christmas do next Saturday."

"What?"

"The Christmas party," Chalmers said. "It's being held at the Grand on Tower Street this year, and it's promising to be a big deal. Mrs Chalmers is doing the decorations."

"Christmas is nearly a month away," Smith pointed out.

"Apparently next Saturday is the only date they had left. You'll be there, won't you?"

"I have no idea. I didn't even know about it."

"Well now you do."

"As much as I've enjoyed this little chat," Smith said. "I have stuff to do."

"I won't keep you much longer then," Chalmers said. "I'll get to the real reason I phoned."

"You didn't call me to remind me about the Christmas thing?"

"You need to make up your mind, Smith."

"I thought I'd made that very clear."

"No," Chalmers said. "You've done no such thing. You're still officially in the employ of York Police, and if you're adamant that you're done with it all there are technicalities you need to consider."

"I'm using the leave that I've accrued," Smith said.

"I'm aware of that, and I'm also aware that you have precisely three days of that leave remaining. After that, you need to make a hard decision."

"I've made my decision."

"You haven't thought about it properly."

"Believe me," Smith said. "I've thought about pretty much nothing else."

"You're a bloody idiot."

"So you keep telling me," Smith said. "I appreciate the concern, but you don't need to worry about me. I've never been happier."

They ended the call, and Smith let the dogs back in. As he watched them make a beeline for the warmth of the living room he was hit with a flashback. The memory came from a place he couldn't understand but it was crystal clear, nevertheless. He was right where he stood now, and he was looking at the backsides of his four-legged friends as they sought out the comfort of a soft, warm sofa to pass out on. Smith had the sudden urge to pick up his phone and call Whitton to find out more about the murder in Badger Hill.

CHAPTER THREE

"How are you feeling?" Whitton said.

She and Bridge were sitting on the two-seater in the living room of the house next door to the one Natalie Grant shared with Sharon Atlee. Natalie was a tall woman with short black hair. Her eyes were the colour of slate and Whitton had found herself staring at them for longer than she should when she first saw them. She'd never seen eyes like them before. There was a man inside the room. He'd introduced himself as Carl Nunn and it was his house. Whitton had decided to let him stay – it was possible he might be able to help them with something too.

"It's not the first time," Natalie said.

"The first time for what?" Bridge asked.

"I found a dead body before. An old man. He wasn't murdered – he'd had a heart attack. That was a few years ago."

"Can you think of anyone who might have wanted to hurt Sharon?" Whitton said.

"Of course not. She was a popular student."

"What was she studying?" Bridge said. "There were law textbooks in her room. Was she doing a law degree?"

Natalie nodded. "She was in her third year. She was strangled, wasn't she?"

"We don't know that yet," Whitton said. "When was the last time you saw her?"

"This morning," Natalie said. "Just after eight. Sharon left before me – I didn't have a class until ten."

"And you found her just before you called the police?" Whitton said. "Is that correct?"

Another nod. "I went for a few drinks with some friends after class."

"We're going to need their details," Bridge said.

"What for?"

"It's just routine." It was Carl Nunn.

Bridge made eye contact with him. Carl held it.

"You need to look into the people who knew Sharon would be alone in the house," Carl said. "Am I right?"

Bridge didn't humour him with a reply.

"It's early days," Whitton said. "And it's important at this stage in a murder investigation that we gather as much information as possible. The majority of that information will be disregarded, but we need to do it anyway. Do you know her boyfriend well?"

"I don't think she has a boyfriend," Natalie said.

"You shared a house with her," Bridge said. "Wouldn't you know if she was seeing someone?"

"She wasn't."

"A minute ago, you said you didn't think so," Bridge said.

"And a man claiming to be her boyfriend arrived just now," Whitton said. "Do you know him or not?"

"Easy now," Carl butted in. "Natalie isn't a suspect here. She's just come home to find her housemate murdered. Could you give her a break?"

"Could you give us a rundown of *your* movements this afternoon?" Bridge said to Carl.

"What?"

"Like I said," Whitton said. "We like to get as many details as possible this early on. You live in the house next door, so it's routine that we'll need to ask you questions like this."

"I got home at around three this afternoon," Carl said.

"Were you alone in the house after that?" Bridge said.

"That's right. The other people I share with have already gone home for the Christmas break."

"Isn't it a bit early for that?" Bridge said.

"They're both doing Humanities. The term ended last week for them."

"It's alright for some," Whitton said. "So, you're alone in the house at the moment?"

"I'm staying in the city. I've got a job at a pub on the Hull Road."

"When will I be able to go back next door?" Natalie asked.

"I can't give you an answer to that?" Whitton said. "Our forensics team are very thorough."

"Is she still there?" Carl said. "Sharon, I mean, has her body been taken away?"

"What are you studying?" Bridge asked to change the subject.

"Psychology," Carl said. "Perhaps I'll join the police after I graduate."

"I wouldn't advise it."

"What did you do when you got home?" Whitton asked Carl.

"I crashed on the couch for a bit," he said. "Checked out some social media and stuff like that. I can show you my activity logs if you don't believe me."

"That won't be necessary," Bridge said. "Was everything quiet next door? Did you see or hear anyone coming or going?"

"I put some music on, and I like to play it loud when I'm alone in the house."

"So, you didn't hear any unusual noises coming from next door?" Whitton said.

"I didn't," Carl said. "How was she killed?"

"She was strangled," Natalie said.

"We don't know that yet," Whitton said for the second time.

"She was," Natalie said. "She had marks on her neck."

"It was probably not premeditated then," Carl said, out of the blue.

"Could you leave the detective work to the people who get paid for that sort of thing?" Bridge said.

"Just thinking out loud. From a historical perspective, strangulation is, statistically speaking not a method favoured by killers who set out to kill. There are exceptions of course, but not many. This looks to me more like an argument that spiralled out of control."

"I think we can wrap things up there," Whitton said.

Carl wasn't quite finished yet. "This was someone she knew. You probably won't find any evidence of forced entry, and there won't be any sign of a struggle inside. Someone saw red and killed her with their bare hands."

"That's all for now," Whitton said. "We may need to speak to you again."

"I could be wrong of course." Natalie had something else to say too. "And I don't know the details of the student who was killed on Sunday, but I think Carl is mistaken if he thinks Sharon's death was a spur of the moment thing. The girl who was murdered in Heworth was also strangled, wasn't she?"

"We can't discuss that," Bridge said.

"It was all over the media," Natalie said. "It also mentioned something about her being a student here in the city. She was studying law too."

CHAPTER FOUR

It was gone nine by the time Whitton got home. The music coming from inside the house told her that Smith was still up. It was some kind of weird Blues music, and it was rather loud. Whitton wondered if her husband was regressing. Was he slowly turning into a teenager again? Ever since he'd announced that he was quitting the police he'd changed drastically. He was spending his days playing the guitar and listening to music, in between the school runs and the shopping trips, and Whitton was starting to get concerned about his state of mind. When she came home from work, he showed no interest in the events of her day and that was troubling. She was worried that he might be on the verge of some kind of breakdown.

Whitton let herself in, hung up her coat and made her way to the kitchen. Smith was standing at the sink, finishing off the dishes. He turned around when he heard her come in.

"Tell me all about it."

"Excuse me?" Whitton said.

Smith dried his hands, walked over to the fridge, and took out two beers. He turned off the music and handed one to Whitton.

"Thanks," she said and took a long drink. "I needed that. Are you OK?"

"I think I am," Smith said. "What was it like?"

"I thought you weren't interested."

"I may not be a detective anymore," Smith said. "But that doesn't mean my brain has been lobotomised. I might be able to help."

Whitton sat down at the table. Smith stood behind her and massaged her shoulders.

"Down a bit," Whitton said.

Smith did as she'd asked.

"The victim was a Sharon Atlee," Whitton said. "Twenty-one. Third-year law student."

"Same as the first one," Smith said.

"I didn't think you were paying attention when I told you about that."

"It's a gift of mine. It looks like I'm not listening, but I am. What else? Was she strangled too?"

"She was," Whitton confirmed. "And she had identical marks on her stomach as Rebecca Stone."

"Any idea what they could mean?"

"We're still baffled by them. It looks like a spike next to two UFOs beaming down light. We have no idea why someone would draw that on the victims."

"What else do you know?" Smith said.

"While we were busy at the scene," Whitton said. "A car pulled up and a very angry bloke got out. Turns out he's the victim's boyfriend and he insisted that he knows who killed her."

"And?"

"I think he was in shock. The name he gave us was Sharon's law professor."

"Has he been checked out, the law professor, I mean?"

"It's on the agenda for tomorrow."

"Why?" Smith said. "If the boyfriend gave you a name, why hasn't he been picked up and interviewed?"

"The DI didn't think it was urgent."

"Well, the DI is wrong. What about the boyfriend?"

"We'll be speaking to him too tomorrow. He was in a bit of a state, and we weren't going to get much out of him tonight."

"What is wrong with the DI?" Smith said. "Both of them should have been hauled in and interrogated tonight."

"Why are you so interested all of a sudden?" Whitton asked.

"Just curious. The band practice today didn't go too well."

Whitton sighed. "There's always tomorrow."

"I don't think I'm going to go to any more auditions. They all want the same thing – some kind of robot, and that's not how I play. Who gives a shit if a song is supposed to be played in E flat major – I reckon giving it a minor twist sometimes makes it more real. And whenever I try to play my own stuff, I'm always cut down before I've even reached the chorus."

"Your songs are a bit out there," Whitton said.

"What's wrong with *out there*? Do you think Pink Floyd were turned down because their stuff was different? No, they weren't."

"Are there any more of these on offer?" Whitton held up the empty beer bottle.

"Coming up," Smith said.

He got two more beers and sat back down.

"Did you leave the girls next door?" Whitton said.

"By the time I got back from band practice they were passed out in front of the TV in Lucy and Darren's house. I thought it was best to leave them."

"Are you doing the school run tomorrow?"

"Darren said he'd do it," Smith said. "It's not like he's got anything else to do."

"I could say the same thing about you," Whitton dared.

"That's not fair. I'm officially on leave."

"Officially," Whitton repeated. "But it seems that you're intent on making that a permanent thing."

"Chalmers phoned me earlier," Smith said.

"What did he want?"

"What do you think? He started off with some bull about a Christmas party. Did you know about that?"

"Of course I did. So did you. We were told about it weeks ago."

"It must have slipped my mind," Smith said. "He started off chatting about the Christmas thing, and then he got to the point. Tried to persuade me to come back to work. He called me a bloody idiot again."

"Hmm."

"I've made up my mind."

"So you keep saying," Whitton said.

"I mean it. It's going to take some adjusting, but I'll figure something out."

"You're not pursuing the rock 'n roll dream anymore then?"

"I don't think that's the life for me."

Whitton stretched her arms and finished her beer. "I'm beat. I'd heading up to bed."

"Me too," Smith said. "What was the name of the law professor?"

"The what?"

"You said the boyfriend of the latest victim was convinced he knew who'd killed his girlfriend," Smith said. "Who does he think it is?"

"Some law professor at the university," Whitton said. "Professor Wild or something."

Smith stared at her with wide eyes.

"What?"

"Herman Wild?" Smith said.

"Do you know him?"

"Know him?" Smith said. "Herman Wild was the reason I did so well when I was doing the law degree. Professor Wild was a guru – the man was a legend."

"He was the one the boyfriend mentioned."

"The boyfriend is talking absolute shite," Smith said. "Utter crap."

CHAPTER FIVE

"Herman Wild was acquainted with both victims," DI Smyth began the morning briefing.

He wrote the law professor's name on the whiteboard in the small conference room.

"According to the faculty of law at the university, he was well acquainted with Rebecca Stone and Sharon Atlee."

"Smith thinks the boyfriend is mistaken," Whitton said.

"Smith no longer has an opinion on the matter," DI Smyth said. "He's made that abundantly clear."

"Professor Wild was a member of the faculty back when Smith did his law degree," Whitton added. "He had a lot of time for the man, and he's convinced that the boyfriend has made a mistake."

"I'll bear that in mind," DI Smyth said. "Sharon Atlee's boyfriend was adamant that he was the one responsible, and we have no choice but to follow it up."

"He should be at work today," Bridge said. "The term is drawing to a close but if I remember correctly from my time at uni, the workload for the law students was much more hectic than most of the others."

"What did you study at university, Sarge?" DC Moore asked.

"That's not important," DI Smyth said.

"Political Science," Bridge replied anyway.

"We'll be speaking to Professor Wild during the course of the day," DI Smyth said. "But before we do I want to go over the forensic findings. Sharon Atlee died as a result of strangulation. The bruises on her neck suggest she was asphyxiated. We're still waiting for confirmation, but it appears that she was strangled with a thick rope. The rope was not retrieved from the scene."

"There didn't appear to be any sign of forced entry to the property," Bridge said.

"There was not," DI Smyth confirmed. "No broken windows or damaged locks. Also, there was no evidence that any sort of struggle took place."

"Surely she would have put up a fight," DC King said.

"It appears not, Kerry."

"Do we know if she was drugged with something?" DC King said.

"It's one of the first things Dr Bean will test for," DI Smyth said.

"She knew her killer," Whitton said.

"Early indications suggest that she did," DI Smyth said. "This was not a case of a killer breaking in and taking his victim off guard. The evidence points to a murderer gaining access by simply knocking on the door. Miss Atlee lets him in, they go to her room, and he kills her."

"Do you think they could have been more than friends?" DC Moore put forward. "She was found in her bedroom, wasn't she?"

"It's possible, Harry," DI Smyth said. "And we'll be exploring that avenue."

"Sharon's housemate was convinced that she wasn't in a relationship," Whitton said. "She didn't even know about the boyfriend."

"That doesn't rule it out. We will be examining every aspect of Miss Atlee's life in detail."

"Are we working on the assumption that Sharon's murder is connected to Rebecca Stone's?" Bridge said.

"We can't ignore the similarities between the two," DI Smyth said. "Both women were law students – both of them were strangled and they both had the peculiar drawings on their stomachs. And we'll move on to that now. Harry."

DC Moore tapped the keypad of the laptop, and a photograph of the strange drawing appeared on the large screen at the back of the room.

"Any thoughts?" DI Smyth said.

"A spike and a couple of unidentified flying objects," Bridge said.

That's exactly what it looked like. In the centre was a thin shape that tapered upwards to form a point at the top. On either side of it were two identical objects that, on first glance resembled the classic idea of what a UFO should look like. And protruding from each of them were similar triangles that appeared to be beams of light shining directly at the ground. The earth was depicted as a single straight horizontal line.

"What if we run it through a Google search?" DC Moore suggested. "See if anything comes up."

"It's worth a try," DI Smyth agreed.

DC Moore did it straight away, but the results were inconclusive. There were a few suggestions that it could represent some kind of alien invasion, but none of the detectives on the team thought that was what the drawing on the dead women represented.

"I suggest we shift the bizarre illustration to the back burner for the time being," DI Smyth said. "This one is rather concerning. We have two women, both of whom were killed in the same manner. Both women were studying law, and they had identical drawings on their stomachs. Rebecca Stone was murdered three days ago and we're no further ahead than we were on Sunday."

"Where's the motive here?" Bridge said. "I thought that, in Smith's absence, someone needed to bring it up."

"Where indeed?" DI Smyth said. "By all accounts neither Rebecca nor Sharon had any enemies. Why did someone want them dead?"

The silence in the room lasted for a while, and it was only broken by the sound of the message tone on Bridge's phone. He didn't check to see who had sent it.

"I'd say we can conclude there," DI Smyth said. "Bridge, you and Harry can go and speak to Sharon Atlee's boyfriend. It's possible that his little outburst last night came from the shock of finding out that his girlfriend was dead. Find out why he was so convinced of the professor's guilt. Whitton, I want you and Kerry to pay Professor Wild a visit. No doubt you'll find him on campus. Do not mention Smith's name."

"I agree," Whitton said. "It was almost twenty years ago, but it's possible he remembers Smith – he was one of his star students."

"You're kidding me," DC Moore said.

"Top five percent," Whitton elaborated.

"And he quit? Just like that?"

"It seems to be a recurring theme in my husband's life," Whitton sighed.

"Off you go then," DI Smyth said. "I want some answers before the end of the day."

CHAPTER SIX

"As promised, now that another term draws to a close, we'll fill the time with something slightly more light-hearted."

Whitton and DC King had been informed that Professor Wild was due to give a lecture in the main hall, and they'd also been told that they were more than welcome to attend. Whitton wasn't sure what to expect – if Herman Wild was a professor when Smith did his law degree, he had to be at least in his mid to late fifties now but the imposing figure addressing a full lecture hall didn't look any older than the DI and he was only forty-six. Professor Wild had a full head of thick, brown hair and he paced up and down with the energy of a man half his age.

Whitton was surprised to see so many people in the lecture hall. She'd expected at least some of them to stay home after the shocking murders of two of their fellow students.

"Most of you have already fulfilled the requirements necessary to pass this term," Professor Wild said. "Jackie Grant, I'm sure you'll get there in the end. Right, let's get started. I asked you to research historical evidence that proves that in essence the law is, indeed, an ass. I'll begin with an old favourite of my own and then I'll hand the floor over to you. This one has always tickled me for its absolute insanity. Were you aware that it is against the law to linger after a funeral?"

A few sniggers could be heard.

"Not only is it illegal to hang around after the final rites have been read, it is a law that was actually enforced as recently as 2015. A grieving husband was fined the sum of one hundred and sixty pounds for staying by his wife's graveside for twenty minutes after the funeral had ended. Can anyone top that?"

A woman in the front row stood up.

"Ah, Jackie," Professor Wild said. "I expected nothing less. Go on."

"According to Section 33 of the Public Health Act, 1985," Jackie said. "It is illegal to travel on public transport if you suspect that you might be infected with the Plague."

This earned even more laughter from the students.

"Even though the Plague was eradicated long before the Act came into being," Jackie added.

Professor Wild nodded. "That is a good one."

"Being annoying is perfectly legal," a man in the back row shouted out. "Unless you happen to be in a library. According to the Library Offences Act, 1998 and 2005, being an irritation in a public library can land you a fine."

"In Alabama it's illegal to wear a fake moustache in church," a man offered.

"We could be here until the end of time discussing the bizarre laws from across the pond, Allan," Professor Wild said. "Let's stick to statutes this side of the Atlantic, shall we?"

"The Postal Services Act of 2000," a woman in the front said. "States that chatting to the postman for longer than necessary is an offence tantamount to purposefully sabotaging the delivery of the mail."

"Who knows what a bored housewife could be charged with for shagging the postie then," a thin man in the middle row chirped.

"Thank you for that, Lloyd," Professor Wild said. "We've got time for one more. I see we have some visitors today, and I get the feeling that they would very much like my attention."

He stared right at Whitton when he said this.

A man at the front put up his hand.

"Let's hear it then, Nigel," Professor Wild said.

"The Madhouses Act of 1774 stipulated that you were only allowed one lunatic per household. People were required to apply for a special permit if they wanted to keep more than one nutcase at home."

"And that is a very appropriate one to finish off with," Professor Wild said. "It is a prime example of how bizarre and wonderful the law actually is. Off you go. Don't do anything I wouldn't do, and if you have to, make damn sure you don't get caught."

Whitton waited for the lecture hall to empty out, and she and DC King made their way up to the front. Professor Wild stood with his hands in his pockets and watched them approach.

"What can I help you lovely ladies with?" he said.

Whitton took out her ID and Professor Wild raised a hand.

"I know who you are."

"Is there somewhere we can talk in private?" Whitton asked.

"We won't be disturbed in here for another thirty minutes. Is this about Rebecca?"

"Partly," Whitton said. "I'm not sure if you're aware but another student was murdered yesterday afternoon. Sharon Atlee."

Professor Wild's eyes faced downward, and he rubbed his face.

"God, no."

"I'm afraid so," Whitton said. "Are you sure you don't want to take this somewhere more private?"

"Follow me," Professor Wild said. "We can talk in my office."

It was a short walk to the office. Professor Wild opened the door and told them to take a seat. There wasn't much inside the room. A desk with three chairs – a small wooden bookshelf and a single filing cabinet was the extent of it.

"Not quite what you imagined the office of a professor of law to look like?" Professor Wild said.

"Not really," Whitton said. "I thought there would be more books."

"Everything I need is on here," Professor Wild tapped the laptop on the desk.

"When was the last time you saw Sharon Atlee?" DC King said.

"Yesterday afternoon," Professor Wild said without hesitation.

"What time was this?" Whitton said.

"Around four I think."

"Here at the university?"

"No," Professor Wild said. "Sharon was absent yesterday. I went round to her house."

"At four in the afternoon?" DC King said.

"Round about then."

"Why did you go to see her?" Whitton said.

"Because she asked me to. She sent me a message asking me to pop round."

"How long did you stay at her house?" DC King said.

"No more than thirty minutes."

"And she was fine when you left?" Whitton said.

"Perfectly."

    Whitton knew she had no choice about what to do next.

"I'm afraid you're going to have to cancel your lectures and seminars for the rest of the day. We're going to have to ask you to come to the station to answer some more questions."

"Not a problem," Professor Wild said.

"You don't seem very bothered," DC King said.

"I'm a professor of law, my dear. I know how it goes. I presume I'm not under arrest yet."

"Of course not," Whitton said.

"That's something at least. Shall we go?"

"Aren't you going to reschedule your workload?" DC King said.

Professor Wild held up a mobile phone. "I can do that on the way."

"It shouldn't take too long," Whitton said.

"You never can tell, can you?"

"Come on then," Whitton said.

"How is Jason, by the way?"

Whitton was taken off guard and she wasn't sure how to reply.

"He was one of the brightest legal brains I've ever come across, you know. He could have been a shining star, but he chose to follow a completely different path. Give him my regards when you see him."

CHAPTER SEVEN

Kevin Miller seemed a lot calmer than he had outside Sharon Atlee's house the previous evening. Sharon's boyfriend answered the door to Bridge and DC Moore and invited them in straight away.

"I've run out of coffee," he informed them in the living room.

"That's fine," Bridge told him. "How are you doing?"

"Not great. It's not every day you find out that your girlfriend has been killed."

"How *did* you find out?" DC Moore said. "You came to the house not long after we did. How did you know what happened so soon?"

"Carl phoned me and told me."

"Carl Nunn?" Bridge said. "The next-door-neighbour?"

"Carl and I have been friends for a few years."

"Are you a student too?" DC Moore said.

Kevin nodded. "I'm in my final year of a law degree."

"Law?" Bridge said.

"Somebody has to do it."

"Are there no lectures today?" DC Moore asked.

"It appears not. I got a WhatsApp informing me that Professor Wild will be absent for the rest of the day, so we were encouraged not to come in."

"Surely Professor Wild isn't the only lecturer in the law faculty," Bridge said.

"Of course not, but all of the classes I had scheduled for today are with him. I've finished most of the stuff I need to do for this term anyway. I imagine he'll be permanently absent now."

"What makes you think that?" DC Moore said.

"I'm not an idiot. The WhatsApp was very vague, but I know what it meant. That bastard is going to get everything he deserves."

"We can't discuss that," DC Moore said. "You said you're in your third year of the degree?"

"That's right. Are you here to talk about my law degree, or was there something else?"

"Both," Bridge said.

He didn't get the chance to elaborate. The sound of a door slamming could be heard and a woman's voice passed by the room. The expletives she was letting out indicated that she wasn't in the best of moods.'

"That's Penny," Kevin said.

"She has an impressive repertoire of oaths there," Bridge said.

"You get used to her after a while."

"We'll get to the reason for the visit," Bridge said. "Last night you seemed convinced that Professor Wild was responsible for Sharon's murder. Can you explain why you thought that?"

"Because I know what's been going on."

"Could you explain what you mean?"

"Everybody knows what a lech Professor Wild is," Kevin said. "Sharon isn't the only student he's seduced with his academic charm."

"Seducing students is a far cry from murder, Mr Miller," Bridge said.

"He had a thing with Rebecca too."

"Rebecca Stone?" DC Moore said.

"And now both of them are dead. Coincidence? I don't think so."

"I'm still finding it hard to understand why you think Professor Wild would kill Sharon," Bridge said. "What reason would he have to do that?"

"To see if he could get away with it?" Kevin speculated. "I don't know. All I know is, it was him that did it. Have you arrested him?"

"We can't talk about that," DC Moore said.

"Where were you yesterday?" Bridge said. "Between four and six yesterday afternoon, say?"

"Why are you asking about where I was?" Kevin said.

"It's just routine," DC Moore said. "We always question those closest to the victim first."

"I was at home."

"You were here?" Bridge said.

"It's the only home I have right now."

"Was anybody else here with you?"

"No," Kevin said. "I was here alone."

"Did you perhaps use the Internet in that time?" DC Moore said. "Maybe make a phone call?"

"How am I supposed to remember that?"

"It might help your case if you could," Bridge said.

"Case?" Kevin repeated. "Am I a suspect in Sharon's murder?"

"We always look at the close relatives and friends first. As my colleague said, it's just routine."

"Well, I don't have an alibi for the time that Sharon was murdered."

"How do you know what time that was?" DC Moore asked.

"Because you've just hinted at it. Between four and six you said."

The door opened and a tall woman with blond hair came into the room.

"We're in the middle of something here, Penny," Kevin told her.

"In the middle of what?" Penny said.

"Please, could you just give us a minute."

"Make sure it's a minute. There's a program I want to watch on soon, and I don't want to miss it."

"Thanks, Penny," Kevin said.

"Fucking liberties," she said. "That's what's being taken here. I pay the same fucking rent as you in case you've forgotten."

With that, she left them in peace.

"She seems lovely," Bridge said.

"She's alright in small doses," Kevin said. "How much longer is this going to take?"

"I'm afraid we have the problem of your lack of alibi, Mr Miller," DC Moore said.

"How long were you and Sharon together?" Bridge said.

"A few months."

"And you got on fine?"

"What the hell is this?" Kevin said. "My girlfriend has been murdered and you're giving me the third degree. I know the law better than most and as I see it, it's not my responsibility to prove my innocence – the onus is on you to establish guilt. Are you going to arrest me?"

"Not right now," Bridge said.

"Then I believe this conversation is over."

Bridge nodded. "You're correct. We will need to speak to you again."

"Although you probably knew that already, didn't you?" DC Moore added.

CHAPTER EIGHT

"Professor Wild was telling the truth about the message," Whitton told DI Smyth inside his office. "He received a WhatsApp from Sharon Atlee at just before four yesterday afternoon asking if he could come to the house she rented."

"Did he elaborate on the nature of the visit?" DI Smyth said.

"No, and I didn't press him. I wanted whatever he said to be on record."

"Good call. The man is a professor of law, and he's going to be a tricky one to interview."

"That's one of the reasons I came to see you before we proceeded."

"Has he been arrested?"

"No," Whitton said. "He didn't resist when we told him we needed him to come in and he hasn't mentioned anything about legal representation, but I'm still not sure how to go about this. It's possible that he was the last person to see Sharon Atlee alive. He's admitted to going to her house and the timeline is bothering me."

"We've got a window of roughly two hours to look at," DI Smyth said. "Sharon was last seen on social media at 16:13 yesterday afternoon. Her housemate came home and found her just after six. Professor Wild told us he was at the house for no longer than thirty minutes, so that doesn't leave much time for someone else to gain access to the place and kill Sharon. Right now, he's looking likely for her murder."

"Where is he now?"

"PC Griffin is babysitting him in one of the interview rooms."

"Poor man," DI Smyth said. "I wouldn't want to be babysat by PC Griffin."

"I don't think he did it, sir," Whitton said.

"A minute ago, you said he was looking likely for it."

"It's just a feeling I get."

"Go on."

"It doesn't feel right," Whitton said. "It's true that he was acquainted with both victims. Rebecca and Sharon were both studying law, but what possible reason would he have to kill them?"

"Murder is a funny old business," DI Smyth said. "You should know that by now."

"How are we going to play it? Do you want me in the interview with you?"

"I would have liked to have Smith on board with this one."

"Smith is too close to the suspect, sir," Whitton said.

"It's been almost twenty years since he did the law degree."

"It's just something Professor Wild said when we were about to leave," Whitton said. "He asked how Jason was, and I wasn't expecting it."

"Interesting. Did you get the impression that he was playing some kind of game?"

"No. I got the feeling he was simply asking about Smith in a friendly manner."

"Right," DI Smyth said. "Don't take this the wrong way, but I think it would be better if you weren't involved in the interview. If the professor is up to something, and he's using Smith as some kind of pawn in this, you, by proxy are also too involved."

"We can't afford to take any chances," Whitton said.

"No, we can't. I'll ask the DCI to join me in the interview room."

"I think Chalmers is a good choice too."

"In the meantime," DI Smyth said. "I want you and Kerry to work with Bridge and Harry to find out everything you can about the two victims. Sharon Atlee's boyfriend claims that Professor Wild was more than just friends with Rebecca Stone too. See how much truth there is to that."

"Will do, sir," Whitton said. "I've got a bad feeling about this."

"It's early days."

"No," Whitton said. "We've got two dead women and everyone we've spoken to so far has sounded warning bells in different ways. Something tells me that this one is going to be different to anything we've ever worked on before. I hope to God that I'm wrong."

She'd barely made it out of the office when her phone started to ring. The screen told her that it was Smith.

She answered it. "What are you up to?"

"Admitting defeat," Smith said. "I've been working on the solo for *Comfortably Numb* and I've come to the conclusion that David Gilmour created that solo in such a way that it would be impossible to replicate. The man is an alien."

"I'm a bit busy right now, Jason," Whitton said.

"Have you spoken to Herman?" Smith said. "Professor Wild, I mean?"

"We brought him in a short while ago. The DI thought it would be best if him and Chalmers carried out the interview."

"While I was busy massacring the greatest guitar solo ever written," Smith said. "I got thinking about something. It was a lecture that Professor Wild gave when I was in my second or third year."

"You remembered something from almost two decades ago?"

"It was a memorable day. It was all hypothetical of course, but I recall Professor Wild putting forward the proposition that getting away with murder was entirely possible within the boundaries of the law."

"That's ridiculous."

"Is it though?" Smith said. "You hear about it all the time. People get away with it because of the confinements set about in law. A search not carried out properly – a suspect not being read their rights, and that kind of thing."

"I really don't think we've got anything to worry about."

"Just be extremely careful with Herman Wild."

"I thought you said he was a legend in his day," Whitton said. "I recall the word *guru* was used."

"He *was* a legend," Smith said. "But he had some fanciful ideas, and he wasn't averse to pushing the boundaries to see how far he could go."

"Thanks for the tip. We need you here, Jason."

"And I'm quite happy here."

"It doesn't appear so to me," Whitton said. "You pretend not to care what's going on at work but it's quite clear that you're talking shit."

"That's not nice," Smith said.

"I know you. You're cutting off your nose to spite your face. Swallow that Aussie pride and get your arse back here where you belong."

"Hmm," Smith said. "Is there anything I need to pick up from the shops?"

"You went shopping yesterday," Whitton reminded him. "And the day before that."

"I'll make something nice to eat later," Smith said. "Or we could treat ourselves to a meal at the Hog's Head."

"We'd better not. We'll need to cut back when we've only got one salary coming in. I'd better go – we're snowed under here."

CHAPTER NINE

Smith stared at his phone as though it might bite him at any moment. Whitton's parting remarks had stung, and he'd been unprepared for them. He tossed the phone on the kitchen table and went outside for a cigarette. The garden had seen better days. The small patch of lawn had turned brown, and Smith knew it would be a good few months before it started to grow again. The roses on the border with the house next door had withered and died a long time ago, and the tree at the end of the garden only had a few more leaves left to shed. Winter wasn't far off.

Smith lit a cigarette and tried to remember more about the lecture he mentioned to Whitton. The subject matter had stuck in his head, but he was finding it hard to recall the details. He closed his eyes and an image of a man in his early thirties came into his head. Herman Wild had been one of the youngest law professors in the country. He'd been offered the tenure not long after his thirtieth birthday, and Smith remembered that it was an incredible achievement at the time.

Herman was a dynamic force, full of energy. He really was passionate about every aspect of the law, and that enthusiasm was contagious. Smith knew for a fact that Professor Wild was the sole reason he'd excelled during his time studying law. Of that, there was little doubt.

He still couldn't recall the ins and outs of the lecture he'd told Whitton about. He wondered if he'd kept any of his study notes from back then. It was just after the turn of the new century and technology was nowhere near as advanced as it was today and the majority of course work was done the old-fashioned way on actual paper.

Smith stubbed out the cigarette and went back inside the house. He made his way upstairs and stopped below the hatch that opened up to the small space above the ceiling that was an attic of sorts. If there was anything left from his time at university this was the only place it could be. The fire that had gutted a lot of the house a few years ago had destroyed most of his possessions but the attic had been spared.

Smith wasn't a short man but, even on tiptoes he was only able to touch the outside of the hatch. He was going to need a ladder if he was going to be able to haul himself up inside the attic space. He went back downstairs and opened the front door. There was an aluminium ladder in the garage next to the house. He opened the garage door and flicked the light switch. Nothing happened. It had been quite some time since he'd been in here – his car was always relegated to the driveway, and he wondered how long the lightbulb had been bust. He found the ladder propped against the wall and carried it into the house.

The first thing that occurred to Smith when he pushed open the wooden board to the attic was the musty odour that hit him. The hatch hadn't been opened for a very long time. He couldn't remember if there was a light up here, but when he felt about for a switch he was in luck. And even better, the light came on when he flicked the switch.

It was like going back in time. Boxes were lined up in rows against the back of the attic, and the sudden déjà vu that Smith experienced brought it all back. He was the one who had brought the boxes up here and he was the one who had stacked them tidily, as per his Gran's instructions. She'd made it clear that he was to stand only on the wooden beams that crisscrossed the floor, and Smith smiled when he remembered her exact words.
Your grandfather fell through those ceiling boards once, and his back was never the same again.

Smith wished he'd brought a torch with him. Even though there was light from the single bulb on the ceiling, it wasn't much to see by and when he got closer to the boxes, he realised that none of them appeared to be labelled. He decided to climb back down. This would be much easier with two people, and Darren Lewis didn't have anything better to do. It was Wednesday, and Darren's parents looked after Andrew on Wednesdays. It was a recent arrangement, and it had been Jenny Lewis's idea. She and her husband, Frankie didn't see much of the baby and Darren was glad to have a break from parental duties while his parents took over.

Smith rang the bell, and Darren opened the door shortly afterwards.

"Are you busy?" Smith asked him.

"Not really," Darren said.

"You are now. I need a hand lugging some boxes down from the attic next door."

"What boxes?"

"I have no idea what's in them, and that's why I need you to help me get them down."

Darren offered to go up into the attic. He would pass the boxes down to Smith on the landing below.

"Make sure you only stand on the wooden beams," Smith warned.

"I have been up in an attic before," Darren said. "I helped my dad fit some lagging in the attic at home. You've got some cool stuff up here."

"Could you just concentrate on the boxes."

"Who do all these medals and trophies belong to?"

"I have no idea," Smith said. "I didn't see them up there. Must be from when my Gran had the place."

"Horace Smith," Darren said. "His name is on a few of them."

"That's my grandfather," Smith said. "What are they for?"

"Boxing, mostly. He must have been really good."

"I never met him. Could you just get the boxes?"

An hour later the living room was a mess. There had to be at least two dozen boxes in the middle of the floor. Two boxes of medals and trophies were amongst them. Smith would go through these later. He thanked Darren and the teenager went back next door.

"Where to start?" Smith said to himself.

He decided to smoke a cigarette before he got stuck in.

He was halfway through the cigarette when his phone started to ring. It was Whitton and she didn't beat about the bush.

"Herman Wild has confessed to the murders of Rebecca Stone and Sharon Atlee."

"You can't be serious?" Smith said.

"I've never been more serious in my life," Whitton said. "But we might have a problem."

"He didn't do it on record, did he?"

"How the hell did you know that?"

"Because of something I've been thinking about all morning," Smith said. "Give me twenty minutes."

"What are you talking about?"

"You were right," Smith said. "I'm not cut out for the house-husband life. I'm coming back to work."

CHAPTER TEN

Jackie Grant was making the best of the time she'd been given to make an attempt at getting back on track with her coursework for the term. The news of Professor Wild's departure from campus, accompanied by two police detectives had caused speculation and rumours to explode all around the university grounds. Jackie wasn't interested in these – she'd been given a lifeline, and she was going to make the most of it.

Jackie had started well. The first year of the law degree had been plain sailing, and she'd ended the final term with grades that put her right at the top of the class. Then, in the second-year things had started to go downhill. She'd met a man, and her priorities changed. Her mother had predicted it, and that was the worst part. Jackie was always loath to give her mum the satisfaction of being right, but Barry Gilbert had come on the scene and the law degree was always going to take a back seat when he arrived. Jackie never thought it would happen to her – it was the kind of cliched thing that other people fell for, but Barry Gilbert had well and truly swept her off her feet and she was besotted with the man. Academically, he was miles behind, but the bad boy feel he exuded had excited Jackie and she'd fallen, hook, line, and sinker for the garage mechanic.

She made some coffee and took it to her room. She put on some music – Angus and Julia Stone always helped her to concentrate, especially at low volume. She woke up her laptop and sipped her coffee. She knew she wouldn't be disturbed for the rest of the day. Emma, her housemate was spending the night with a friend and Jackie would have the house to herself.

The screen of the laptop told her it had warmed up sufficiently to begin. She would work through the coursework systematically and she predicted that she would be able to get back up to date in two or three days. Barry was just going to have to accept it.

Her mobile phone beeped on the desk. After glancing at the screen Jackie ignored it. She would read the message when she was happy that she'd done enough for the day.

The first item on the agenda was *Johnson vs Vernon*. It was a complicated case and that was one of the reasons that Jackie had lingered over it. It involved an incident where a woman, Katherine Johnson had caused injury to Lionel Vernon when she drove her car over his foot. The defence argued that to be guilty of an offence there needs to be an unlawful act, accompanied by a guilty state of mind. The purpose of the assignment was to discuss whether Mrs Johnson could actually be charged with the crime she was accused of, when it was clear that it was an accident – nothing more, nothing less.

The prosecution argued that whether the incident was an accident or not wasn't the issue. The fact that Mrs Johnson had made no effort to remove the car from Mr Vernon's foot was grounds for an assault charge. The defence countered this with a claim that because Mrs Johnson had no criminal intent at the time the car first went over Mr Vernon's foot she could not be found guilty of assault, even if she made no attempt to drive the vehicle off his foot afterwards.

Jackie concluded that Mrs Johnson was indeed guilty of assault with intent. The fact that she made no effort to drive the car off Mr Vernon's foot demonstrated act and intention, after the initial fact, and therefore she was guilty of the crime. Jackie reinforced this opinion with a similar case from the sixties where a court found a man guilty of assault on a police officer for accidentally causing injury with a vehicle and not doing anything to move the vehicle afterwards, thus exacerbating the injuries.

Jackie stretched her arms and finished the coffee in the cup, even though it had gone cold. The music had also stopped and when Jackie glanced at the clock at the bottom of the laptop, she was surprised at how much time had passed without her realising it. She'd been so engrossed in her work that she hadn't felt the passing of time. It felt good. She felt like she was back on track, and she was confident that she would be able to catch up before the deadlines that had been set.

The next case involved a woman who had tried to sue the manufacturers of a soft drink after finding what appeared to be the remains of a slug in the bottom of the bottle. She had been given the bottle of ginger beer by a friend. She'd claimed damages for shock and the sickness that followed. Jackie decided that this was the ideal time to take a break. She would tackle the legal implications of gastropod poisoning later.

She used the bathroom and went downstairs to the kitchen. She felt like a drink, but she'd forgotten to restock with wine. She wondered whether Emma had a bottle or two stashed away somewhere. After opening every cupboard, she realised that she was out of luck. There wasn't a drop of alcohol to be found. The sound of her ringtone could be heard upstairs and shortly afterwards the doorbell rang.

Jackie ignored both. Instead, she went outside to the small patch of gravel that passed for a back yard. She breathed in the crisp air and closed her eyes.

"Woman versus slug juice," she said out loud and chuckled.

A noise close by caused her to open her eyes. It sounded like it came from inside the house. Then everything was quiet again.

"Woman versus slug juice," she said once more. "No case to argue. The ginger beer was purchased by a friend, and it was the friend who gave her the drink. Ergo, no contract was entered into with which to sue."

All of the assignments the students were given were actual cases, but the students weren't privy to the outcome of these cases. Their task was to dissect them and pick holes in anything they thought was important. Jackie was right on the money with her prediction of the outcome of the *Johnson vs*

Vernon case. Katherine Johnson was found guilty of assault with intent because it was ruled that her failure to remove the car from Mr Vernon's foot constituted act and intention. She was given a suspended sentence and fined five-hundred pounds.

The outcome of the slug juice affair was going to remain a mystery to Jackie Grant. She was never going to learn that the court would extend the law of negligence in this instance. It would be extended to require reasonable care towards those likely to be affected by a company's actions. Jackie would never be aware of this.

She went back inside the house to find someone in the kitchen.

"Christ," she said. "You gave me a heart attack. How did you get in?"

"Front door was open. I brought wine."

"You are a lifesaver," Jackie said.

She probably would have rephrased this if she'd been able to see the figure lurking behind the door with the thick rope tucked into his belt.

CHAPTER ELEVEN

"What has he said?" Smith said.

"Hold your horses," DI Smyth said. "You can't just barge into my office and start acting as though you work here."

"I do work here."

"That's not the impression I got."

"Come on, boss," Smith said. "I'm back. I thought that's what you wanted."

"What I want," DI Smyth said. "Is for you to stop acting like a baby and come back down to earth."

"I'm back. I lost the plot for a while back there, but I'm definitely back. Where is he?"

"He's in one of the holding cells."

"Whitton said he confessed," Smith said.

"He told the duty sergeant that he couldn't take it anymore. He claimed that he was the one who killed Rebecca Stone and Sharon Atlee."

"Fuck it."

"My sentiments exactly. Nothing he said down there in the custody suite can be used as evidence."

"And he damn well knows it. He offered up a confession before he was even under arrest. He hadn't even been interviewed yet. What's your plan?"

"I really don't know," DI Smyth said. "We're going to need to put our heads together to figure out how to play this one. I was planning on interviewing him with the DCI by my side."

"No offence to Chalmers," Smith said. "But he isn't the right bloke for this. Herman Wild is possibly the finest legal brain in the city, if not the whole country. The man became a professor at the age of thirty, for fuck's sake."

"Do you have any suggestions?" DI Smyth said.

"Not off the top of my head," Smith said. "Do we have grounds for an arrest based on what we know about him?"

"Disregarding the confession?"

"That confession is about as much use as Uncle Jeremy at a press conference, boss."

"That's enough."

"I'm serious. Tell me everything we've got on him?"

DI Smyth did. He told Smith about the message from Sharon Atlee asking Professor Wild to come to her house. He also mentioned Sharon's boyfriend's claim that the professor was romantically involved with not only Sharon, but Rebecca Stone too.

"The WhatsApp is interesting," Smith decided. "But the word of the boyfriend is hardly evidence worthy. It's his word against Herman's, as is the confession to the duty sergeant. Fuck it. I don't like this, boss. I want to speak to the duty sergeant."

"Sergeant Finch is an experienced officer."

"I don't doubt that, but I want to know what was said down there."

Sergeant Jack Finch was a short, stocky man with a shaved head. He was relatively new to the post in York and Smith hadn't had many dealings with him. DI Smyth told him to take a seat inside the office.

"You know DS Smith?"

"Who doesn't know Smith?" Sergeant Finch said.

"What did Professor Wild say to you?" Smith got straight to the point.

"He said he couldn't take it anymore, and he wanted to confess to the murders of Rebecca Stone and Sharon Atlee."

"Why do you think he did that?"

"How should I know?"

"Because you were the one talking to him," Smith said. "You do realise that nothing he said to you can be used against him."

"You say that like it's my fault."

"Did you at least advise him not to say anything?" Smith said.

"I'm not his lawyer," Sergeant Finch said. "Have I done something wrong? Do I need to get in touch with my union rep?"

"Let's calm down a bit," DI Smyth said. "How did Professor Wild appear to you before he made the confession?"

"What do you mean?"

"Did he look like a man who was about to make a revelation that had the potential to destroy his life?" Smith said.

"I don't like what you're implying here," Sergeant Finch said. "I was in this job while you were still wearing short pants."

Smith wondered whether to tell him that many Australians wear short pants for most of their lives, but he didn't think it was a great idea.

"I'm not implying anything," he said. "I want to know why a man who isn't under arrest for anything decides to admit to two murders."

"Look here," Sergeant Finch said. "I don't have to take this. What a suspect does or does not say to me in the custody suite is nothing to do with anything I've done. I've had some who've asked for priests - some like to show me photos of their kids and others ask what the food is like in prison."

"DS Smith isn't implying that it's your fault he confessed," DI Smyth said. "His concern is that the confession is null and void."

"Unless someone was there with you," Smith said.

"I was on my own," Sergeant Finch said.

"This couldn't get much better, could it?"

"I'm not scared of you."

"Glad to hear it," Smith said. "Were you alone in the custody suite the whole time Professor Wild was in the holding cell?"

"People come and go," Sergeant Finch said. "You know the drill."

"But when the professor made his confession, it was just you and him?"

"I thought we'd already established that."

"I like to get the full picture," Smith said. "I hate it when there are pieces missing. So, a man who was brought in for a simple interview decides to confess to two murders. Hold on, why was he in the holding cells in the first place? He wasn't under arrest, so why was he even locked up?"

CHAPTER TWELVE

"This is a balls-up of the first order?"

Smith was sitting opposite Whitton in the canteen.

"You and Kerry brought him in. Why didn't you keep an eye on him?"

"I wanted to speak to the DI about how to proceed with the interview and he was happy to wait for us. PC Griffin was keeping an eye on him."

"And Griffin just took it upon himself to lock him up," Smith said. "This is just beautiful."

"PC Griffin was misinformed by Professor Wild," Whitton said. "The professor told him he was under arrest and PC Griffin had no reason to doubt him. Why would someone make up something like that?"

"So, the prof gets wrongly imprisoned," Smith said. "And then he decides to confess to a couple of murders to a duty sergeant who doesn't know his arse from his elbow. It just gets better and better. A suspect in a double murder now has enough ammo to make our lives extremely unpleasant. He could sue for this, and the man damn well knows it."

"Surely it's not that bad."

"It's worse," Smith said. "If he goes to the press with this we'll be crucified. And I know for a fact that that's exactly what he's planning on doing."

"You don't know that."

"It was in the lecture he gave twenty years ago," Smith said. "I remember it now. One of the tactics to muddy a case against you is to use the press to swing favour in your direction."

"If you're right," Whitton said. "Why is he doing this?"

"Because he believes he can get away with it."

"What are we going to do?" Whitton said.

"Carry on regardless," Smith said. "He's got the upper hand at the moment, but there are ways to change that."

"Such as?"

"I'll let you know when I've figured it out. In the meantime, we need to release him – tell him he's free to go home."

"You can't be serious?"

"I am. It's the last thing he'll be expecting, and it will catch him off guard."

"He's just confessed to two murders," Whitton reminded him.

"He won't repeat it on record, so it's a useless confession. We let him go and, if he did actually kill those women, we find evidence to prove it."

Smith got to his feet.

"Where are you going?" Whitton said.

"I need to let off a bit of steam," Smith said. "I'm going to have a quiet word with PC Griffin and then I might smoke a cigarette."

"Smoke the cigarette first," Whitton advised.

Smith found PC Griffin by the front desk. He was talking to PC Baldwin about something.

"A word please," Smith said. "Outside, if you don't mind."

"I'd prefer it if you could say what you have to say in here," PC Griffin said.

Smith observed the self-satisfied grin on his face. From the onset, he'd taken a dislike to the man. His overall unpleasant appearance aside, he was a man for whom nature hadn't been kind in the personality department either. He really was a horrible specimen of a human being.

"Outside," Smith said. "I insist."

"I would really prefer it if there were witnesses present, Sarge."

Smith nodded to Baldwin.

"I didn't see anything," she said and grinned.

"This is outrageous," PC Griffin said.

"Relax, man," Smith said. "I just want a quiet word."

Smith lit a cigarette as soon as they got outside. He took a long drag and breathed out a cloud of smoke.

"Right," he said. "Can you tell me how someone who wasn't under arrest ended up in one of the holding cells?"

"He told me he'd been arrested," PC Griffin said. "DS Whitton just asked me to keep an eye on him – she didn't tell me he wasn't under arrest."

"OK," Smith said. "What exactly did Professor Wild say to you? Word for word if you can remember."

"He was extremely courteous, Sarge. He told me that his lawyer was going to be at least three hours, and he asked why he wasn't being detained in one of the cells."

"So, you locked him up?"

"It was his idea."

Smith sighed. "I bet it was. You're a fucking idiot."

"Am I going to get into trouble for this? Will it go on my record?"

"It should do," Smith said. "How could you be so stupid? You locked up a man for no reason. Once the press gets hold of this, heads are going to roll. And they will get wind of it; it's just a matter of time. If I were you, I'd prepare yourself for the wall of shit that's heading your way."

"I'm sorry," PC Griffin said. "He really fooled me. Why would he do that?"

"That's not your concern. I suggest you fuck off now before I do something we'll both regret."

"But Sarge."

"Now please."

Smith lit another cigarette and rubbed his eyes. He tried to make some sense out of Professor Wild's actions. He was definitely playing some kind of game, but Smith couldn't work out what game it was. He wondered if he might get some answers from the pile of boxes in the living room at home and he made a mental note to go through them as soon as he got home.

He ran through the series of events in his head. He hadn't been involved in the initial stages of the investigation, but Whitton had kept him pretty much up to date. Rebecca Stone had been killed at home on Sunday. She'd been strangled with something – possibly a thick rope. Rebecca had a drawing on her stomach of something none of the team had managed to figure out. Forensics found no evidence of forced entry and no sign of a struggle. Sharon Atlee's murder was a carbon copy of Rebecca's, right down to the peculiar drawing on her stomach. Both women were students of law at the university, and both of them were acquainted with Professor Wild.

Smith decided that there was only one logical course of action to follow. Professor Wild couldn't be trusted. Smith didn't think they could rely on anything he told them, so they needed to let the evidence do the talking for him. People lie – evidence doesn't.

CHAPTER THIRTEEN

"We've got a full team again," DI Smyth said.

The afternoon briefing had just begun, and Smith had asked for a rundown of what they had so far. It hadn't taken long, and there wasn't anything that Whitton hadn't already told him.

"Professor Wild has been allowed to go home," DI Smyth said.

"I thought he confessed," DC Moore said.

"It was a trick," Smith said. "He told the duty sergeant that he killed those two women because he knew we couldn't use it against him."

"How can you be so sure?" DC Moore said.

"Because I attended a lecture during my time at university," Smith said. "And he put forward a hypothesis containing something similar. It was a lecture discussing getting away with murder. Killing someone and using the restrictions put in place within the law to get away with it."

"That's insane," Bridge said.

"It's been done before," Smith said. "Google it."

"What do we do now then?" DC Moore said.

"Use the evidence to prove guilt," Smith said. "And make damn sure everything is done in accordance with the law. Every step of the investigation, going forward needs to be beyond contestation in a court of law."

"You're starting to sound like a lawyer yourself now," Bridge said.

"Are you seriously suggesting that this is some kind of sick game?" DC Moore said. "Because I find that really hard to believe."

"I'm not a hundred percent sure of it," Smith said. "But there are far too many similarities between the things that were discussed in that lecture and the recent events."

"What do you suggest we do about it?" DC King said.

"Examine the evidence," Smith said. "A confession is all very well, but we all know how unreliable a confession can be, not to mention it being pretty flimsy in terms of evidence. Any lawyer worth his stripes will argue away a confession in a flash. We need hard proof. Something that cannot be disputed. Firstly, we need to check out Professor Wild's movements, specifically around the times of the murders he's conveniently admitted to."

"We know he was at Sharon Atlee's house between four and half-past yesterday afternoon," Whitton said. "Sharon was found not long after that."

"Then we focus on what we don't know. When was Rebecca Atlee's body discovered?"

"Just after two on Sunday afternoon," DS Smyth said. "Her housemate found her."

"And when was Rebecca last seen before that?"

"The housemate went out for an early lunch at eleven that morning," DI Smyth said. "So, we have a window of three hours."

"Check it out," Smith said. "Find out where Professor Wild was at that time. If we can put him somewhere else, we'll be able to confirm that his confession is a sham."

"I'm still finding it hard to get my head round this," DC Moore said. "If this is some kind of sick game, what is the prof actually getting out of it?"

"You don't know the man, Harry," Smith said. "He likes to push boundaries, and he likes to push them as far as he can."

"Let's crack on with what we have," DI Smyth said. "In both instances Forensics found no evidence of forced entry and no indication that a struggle took place. We have the initial pathology report back and neither Rebecca Stone nor Sharon Atlee had any traces of narcotic in their systems. Dr Bean also confirmed that they both died due to asphyxiation. Traces of fibres from rope strands were found on the necks of both women. The rope itself is rather unusual – it's made from hemp and it's relatively uncommon these days."

"Is it worth looking into suppliers of that kind of rope?" DC Moore asked.

"Of course it is, you fool," Smith said.

"It was just a simple question, Sarge," DC Moore said.

"It was a dumb one."

"I preferred it when you were retired," DC Moore dared. "At least I didn't have to put up with the insults."

"Enough," DI Smyth said. "Harry, check out suppliers of that particular rope. I doubt there are many outlets in the city."

"Look at online suppliers too," Smith said.

"Is Professor Wild our only suspect?" DC King said.

"That's a very good question, Kerry," Smith said. "And we'll examine it in more detail when we have confirmation that he doesn't have an alibi for both murders."

"What if he does?" Bridge said.

"Then we'll have to come up with a change of plan," Smith said. "Because if that's the case it means he's not working alone, and I really hope that's not the case."

"This really is insane," DC Moore said. "We've never come across anything like it."

"Think of it as a challenge," Smith said. "A deviation from the norm is always good for clearing out the cobwebs in a stagnant brain."

"You've got weird since you came back from early retirement," Bridge said.

"Smith has always been weird," Whitton pointed out.

"I want to discuss the drawings on the women's stomachs," Smith said. "The fact that they're identical suggests that they're important."

"We've been unable to figure out what they actually are," DC Moore said.

"Two UFOs and some kind of spike," Bridge said.

"Do we have a photo we can put up on the big screen?" Smith said.

"Harry?" DI Smyth said.

DC Moore did the honours again. He tapped the keypad of the laptop, and the photo of the strange drawing appeared on the white screen.

"This is the one from Sharon Atlee," he said. "It's exactly the same as the drawing on Rebecca Stone's stomach."

"It really does look like a couple of unidentified objects beaming light onto the ground," Bridge said. "It's possible its sole purpose is to throw us off track – it might mean nothing at all."

"No," Smith said. "It means something."

He walked to the back of the room to get a closer look. He tilted his head and studied the photo from different angles.

"I don't think it has any significance," DC Moore said. "It's possible that the killer is playing more games with us."

Smith stood up straight again. "I know what it is."

He returned to his seat.

"Are you going to enlighten us?" DI Smyth said.

"Can you invert it?" Smith said.

DC Moore tapped the keypad and the photograph on the screen was shown upside down.

"Bloody hell," Bridge commented.

Smith nodded. "Can you see what it is yet? Sorry, I couldn't resist."

CHAPTER FOURTEEN

"It's an inverted depiction of the sword and the scales of justice."

Smith took no satisfaction in being the one to figure this out. If anything, it actually made everything in the investigation much more complicated.

"The law is an ass," he added. "That's the point that they're making here."

"We don't know that," DC Moore said.

"Come on, Harry," Smith said. "What else could it mean? This is the symbol of justice. It's the sacred representation of Lady Justice – everything that law and order is based on has been turned on its arse. Whoever came up with this has no respect whatsoever for the law."

"This doesn't strike me as something a professor of law would draw, Sarge," DC King said.

"No," Smith agreed. "No, it doesn't, and that just makes it all the more puzzling. I'm still finding it hard to digest. Professor Wild's confession leaves little doubt as to whether he's involved somehow, but the drawings are at odds with everything he stands for."

"People can change, Sarge," DC King said. "Perhaps he's had a change of heart – perhaps he's become somewhat disillusioned with the law, and this is the result."

"You might have a point there," Smith said.

"We're going round in circles," DI Smyth said. "We have no way of knowing what the drawings are supposed to represent, so we won't waste time discussing it."

"I disagree, boss," Smith said.

This earned a smile from DI Smyth. "I thought you might."

"Those drawings are important. The relevance of them will get us closer to the motivation behind the murders."

"Here we go," Bridge said.

"Motive is the key element in every murder investigation. That's just the way it is."

"Right," DI Smyth said. "First things first. I want the details of Professor Wild's movements during the times of both murders."

"We know he went to Sharon Atlee's house between four and half past yesterday afternoon," DC Moore said.

"Do we?" Smith said. "From what I've gathered we only have the WhatsApp that was sent from Sharon's phone. We have no real proof that the professor actually went there. And isn't it also possible that Sharon wasn't the one who wrote the message."

"It was sent from her phone," DC Moore said.

"What's your point, Harry?"

"Oh," DC Moore said. "I see what you're getting at."

"The time off seems to have sharpened your mind somewhat, Smith," DI Smyth said. "It's good to have you back on board."

"It's good to be back, boss," Smith said. "I suggest we stop talking and start acting. This has all the elements of a nasty case, and I've got a feeling we're in for a long, hard slog, but it's nothing we can't handle. Harry – get onto those rope suppliers. Kerry, you and me are going to head over to the university. I'm not a big fan of the place, but I want to get an idea of what our devious professor has been up to since I last saw him. Bridge, I suggest you and Whitton occupy your time looking into Professor Wild's movements over the past few days."

"Are you quite finished?" DI Smyth said.

"Sorry, boss," Smith said. "I'm getting carried away, aren't I?"

"A little bit."

"I suppose I'm making up for lost time. I didn't mean to take over."

"I wouldn't expect anything else," DI Smyth said. "A quick word in private if you don't mind. The rest of you can get to work."

"Boss?" Smith said when he was alone with DI Smyth.

"Are you alright?"

"Never been better," Smith said.

"Your behaviour seems a bit manic."

"Manic?" Smith repeated.

"I've seen you animated before," DI Smyth elaborated. "But when you rattle off stuff like that at full speed it makes me concerned."

"The law was my passion, once upon a time and I still hold it in high regard. So, when I suspect that someone is making a mockery out of the very thing that holds society together it tends to get me a bit rattled. I'll try and tone things down a bit."

"There's no need for that," DI Smyth said. "It's good to have you back."

"It's good to be back," Smith said. "And I never thought I'd say that. And now I need to see how I can get out of slow dancing with Uncle Jeremy."

"Excuse me?"

"Ask Chalmers," Smith said. "I'd better get to work – I don't want to keep Kerry waiting."

Something was happening when Smith reached the front desk. Baldwin was arguing with a group of men and women. One of them, a man Smith vaguely recognised spotted Smith and made a beeline for him.

"You've been back barely five minutes," he said. "And already we've got a scoop. Do you have a comment on how an innocent man ended up locked in one of your cells?"

Smith had expected Professor Wild to go to the press with his story, but he hadn't expected him to do it so quickly.

"I have no idea what you're talking about," he said.

"Can I quote you on that? Not only is an innocent citizen banged up for no reason, York CID's most high-profile copper doesn't even know about it."

"You're wasting your time," Smith said. "You're not going to get anything here."

"Are you worried that Professor Wild is going to sue?" one of the other people asked.

She looked Smith right in the eyes when she asked the question.

"You'll have to ask him that?" Smith said. "Now, I would advise you to leave before we talk about wasting police time."

"We'd better scarper, Hillary." It was the first man. "We wouldn't want to get locked up for bugger all – they seem to make a habit of it in this place."

   "When did they come in?" Smith asked Baldwin when the journalists had gone.

"About five minutes ago. I heard about the mix up with PC Griffin and the suspect. How did the press find out about it so soon?"

"It was all part of Professor Wild's game, and I've got the feeling that he's far from finished."

"Are you saying that this isn't the end of it?"

"Not by a long shot," Smith said. "But if it's a war he wants, he's going to get it, and he's made the mistake of declaring war on the wrong people."

CHAPTER FIFTEEN

"Does this bring back memories, Sarge?" DC King said.

"I had some good times here, Kerry," Smith said. "I really thought the law was going to be my whole life."

"It still is," DC King said. "Just in a different way. What caused the change of heart – what made you decide to join the police? Whitton said you were top of the class."

"It's actually ironic," Smith said. "The decision was born from a feeling I had – an epiphany if you like. I thought the life of a lawyer was the life for me. I'd just got my year-end results, and I took my Gran out to celebrate. We'd had a really nice lunch, and we were passing the Minster afterwards when a yobbo robbed my Gran. He grabbed her handbag and knocked her to the ground."

"That's horrible."

"I chased after him," Smith said. "I probably should have stayed with my Gran, but I was pretty fit back then and I caught him in no time. He was arrested, and my Gran got her handbag back. I didn't know that she'd broken her hip in the fall. She developed pneumonia, and she died soon afterwards in hospital."

"I'm so sorry."

"That wasn't the end of it. The scumbag somehow got himself a hotshot lawyer who got him off with no more than a slap on the wrist."

"And that's why you joined the police?"

"It seemed like the right thing to do, Kerry," Smith said. "It was one of the defining moments in my life – watching that smart Alec in a suit talk his client out of what he really deserved. Justice was not served that day, and I was fucked if I was going to be a part of a profession that could allow that to happen. I reckon I would have made a shit lawyer anyway – I'm too honest."

DC King laughed. "You're probably right. Do we know who to speak to?"

Smith raised a hand to his temple as a white-hot pain exploded inside his head.

"Are you OK, Sarge?" DC King said.

"Shit," Smith said. "I don't know where that came from. I'm fine – it's gone now."

The law department had changed drastically since Smith had studied there. Everything seemed to have been given a modern facelift, and Smith didn't recognise any of it. He found the office for the head of admissions, and decided it was as good a place as any to start. The door was open, so Smith and DC King went straight it.

A middle-aged man was alone in the office. He looked up from the desk when he saw Smith and DC King.

"Can I help you?"

"Police," Smith said. "We need to talk to someone about Professor Wild. Would that someone be you?"

"I very much doubt that. I'm a lowly IT guy. Malcolm Williams. I was brought in to sort out some gremlins in the system. Rachel just popped out for a bit of lunch. She shouldn't be long."

"Rachel?" DC King said.

"She's the head of admissions," Malcolm said. "Rachel Bright. She's been here longer than anyone if I heard right."

Smith didn't recognise the name. "Do you mind if we take a look around while we wait for Mrs Bright?"

"I can't see it being a problem. I'll let her know you're looking for her when she gets back."

Smith thanked him and headed for what he remembered to be the main lecture hall. He stopped outside the door and listened. There didn't appear to be a lecture in progress, so he pushed open the door and stepped inside. The hall hadn't changed at all. It even smelled the same – like mothballs and old perfume, and Smith breathed it in.

"This is where young people come to be disillusioned, Kerry."

"That's a bit cynical, isn't it, Sarge?" DC King said.

"Very," Smith agreed. "But it's the truth. Bright young folk come here with hopes and dreams of making a difference. They want to be part of something meaningful – they want help to maintain something sacred. They spend three years believing that what they're doing actually means something, and then they head out to the real world and get those dreams smashed to pieces as soon as they realise that the law is something completely different to what they expected it to be."

"You really don't like lawyers, do you, Sarge?"

"I get a bit irritated with the hypocrisy, Kerry. He looks promising."

He nodded to a man at the side of the stage. He was dressed in overalls, and he was pushing a mop around.

"The cleaner?" DC King said.

"You'd be surprised what lowly workers can tell us. Nobody pays them any attention, and they often hear things they shouldn't. Come on."

They walked to the front and Smith coughed to get the cleaner's attention.

"There are no lectures scheduled until tomorrow," the cleaner told them.

"What did I tell you?" Smith whispered to DC King.

He took out his ID and held it up.

"Your lot were here snooping around earlier."

"Can we have a quick chat?" Smith said.

"I suppose I can take a bit of a breather."

The cleaner introduced himself as Doug. He didn't offer a surname.

"Is this about the two dead girls?" he asked.

"You heard about that then?" Smith said.

"There isn't much goes on in this place I don't know about," Doug said. "People have been talking about nothing else. They're saying that Professor Wild was arrested."

"They're misinformed," Smith said. "Professor Wild was helping us with our enquiries, but he was allowed to go home."

"Bit hasty if you ask me."

"What do you mean by that?" DC King said.

"Like I said," Doug said. "I hear things. Don't get me wrong – I'm not some kind of eavesdropper; it's just people tend to forget I'm here most of the time."

"I see," Smith said. "What exactly have you heard?"

"Is this going to get me into trouble?"

"Whatever you tell us won't go any further," Smith promised.

Doug scanned the room, and his eyes fell on Smith.

"They're saying Professor Wild had more than just a professional relationship with the dead girls, if you know what I mean."

"Who said this?" Smith said.

"It's the general consensus."

"How long have you worked here?" DC King said.

"Six years," Doug said.

"Do you know Professor Wild well?" Smith said.

"As well as any cleaner can know a professor."

"What do you think of him?"

"I like him. He's never treated me badly."

"Do you believe the rumours to be true?" DC King said. "Do you think it's possible that Professor Wild was in a relationship with some of his students?"

"It's nothing new, is it? And the students here are old enough to know what they're getting themselves into. I'd better get back to work. If the dragon finds me slacking, I'll be in trouble."

"Dragon?" DC King said.

"Miss Bright."

"The admissions woman?" Smith said.

"She's the polar opposite of Professor Wild," Doug said. "Treats me like dirt. Then again, she treats a lot of people like dirt. Bitterness can do that to a person."

"Why do you think she's bitter?" DC King said.

"It's no secret," Doug said. "She couldn't hack it as a lawyer, so she did the next best thing. She got a bit of power in the end, didn't she?"

"She gets to decide on who becomes future lawyers."

"Got it in one," Doug said. "And speak of the devil. I really must get back to work."

Smith turned around. A red-haired woman who looked to be in her fifties was making her way towards them, and Smith had a sudden urge to take a few steps back. She walked with purpose and the expression on her face was one he wouldn't want to look at for very long.

"Douglas," she said. "You're not paid to chit chat. If you've finished in here, you can make a start on the seminar rooms. Most of them will be vacant for the rest of the day."

Doug nodded and went to retrieve his mop and bucket.

CHAPTER SIXTEEN

"We might have a problem."

Bridge had just finished talking on the phone with a man by the name of Brian Flint. Brian was an old friend of Professor Wild's and the information he'd given Bridge wasn't what the detective was hoping for.

"According to Brian," he said. "Professor Wild was with him on Sunday. They had lunch at the Meaty Pig on Murton Lane and Brian claims they were there between noon and three."

"Rebecca Stone was killed between eleven and two," Whitton said. "Her housemate last saw her at eleven and she was found when the housemate returned from the pub at two. It's still possible that Professor Wild killed Rebecca before he met his friend at the pub."

"That's the problem," Bridge said. "According to Brian Flint, they didn't meet at the pub. Professor Wild was with him from ten that morning. He can't be the one who killed Rebecca."

"The friend could be lying," Whitton said. "And why confess to a murder you have an alibi for?"

"It makes no sense whatsoever," Bridge said.

Whitton picked up her phone and brought up her Google.

"There's a number for the Meaty Pig here on their website," she said.

After a brief conversation it was confirmed that Professor Wild was indeed at the pub on Sunday. According to the bar manager, he had been a regular there for three years and he rarely missed a Sunday lunch.

Whitton was baffled. "I'm finding it hard to get my head round this. We've got two dead women, both of whom were students of Professor Wild's. Both were strangled, and the crime scenes were identical. The boyfriend of one of the women is convinced that Professor Wild was responsible and soon afterwards he confesses to both murders."

"Even though he has an alibi for at least one of them," Bridge said. "We still don't know where he was when Sharon Atlee was killed."

"Sharon was discovered at around six yesterday," Whitton said. "She was last seen on social media at four-fifteen. Professor Wild received a WhatsApp from her asking him to pop round to her house. That was at four o'clock, and we still have no proof that he actually did go to her house."

"We shouldn't have released him," Bridge said.

"Smith thought it was the only thing we could do," Whitton said.

"The man confessed to two murders. I'm surprised the DI went along with it."

"Smith thinks Professor Wild is playing some kind of elaborate game and I'm inclined to agree with him. We need to look more closely at who else could be involved."

"So, you suspect that the prof is still a part of this?"

"Definitely. It's possible that he's the puppet master here. He's pulling the strings, but someone else is carrying out the murders. And you know how complicated things can get when we've got more than one killer working together."

"Is Smith alright?" Bridge asked.

"Where did that come from?"

"He got a bit carried away earlier. I was worried he was about to have some kind of manic episode."

"He's very passionate about the law," Whitton said. "And I think this case is already getting to him."

"He's only been back five minutes."

"You know what he's like."

DC Moore came into the office and the grin on his face meant he'd found something important. He had a laptop bag over his shoulder.

"Out with it then," Bridge said.

"Out with what?" DC Moore said.

"That smug face of yours is starting to make me feel a bit ill. What have you got for us?"

DC Moore put the laptop on the table and sat down next to him. "I trawled the net for suppliers of the type of rope that was used to kill the two students. There are a few online shops that stock it, but unfortunately, they're all located abroad, and it'll be tricky to get any info from them."

"Could you just get to the point?" Whitton said.

"There's a place right here in the city," DC Moore said. "A shop called *Hemporium* on James Street. According to the pathology report the abrasions on Rebecca's and Sharon's necks suggests that they were strangled with a relatively thick length of rope – fourteen or sixteen millimetres, and *Hemporium* happens to stock that thickness of hemp rope."

"What does someone use that kind of rope for?" Bridge said.

"It's usually used for decorative purposes," DC Moore said. "Macrame, scrapbooking and that sort of thing. The thicker stuff can be used to hang ornaments and garden decorations. It's a pretty versatile rope."

"So we've seen," Whitton said.

"What you've told us still doesn't explain the disturbing grin on your ugly mug," Bridge said.

"I'm not finished," DC Moore said.

He opened the laptop and woke it up with a swipe on the keypad.

"Give it a second to warm up," he said. "I spoke to a fellow Londoner at *Hemporium* – a lovely woman I just happen to be hooking up with after work, and she was more than happy to check the sales of hemp rope for me."

"You're going on a date?" Bridge said.

"It's not really a date," DC Moore said. "We seemed to click, and she asked me what I was doing after work – I said not much, and she suggested a drink."

"It's about bloody time," Bridge said. "Let me know how it goes."

"I'd rather not, Sarge."

"Boys," Whitton said. "Could we perhaps focus on the task at hand?"

"Sorry," DC Moore said.

He tapped the keypad a few more times and a grainy black and white image appeared on the screen.

"What's this?" Bridge said.

"Not only did Lorraine get me the details of the recent sales of hemp rope, she also sent me copies of the CCTV of when the transactions were made. Luckily, there weren't many to go through. Do you recognise this bloke?"

He started the footage and paused it fifteen seconds later.

"Bloody hell," Bridge said. "That's our professor."

"It certainly is," DC Moore said. "According to the lovely Lorraine, Professor Wild purchased fifteen metres of 14mm hemp rope on the 16th of this month."

CHAPTER SEVENTEEN

Rachel Bright asked Smith and DC King to take a seat in her office and closed the door. She'd told the IT man to leave them in peace and Smith got the impression that Malcolm Williams was happy to get out of there. His initial impression of the head of admissions wasn't a positive one. Her fierce appearance aside, her abrupt manner suggested that she did not suffer fools. She didn't offer them anything to drink.

"As you can imagine," she said. "The university and the faculty of law in particular is still in shock."

"We appreciate that," Smith said. "I'm actually surprised to see that it's business as usual."

"What else can we do?" Rachel said. "Life goes on."

Smith was tempted to remind her that life had stopped abruptly for two of her students, but he reckoned it probably wouldn't go down well.

"Did you know Rebecca and Sharon well?" he asked instead.

"As well as I know any of the students," Rachel said. "In an average year we process up to two hundred new admissions. I've been at the university for almost two decades so you can imagine how many students I've had the pleasure of meeting. Can I ask you about Professor Wild?"

"I was hoping to ask *you* about him," Smith said.

"What I meant, is will he be returning to the university? He rescheduled his workload for today so I assume that means he will be back to carry on soon."

"Professor Wild was simply helping us with our enquiries," Smith said. "He wasn't charged with anything, and he wasn't arrested, so I see no reason why he can't return to work. Do you know him well?"

This was met with a snort of derision. "Of course, I know him well. I'm head of admissions and he's in charge of the department. What kind of a question is that?"

"Professor Wild has been at the university for a long time, hasn't he?" DC King said.

"Longer than anyone else on the faculty," Rachel said.

"Is he a popular professor?" Smith said.

"If you're alluding to the ridiculous rumours about Herman's inappropriate relationships with his students, I'll stop you right now. It's nothing but idle gossip – unfounded allegations."

"I wasn't alluding to anything," Smith said. "I asked if Professor Wild is popular. I had the pleasure of learning from him during my time here, and I held him in high regard."

"You're an alumnus of St Johns College?"

"A long time ago," Smith said. "Before your time it appears."

"The answer to your question is yes. Professor Wild is a popular member of the faculty. Popular among colleagues and students alike."

Another sharp pain stabbed Smith over his left eye, and he winced. He hoped this wasn't a warning about an impending migraine. He could do without it right now.

"Are you feeling OK?" Rachel asked him.

"I'm good," Smith said. "I suffer from migraines, but I don't think this is going to be one of them."

"Join the club," Rachel said. "Mine are often debilitating. I take sumitriptan as soon as the warning signs materialise. I always make sure I have some on hand. Do you want me to get some for you?"

Smith recognised the name. He was sure those were the same painkillers he'd been prescribed.

"I'll be fine," he said.

"How many lecturers do you have in the law department?" DC King said.

"Around a dozen," Rachel said.

"We're going to need a list," Smith said. "Could you arrange that for us?"

"Do you believe the murders to be connected with the university?"

"Both women were students here," Smith said. "We have to look at every connection we find. It's possible that it won't come to anything, but we still need to check. We're also going to need a list of students."

"You cannot be serious?"

"I'm serious," Smith said.

"I don't think I'm actually allowed to give out that kind of information. I'm going to need to check first."

"You do that," Smith said. "We're not going anywhere."

Rachel shot up from her chair so quickly that Smith jumped. She glared at him and marched out of the room.

"Is it just me that thinks something weird is going on here?" DC King asked.

"She does appear overly defensive," Smith said. "And the fact that the department is carrying on as though nothing has happened strikes me as suspicious."

"I imagined the place to be deserted," DC King said. "Two female students have been murdered, but you wouldn't think so walking around campus. If this was in the movies there would be cancelled classes – security would be jacked up, and women would be advised to take extra precautions. This just doesn't feel right."

"This isn't a movie, Kerry," Smith said. "This is the real world, if you can call the faculty of law the real world."

Rachel Bright returned with two sheets of paper and sour expression on her face. The head of admissions was clearly not a happy woman.

She placed the papers in front of Smith. "This is a list of faculty members."

"What about the students?" Smith said.

"That part is explained on the second sheet," Rachel said.

Smith glanced at it and nodded. He had expected as much.

"In case you need some translation," Rachel said. "That is a document explaining the position of the university from a legal perspective. There is no general legal obligation for universities to disclose information about its students. We have a responsibility to protect the privacy of our students, and the police cannot force us to divulge this information without a warrant ordering us to do so. Do you understand?"

Smith didn't humour her with a reply to this.

"We're going to need that list, Miss Bright," he said. "I assume it is *Miss* Bright?"

"It is," she confirmed. "Did you not fully understand what I just told you?"

"I understood it perfectly well," Smith said. "Under normal circumstances the university wouldn't divulge any information about its students, but these are not normal circumstances, are they? I'm sure you're aware of the concept of specific grounds. In the case of there being an immediate threat to public safety we, the police can request such information without producing a warrant."

"This is..."

Smith held up his hand. "I'm not finished. Furthermore, under the specific grounds clause, the police are also authorised to demand specific information if we believe that information to be relevant to the investigation of a serious crime. I'm sure you'll agree that a double murder is about as serious as it gets."

Smith thought the expression on Rachel Bright's face now was very similar to a fish he remembered from a documentary he'd once seen. The head of admission's mouth opened wide as though she was starved of oxygen.

CHAPTER EIGHTEEN

"We're in the process of obtaining a warrant to search Professor Wild's property," DI Smyth said.

The team had gathered for the afternoon briefing.

"Be very careful," Smith warned.

"A search of a property is cut and dry, Smith," DI Smyth said. "We get the necessary paperwork, and we carry out the search as we've done hundreds of times before."

"We didn't have the sharpest legal brain in the country to worry about during those searches, boss," Smith said. "Every aspect of the search has to be done right. No mistakes."

"What mistakes can you make during the search of a house?" DC Moore wondered.

"You'd be surprised," Smith said. "The warrant itself has to be squeaky clean. One spelling mistake or piece of vague language and the entire search and anything it turns up can be thrown out. The signature at the bottom needs to be legible and legitimate. We're looking specifically for anything that might implicate Professor Wild in the murders of Rebecca Stone and Sharon Atlee, and that needs to be made clear in the warrant."

"We have done this before," Bridge said.

"No," Smith said. "We've never come up against anyone like Herman Wild before. He will pick apart every word on that warrant. And he will be watching the officers who carry out the search like a hawk. One blunder, no matter how insignificant it may seem, and he will spot it. Not only that, he'll rip it to pieces until there's nothing of evidence value left to it."

"You're doing it again," Whitton said.

Smith frowned. "Doing what?"

"This new manic thing of yours. Calm down."

"I am calm."

"Then slow down," Whitton said. "You're starting to scare me."

Smith opened his mouth to speak but the sound of DI Smyth's mobile phone stopped him.

"We've got our warrant," DI Smyth said after a short conversation. "Bridge, you can do the honours. Webber has been told to be on standby, so he and the forensics officers should be ready to go. Smith, no offence."

"None taken, boss," Smith said. "I still think Professor Wild is playing a game with us, and me in particular and it would be a bad idea for me to be a part of this. A game only works if everybody is willing to play."

"I'll pretend I understood that."

"I didn't really understand it myself," Smith said. "Fuck."

His hand shot to his forehead.

"Are you OK?" Whitton said.

Smith didn't reply. His eyes narrowed and closed when an explosion of pain detonated over them.

"Are you having a migraine attack?"

It had been a long time since the migraines had plagued him. The worst one had resulted in a stay in hospital and he'd been prescribed medication to keep them under control, but once again Smith hadn't remembered to keep some sumitriptan on him, and he knew that once the aura began to blur the vision in his left eye, it would grow in size until everything he looked at would take on an otherworldly aspect.

"Jason."

Whitton's voice sounded like it was coming from far away. Another voice could be heard but Smith couldn't make out who it belonged to. The aura was intensifying now and even when he closed his eyes, it was still there.

"I need sunglasses and painkillers," he managed.

"Has he lost his mind?"

Smith recognised this voice – it was DC Moore's cockney twang.

"He needs some paracetamol," Whitton said. "Or Ibuprofen would be better."

Smith was vaguely aware of someone placing a glass in his hand, and then he was given two tablets.

"Take these," Whitton said.

Smith crunched the tablets between his teeth and took a sip of water. He got to his feet and managed to stay up.

"I'm going to find somewhere to lie down."

"Let me help you," Whitton said.

Smith shook his head and instantly regretted it when a sledgehammer slammed into his temple. He staggered out of the small conference room with Whitton close behind.

She returned soon afterwards.

"Is he going to be OK?" DC King asked.

"He'll be fine," Whitton said.

"Does he need medical attention?" DI Smyth said.

"Even if he did," Whitton said. "Do you want to try to force him to get it?"

"Where did he go?"

"He's sleeping it off in one of the holding cells."

"He'd better make sure that Sergeant Finch doesn't lock him in and throw away the key," DI Smyth said. "The duty sergeant isn't Smith's biggest fan at the moment."

"We found out something interesting from the cleaner at the university," DC King said. "He's been there for six years, and he hears things that people don't realise. Professor Wild is a bit of a Romeo by all accounts. It's common knowledge that he's a bit of a player on campus."

"What else did this cleaner tell you?" DI Smyth said.

"That was about all we got before the admissions woman told him to get back to work. And she is not someone I would care to meet again in a hurry.

Something is going on at that university – something sinister. Two of their students have been murdered and they're carrying on as if nothing is wrong. Nobody seems to care. I've never felt such a cold atmosphere before."

"I suggest we finish up there," DI Smyth said. "Bridge, go and see what you can find at the Lothario professor's house."

CHAPTER NINETEEN

Smith was not sure if he was dreaming or not. He'd been slipping in and out of sleep for the past couple of hours - the two states were starting to merge, and he was finding it hard to differentiate between the two. When he first made himself as comfortable as it was possible to get on the hard bed in the holding cell, a man's voice could be heard. He was expounding about piglets, and he was doing it very loudly. One snippet of his soliloquy stayed in Smith's head.

The piglets are let out on the streets before they've even been fully weaned these days.

Smith had no idea what he was talking about.

And now, as he sat up inside the cell, he wondered if this was part of a dream he was having. He couldn't recall the reason for him being locked in a prison cell. The migraine from earlier had eased and been replaced by a dull headache. The attack had wiped him out, but the migraines always did. Smith knew he would be exhausted for the rest of the day.

"Hello," he called out. "Is anyone there?"

"Is anyone there?" a man's voice repeated.

It was piglet man.

"Anyone?" Smith shouted.

Shortly afterwards, footsteps could be heard, and a figure appeared on the other side of the bars of the cell. Smith was now wide awake – it was Sergeant Jack Finch and the grin on the duty sergeant's face told Smith that he was enjoying this.

"Could you let me out?" Smith said.

"It's not locked," Sergeant Finch told him. "Why would I lock you in?'

Smith got off the bed and pushed the cell door open.

"How are you feeling?" Sergeant Finch said. "You were in a bit of a state earlier."

"I've been better," Smith said. "Sorry about before. I got a bit carried away, and I have a habit of taking it out on the wrong people."

"No hard feelings."

The duty sergeant held out his hand and Smith shook it.

"My wife suffers with migraines," Sergeant Finch said. "And I feel for you. I thought they mostly affected women."

"I'm one of the unlucky few."

"I bet you've never spent time in a prison cell before."

"This isn't the first time," Smith said. "And I doubt if it'll be the last. Thanks again."

He left the custody suite and walked down the corridor towards the small conference room. A quick glance inside told him there wasn't a briefing in progress. He wondered what the rest of the team were up to. He wasn't even sure what time it was. It was difficult to tell after a migraine. The haze it brought with it could zap minutes or hours and it was impossible to predict.

Smith's next port of call was the car park. Often the ache in his head left in the wake of a migraine attack could be relieved with nicotine. He lit a cigarette and took a long drag. It was bitterly cold and there wasn't a cloud in the sky. The sun was already setting behind the buildings in the west and Smith knew that the darkness would cause the temperatures to plummet even further.

He was halfway through the cigarette when his phone started to ring in his pocket. The ringtone told him that it was DI Smyth. Elvis Costello was telling him that Oliver's Army was here to stay.

"Boss," Smith answered it.

"How are you feeling?" DI Smyth said.

"Better."

"Do you need some time off?"

"I'm fine," Smith lied. "What's new?"

"We've just finished with the search of Herman Wild's house, and before you say anything, everything was done by the book. The prof didn't even request to be present when the search was carried out."

"Please tell me he was given the option."

"Do I really need to answer that?"

"Sorry, boss," Smith said. "My head is still a bit groggy. Did they find anything?"

"Rope. Five metres of 14mm hemp rope. Harry got lucky with the shop we believed Professor Wild purchased the rope from. It's a place called *Hemporium* on James Street, and we have the professor on CCTV buying fifteen metres of the stuff on the 16th of this month."

"What happened to the other ten metres?" Smith said.

"That's a very good question. And it's one we'll be putting to Professor Wild when we interview him either later today or tomorrow."

"Has he been arrested?"

"The rope was enough to warrant it," DI Smyth said.

"Where did you find it?"

"What?"

"The rope," Smith said. "Where was it?"

"On the table in the living room."

"Hmm."

"What are you thinking?"

"Something doesn't feel right," Smith said.

"The migraine has clouded your judgment. You're not thinking straight."

"My head is as clear as always, boss," Smith said. "Surely you must see that this is suspicious."

"Webber has promised to prioritise the rope. If the fibres retrieved from the necks of the dead women match the fibres from the remaining rope in Professor Wild's house, we've got him."

Smith's cigarette had gone out. He relit it, inhaled and breathed out a cloud of smoke.

"He's going to come up with a perfectly plausible explanation for this," he said. "You do not leave something as damning as a length of rope in plain sight when you know it can be linked to two murders."

"I'm not suggesting that Professor Wild was the one who killed Rebecca and Sharon," DI Smyth said. "He has an alibi for one of the murders anyway, but he's involved somehow, and that's what we're going to focus on."

"Where is he now?"

"Still at the house. He's been arrested, and he'll be brought in. Are you up to the interview?"

"Hold off on that until tomorrow," Smith said. "It's getting late, and I want to have a long hard think about this before I go into that interview room. Perhaps a night in a holding cell will do us some favours."

"I agree," DI Smyth said. "Get off home – get some rest, and we'll face whatever tomorrow brings with fresh heads."

CHAPTER TWENTY

Theakston and Fred were unusually calm when Smith went inside his house. The dogs clearly sensed that he wasn't feeling too great and they gave him a rather gentle greeting.

"It's alright, boys," Smith said to the rotund Bull Terrier and the grotesque Pug. "I'll be right as rain after a good night's sleep. Where are the girls?"

Right on cue the front door opened, and Laura and Fran came in with Lucy. The girls ran straight upstairs.

"You're home early," Lucy said. "Are you alright – you don't look well."

"Migraine," Smith said. "It wasn't as bad as some of them."

"What time will mum be home?"

"She shouldn't be long," Smith said.

"Are you officially back at work?"

"Apparently so."

"It's about time. What are your plans for food?"

"I hadn't thought that far ahead," Smith said.

"Darren made a casserole," Lucy said. "And it's more than enough to feed all of us."

"Darren? I didn't know he could cook."

"He's been learning, and he's getting quite good. We can bring it round later. It just needs warming up."

"That sounds great. I'll let you know when Erica gets home."

"Are you trying to get rid of me?"

"Of course not," Smith said. "I just imagined you had things to do."

"Something is bothering you, and it's not just the migraine. I know that pained look."

"Let's sit somewhere more comfortable," Smith said.

He suggested they sit in the living room, forgetting all about the boxes he and Darren had left there earlier.

"What happened in here?" Lucy asked. "It looks like someone broke in and dumped a load of old boxes in here."

"Me and Darren got them down from the loft," Smith told her. "I'm hoping there's some stuff from my time studying law in there. Something that's relevant to the case we're working on. Will you give me a hand shifting them out of the way? Whitton will skin me alive if she sees the mess."

It didn't take long – ten minutes later the boxes were stacked against one of the walls.

"Out with it," Lucy said. "What's got you so worked up?"

"It's this case we're working on," Smith said.

"The murdered students?"

"News travels fast. We've got two dead women, both of whom are studying law at the university. The crime scenes are identical, right down to the last detail and it's very obvious that the same perpetrator carried out both murders."

"How were they killed?" Lucy asked. "Or can't you talk about that."

"It'll come out sooner or later," Smith said. "Both women were strangled with a rope. Strands of hemp rope were recovered from the scene of the second murder."

"Do you have any suspects?"

"One," Smith said. "A very likely one. He's a professor of law, he was well acquainted with both women, and he's confessed to killing them."

"Where's the problem?"

"I think he's playing some kind of game. He confessed to two murders, but the confession cannot be used against him because it wasn't done on the record, and it will boil down to his word against the person he confessed to. And we now know that he has an alibi for at least one of the murders."

"Interesting."

"I'm glad you think so," Smith said. "To complicate matters further we found CCTV footage of him buying an identical length of rope to the one used, and when we searched his property, the rope was there in plain view. Everything about this investigation has been too convenient. And the confusion he's thrown into the mix with the confession and subsequent alibi has got us all baffled."

"It does sound unusual. You say he's a professor of law?"

"He was my professor of law back when I was doing the degree, and the man is a highly respected academic. I haven't been able to figure out why he's doing this."

"You will," Lucy said. "You always do."

"This one feels different," Smith said. "I'm starting to wonder if I'm going to meet my match in Professor Wild. He knows more about the law than anyone I've ever met, and if this game of his really is something to do with committing murder and getting away with it, I don't think we're equipped to deal with it."

The door opened and Laura and Fran came in. Smith noticed that Laura's jumper was back to front again. She'd gone through a stage where she preferred to wear her jumpers inside out or back to front and for a while she'd started to dress properly, but she'd clearly decided that it was more fun this way.

"What's for tea?" she said.

"Darren's made a casserole," Lucy said. "You were there when he was making it."

"That thing with carrots and weird turnips?"

"They're called Swedes," Lucy said. "You'll enjoy it."

"Yuck," Fran offered.

"Can we watch television?" Laura said.

"Sure," Smith said. "I'm going outside for a smoke anyway."

"Focus on why he's doing it," Lucy said.

Smith smiled. He was getting advice on murder from a seventeen-year-old, and she was quoting him word for word.

"I'll give it some serious thought," he said.

CHAPTER TWENTY ONE

"Hello."

It was the third time Professor Wild had tried to get the attention of someone in the custody suite and once again he was met with silence. When he was brought in a few hours earlier he'd been asked if he required the services of a legal representative, and he'd politely declined. Sergeant Jack Finch had been warned about the professor of law, and he'd passed on the warnings to Sergeant Bill Plant when he arrived to relieve him in the custody suite. The duty sergeant had been briefed and told to be on his guard. This was no ordinary prisoner, and everything had to be done carefully. One mistake could cost them dearly.

When Professor Wild was brought in, Sergeant Plant made sure he was not left alone for one second. He'd discussed the details of the arrest with DS Bridge – he was the arresting officer and determined that the evidence they'd uncovered warranted detention. The CCTV footage of Professor Wild purchasing the hemp rope, and the discovery of a third of that rope inside his house more than justified holding him for the maximum time allowed, in accordance with the law.

Professor Wild was then searched, and his belongings were signed for and stored. His fingerprints were taken, and he was asked if he would agree to submit a DNA sample.

"I'd rather not," he'd replied.

Sergeant Plant hadn't pressed the matter. The professor was booked in and escorted to the holding cell. He was offered refreshments, and he'd declined these too. The duty sergeant was satisfied that every part of the booking in process had been carried out to the letter. His job had been carried out, and the baton had now been passed to the detectives in the employ of York Police.

"Hello," Professor Wild shouted. "I need to speak to someone."

"They're no more than suckling pigs, mate."

Professor Wild had been placed in the same cell where Smith had slept off his migraine earlier, and he had the pleasure of piglet man as a neighbour. "They don't train them like they used to. Straight out of school, some of them are and you know what schoolkids are like these days. Times have changed. What are you in for?"

"Perverting the course of justice," Professor Wild said.

"Whatever the fuck that means. Solidarity, brother."

Sergeant Plant appeared on the other side of the cell.

"Is there something you need?" he asked Professor Wild.

"I imagine moving me away from the delusional fool next door would be too much to ask for?" the professor said.

"I'm afraid so."

"Then perhaps you could arrange medical assistance."

"Are you not feeling too good? Was it something you ate?"

"It's nothing of the sort," Professor Wild said. "Are you a doctor?"

"No, I'm not."

"Then I suggest you find someone who is."

"It might take a while."

"I'm not going anywhere. And while I wait, I would like to make a phone call, if I may. I'm entitled to a phone call, and I don't recall being given the option when I was brought in. I expect you were caught up in the moment."

"I'm not scared of you," Sergeant Plant said.

"I wouldn't expect you to be."

"I don't know what your game is, but I've been doing this a long time, and I've come across worse than you – much worse."

"I would really like to see a doctor now," Professor Wild said. "And perhaps, that phone call."

"Wait here," Sergeant Plant said and started to laugh. "Sorry, it's an old duty sergeant joke."

"He should do stand-up," piglet man said.

"Please stop talking," Professor Wild said.

"There's no need to be rude. I'm only trying to be friendly. You haven't even asked what I'm doing here."

"I imagine you broke the law, and you were caught."

"I give up. You and that Hitler duty sergeant should consider forming a double act. I'll be out of here in the morning – I get the feeling that you're not going to be so lucky."

"You'd be surprised," Professor Wild said. "I'll be leaving this cell before the clock strikes midnight."

"We'll see."

He sat back down on the bed and stretched his arms. The ache in his chest told him that he still had time. After a brief internal debate, he started the breathing exercises the doctor had suggested. He closed his eyes and focused all his attention on the deep breaths he took. He visualised the lungsful of oxygen as they entered the bloodstream and made their way around the body.

Breathe in, he told himself. *Count to five and let the air out slowly.*

He repeated this ten times and concentrated on breathing normally again.

The first angina attack had struck when Professor Wild was driving home after a long day at the university three years ago. He'd managed to find a place to stop the car and immediately called an ambulance. He thought he was having a heart attack. The tightness in his chest was like no pain he'd ever experienced before and when his throat became constricted, he was worried that he was going to die, right there in the car park of the local Sainsburys. The pain spread until he could feel it in his teeth and temples and then, just as soon as it had arrived it was gone, leaving a dull ache in its wake.

After explaining the symptoms to the paramedics and feeling somewhat stupid, he was checked over and taken to hospital, where the doctor who treated him immediately diagnosed angina. After a lecture about his unhealthy lifestyle, he was told how to recognise the early warning signs, and prescribed medication to prevent further attacks. He was also advised to keep some nitroglycerin at hand at all times, in case of surprise attacks. Professor Wild had followed the doctor's advice – he'd cut down on his alcohol intake and started eating healthier foods, and he made sure he had some nitroglycerin on his person at all times.

This time was no different, but the medication was now locked away with the rest of his possessions in a locker in the custody suite. Professor Wild knew he was playing a dangerous game here, but this was a necessary part of it. The card he was about to play was an essential one. And when Sergeant Plant returned to inform him that the doctor was on his way, and he was allowed to make a phone call, Professor Wild allowed himself to be escorted to the telephone at the end of the row of cells. He wasn't planning on phoning a family member or a friend. He hadn't changed his mind about legal representation – he dialled the number he knew off by heart. It was the mobile number of the crime correspondent of the Daily Mail. Edwina George had been waiting for the call, but Professor Wild knew that what he was about to give her was worth the wait.

CHAPTER TWENTY TWO

If Smith thought he was going to ease into the next day at work with a coffee from the canteen, followed by a cigarette in the car park he was going to be sorely disappointed. He and Whitton were pounced on the moment they set foot inside the station. DI Smyth looked like he'd been waiting for them, and he was not a happy man.

"Follow me," he said and walked down the corridor in the direction of his office.

Smith and Whitton had no choice but to follow him.

"We have a serious problem."

DI Smyth didn't waste any time.

Smith sat down opposite him. Whitton took the seat next to her husband.

"What's happened?" he asked.

"Herman Wild was taken to hospital last night," DI Smyth said.

"I see."

"You don't seem too concerned."

"I'm extremely concerned," Smith said. "And not for Professor Wild's health. I was half-expecting him to pull a stunt like this."

"And you didn't think to share your concerns with the rest of us?"

"There wasn't much point," Smith said. "As long as we've done everything by the book, there isn't much to worry about."

"There is everything to worry about. Professor Wild started complaining of chest pains, he asked for medical attention, and he was taken away in an ambulance as a precaution."

"I still can't see what the fuss is about," Smith said. "Hold on…"

"What is it?"

"The duty sergeant did ask him if he had any underlying health issues, didn't he?"

"Therein lies the problem. Sergeant Plant claims that he did, but Professor Wild says he didn't. And there is nothing in the paperwork that was completed when he was booked in that mentioned Professor Wild's angina. It's another case of the professor's word against Sergeant Plant's."

Smith shook his head. "It's still not a problem. Whether Herman disputes Sergeant Plant's version of events is irrelevant – he had every opportunity to read the paperwork, and if he signed his name at the bottom, he doesn't have a leg to stand on."

DI Smyth rubbed his eyes, and Smith knew straight away what he was about to say next.

"He didn't sign the fucking paperwork, did he?" Smith got there first.

"What are the implications of this?" Whitton said.

"Legally," DI Smyth said. "It probably won't go much further than a slap on the wrists for the duty sergeant. It was a blunder on Sergeant Plant's part, but it was no more than human error, and luckily for us Professor Wild's medical condition wasn't life-threatening. He suffers from angina and, in hindsight he could have simply asked Sergeant Plant to fetch the medication he'd been prescribed. It was booked in with the rest of his possessions."

"But he didn't," Smith said.

"No, he didn't."

"It's a balls-up," Smith said. "But it's a minor one."

"It would have been," DI Smyth said. "If it wasn't already streaming live on the Daily Mail's online site. No doubt it will be in print too by now."

"Fuck," Smith said.

"Precisely."

"How? How did they find out so quickly?"

"According to Sergeant Plant, Professor Wild asked to make a phone call. It's his right, and it looks like the person he called was someone from the Daily Mail. Sergeant Plant checked the call log, and when he phoned the number, someone called Edwina George picked up. She's the crime correspondent with the Mail."

"What are they saying?" Whitton said.

"In a nutshell," DI Smyth said. "A respected academic was badly mistreated at the hands of the police officers of York. He explained about his medical condition, and he wasn't given the option of medical attention when he was brought in. The professor suffered an angina attack in custody, and he nearly died."

"That's bullshit," Smith said.

"We know that," DI Smyth said. "But that's irrelevant. The story is already out there for millions of people to see."

"What's the plan?" Whitton said.

"Damage control," Smith said without thinking. "And the last time I checked, we had people especially trained to deal with shit like that. I'd quite like to get on with what I've been trained to do if that's alright."

He got to his feet.

"Not so fast," DI Smyth said.

"What?" Smith said.

"I've been summoned to a meeting with top brass," DI Smyth said. "And we are to hold back until it's decided how to proceed with this."

Smith nodded and sighed deeply. "How long are we talking about?"

"As long as it can take the officers with the pips to come up with a solution."

"Fair enough."

"Why am I smelling a rat?"

"I can't smell anything," Smith said.

"You're far too calm under the circumstances."

"How many times do I have to tell you, boss?" Smith said. "This is the all-new improved Smith. I've grown up and I've come to realise that it's pointless trying to fight a system that you can't beat. You won't object if I go and get myself a coffee from the canteen."

"Don't do anything you might regret, Smith."

"Wouldn't dream of it," Smith said. "I'll choose a decaf coffee from the machine, just to be on the safe side."

He went upstairs to the canteen and selected the strongest coffee the space age machine had to offer. He'd no sooner sat down when Bridge and DC Moore came in. They joined him at his table.

"I suppose you've heard," Bridge said.

"The boss just told me," Smith said. "I don't know what all the fuss is about. Shit like this happens all the time."

"Have you read the stuff they're saying online?" DC Moore said.

"Nope."

"It's not pretty," Bridge said. "And the comments are even worse. They're making it out like it was our fault that a frail old man nearly died in custody."

"Frail old man, my arse," Smith said.

"You haven't seen the photo they put out, Sarge," DC Moore said. "It makes the prof look like he's on death's door."

Smith sipped the coffee and smiled. It was good coffee.

"He's not going to win this game."

"He's kicked our backsides so far," DC Moore said.

"That's because he knows everything there is to know about the law, Harry," Smith said. "He's using it to hide behind, but there are limits, and he's going to reach his sooner or later."

"I wish I shared your optimism," Bridge said.

"I know a bit about the law," Smith said. "I'm not in the same league as Professor Wild, and I never will be, but we will catch him out."

"What makes you so sure?" DC Moore said.

"He might be streets ahead in the legal stakes, but he knows nothing about detection. His expertise is crime after the fact. That's how we're going to beat him – we're going to have to rethink how we work, but we will catch him out eventually."

Whitton came in with DC King.

"Drink up," Whitton said. "We've got another one."

"Another student, Sarge," DC King said. "Her name is Jackie Grant and she's one of Professor Wild's law students. Early indications suggest that she was strangled, and she has the same drawing on her stomach."

"And it looks like she was killed while Professor Wild was in police custody," Whitton added.

CHAPTER TWENTY THREE

Smith's first impression when he went inside the house was it didn't feel like this was a crime scene. If it wasn't for the white-suited forensics officers going about the motions inside number 26 Jordan Terrace, he wouldn't suspect that a serious crime had been committed there.

He took it all in. The property was an average three-bedroom terraced house in the middle of a row of identical houses. The front door opened onto a narrow hallway that ran the entire length of the property. There were two rooms on the left – one was the living room and the other was a similar sized dining room. The staircase was at the end of the hallway and upstairs were the three bedrooms. At the end of the hallway was a kitchen that opened out to a tiny back yard.

Jackie Grant had been found in the kitchen. Her housemate had come to collect some coursework after spending the night at a friend's house and she'd discovered Jackie on the floor next to the back door. She'd tried to wake her up and that's when she'd seen the welts on Jackie's neck. She called the police soon afterwards.

The SOC suit was making Smith itch, and it was an itch he was unable to scratch. He debated whether to rub up against one of the walls but decided not to. Grant Webber wouldn't thank him for erasing possible evidence. The Head of Forensics was barking orders in the kitchen. Smith pushed open the door to the living room and peeped inside.

"We haven't even started in there," Billie Jones informed him.

Webber's assistant shook her head when she spoke.

"No worries," Smith said. "What do we know so far?"

"Her name is Jackie Grant," Billie said. "The housemate found her shortly before she called it in."

"It's the same as the others, isn't it?"

"Definitely. She was strangled, and she had the same drawing on her stomach."

"Do you know if a rope was used?" Smith said.

"We don't know for certain, but it looks like it."

"Any sign of forced entry?" Smith said. "Indications of a struggle?"

"Nothing," Billie said. "It's a carbon copy of the others. There are two wine glasses on the draining board in the kitchen and both glasses have wine residue in them, so we might get lucky with those."

"She knew the person who killed her."

"I think so too. The locks on the front and back door are intact. There are no broken windows, so unless the killer got lucky and found the door open, I'd say they were acquainted."

"They were," Smith decided. "She invited them in, they shared a bottle of wine, and she was caught off guard."

"I'd better get back to work," Billie said.

"Just one more thing," Smith said.

"You need to stop saying that. That's not your line. What is it?"

"Could you scratch my back for me?"

"What?"

"This suit is itchy as hell, and I can't reach the itch."

Billie smiled and placed her hand on his back.

"Up a bit," Smith directed. "There. That's the spot. Don't be shy."

Billie scratched hard and the relief was instant.

"I hate to interrupt whatever this is." Webber had come into the hallway. "I want to show you something."

"Thanks, Billie," Smith said. "You've got good strong hands there."

She shook her head and went inside the living room."

"Do I want to know what that was all about?" Webber said.

"Not really," Smith said. "What is it you want to show me?"

He followed Webber into the kitchen. Pete Richards was taking photographs of the body on the floor. He didn't even look up when Smith and Webber came in.

"We found this upstairs," Webber pointed to something in an evidence bag on the kitchen worktop.

It was a mobile phone.

"Hopefully the tech team will be able to get something from it," Smith said.

"We've already got something from it," Webber said.

"Wasn't it locked? Jackie Grant can't be long out of her teens – surely a woman her age will have all sorts of security measures in place."

"Not only was the phone not fingerprint protected," Webber said. "It didn't require a password either."

"Sounds suspicious to me. What woman Jackie's age leaves her phone wide open?"

"That's up to you to decide. This is what I wanted to show you."

Webber managed to bring the phone to life through the plastic of the evidence bag.

"Miss Grant received a WhatsApp at just before five yesterday afternoon."

"Are you at home?" Smith read.

"And shortly after that," Webber said. "She had a missed call from the same number."

"Do we know who called her?"

"I'm coming to that," Webber said. "Whoever it was isn't in her list of contacts. And this is the interesting part. There was no further activity on the phone after that. No calls, messages, or Internet browsing. She didn't look at social media and that leads me to conclude that she was killed shortly after she received that phone call."

"I'm inclined to agree with you," Smith said. "It should be easy enough to find out who that number belongs to. Thanks, Webber."

Smith turned to go.

"I'm not finished," Webber said.

Smith turned back around. "Go on."

"We know who called her."

"Why didn't you just tell me that in the first place?" Smith said.

"Where's the fun in that? A bit of suspense never hurt anyone."

"You've become really weird in your old age," Smith said. "Out with it then."

"Billie called the number. Sometimes, that's all it takes. And the call went to voicemail. But the message on the voicemail made it clear who that number belongs to. It's your law professor. The WhatsApp and the phone call came from Herman Wild."

CHAPTER TWENTY FOUR

"We are to carry on as normal," DI Smyth said in the small conference room. "But we are to proceed with caution."

"How did you manage that?" Smith asked.

"Don't look at me. Chief Constable Cartwright was all for us keeping away from Professor Wild until such time as the madness in the press calmed down, but DCI Chalmers somehow persuaded him otherwise."

"Good old Chalmers," Smith said. "We've had a huge development. Professor Wild tried to contact Jackie Grant just before she was murdered yesterday. He sent her a message asking her if she was at home, and when she didn't reply he phoned her."

"What time was this?"

"Around five yesterday afternoon."

"That means Professor Wild has yet another beautiful alibi," DI Smyth said. "That was when we were carrying out the search of his property, shortly before he was arrested and detained. He can't possibly have killed Jackie."

"I thought we'd already established that he doesn't kill them, boss," Smith said. "Someone else carries out the dirty work, and he controls the action behind the scenes. The WhatsApp and phone call were all part of his game. He gives himself the perfect alibi and someone else moves in for the kill. We need to do a thorough forensic on his phone."

"Already set in motion," DI Smyth said. "The professor's mobile phone has been handed over to the tech team and we'll have a detailed report before the end of the day."

"Hold on," Smith said.

"Here we go," Bridge said.

"Who was the arresting officer?"

"That will be me," Bridge said.

"Did Professor Wild make a phone call while you were carrying out the search of his house?"

"It's possible."

"Did he make a phone call or not?"

"I said it's possible," Bridge said. "I wasn't with him the entire time."

"What are you thinking?" DI Smyth said to Smith.

"I'm not quite sure," Smith said.

"Forensics didn't find anything at the scene of Jackie Grant's murder to suggest that she was taken by surprise," DI Smyth said. "On the contrary. It appears that Miss Grant let her killer in, they drank some wine, and everything was fine before she was killed."

"There were two wine glasses in the kitchen," Smith said. "And the wine in the bottom hadn't quite dried. Jackie Grant's killer drank from one of those glasses. It's quite possible we'll get some prints and DNA, but without anything to compare it too, it's useless."

"We could get lucky," DC Moore said.

"We're not going to win this game by getting lucky, Harry. You know as well as I do that a wine glass is a perfect receptacle for evidence, especially when we get residue, but we're not going to get anywhere because neither the DNA nor the prints of the killer's are on file. No, this is a strategic game, and we need to play it accordingly."

"This is not a game, Smith," DI Smyth said. "Three young women are dead – this is definitely not a game."

"That's precisely what it is, boss. It's a game where the tactics have been considered well in advance. And that's why it might be worth thinking about bending the rules a bit."

"I don't like the sound of this. What did you have in mind?"

"He'll let you know when he's figured it out, sir," Bridge said.

Smith nodded. "What Bridge said."

"I've been told to inform you that there will be a press conference," DI Smyth said. "And you'll be relieved to hear that it does not concern any of us. The reason for the press conference is to dispel the guff the press has been churning out, and we will not be divulging anything about the progress of the investigation at this stage. That might change, but as of right now we will be allowed to carry on in peace."

"Leaving Professor Wild out of the equation?" DC King said.

"Unfortunately, yes," DI Smyth said.

"It doesn't matter," Smith said. "I'm sick of the sight of him anyway. We need to focus on his friends and colleagues. The person who killed those three women is not a complete stranger to him – it's someone he knows well, and it'll be someone he trusts implicitly. How soon will we have the stuff from his phone?"

"Before the end of the day," DI Smyth said. "I've already told you that."

"I just wanted to confirm it."

He felt a twinge in his head just above his left eye and he winced.

"Are you alright?" Whitton said.

"I'm perfectly fine," Smith said. "It happens sometimes when my brain is in the process of rearranging facts into some semblance or order."

"I suggest we concentrate on the friends of the victims," DI Smyth said.

"We're on the same page, boss," Smith said. "Rebecca, Sharon and Jackie knew the person who killed them. The most obvious assumption to make is the killer is someone studying law too, so I say we go the Occam's Razor route first, and if we exhaust that avenue, we look at some more bizarre hypotheses."

"Occam's Razor?" DC Moore said.

"William of Occam," Smith elaborated. "He was a monk and philosopher who advocated that the simplest solution to anything is usually the best.

Basically, it means we should choose the explanation that makes the fewest assumptions first. It was a dentist who brought this to my attention."

"What happens when we realise that this problem doesn't have a simple solution to it?" DC King said.

"We look at it from other angles," Smith said. "In my experience, it's very rare that old Occam's theory has any substance to it. Murder is rarely that simple."

"Then why bring it up in the first place, Sarge?" DC Moore wondered.

"Because if it later came out that we'd overlooked the most obvious scenario because it seemed too obvious, we would look like complete dickheads, Harry."

"Where do we stand with Professor Wild?" Bridge said. "Is he still under arrest?"

This question was addressed to DI Smyth, but Smith replied for him.

"The arrest warrant was legit. We had more than enough justification to bring him in and detain him, and he damn well knows it. No, Professor Wild won't be able to find a way to wrangle his way out of that one. And when we get the info from his phone, I know for a fact that we're going to be a step closer to putting an end to the sick game he's playing."

CHAPTER TWENTY FIVE

Emma Wilson was a plump woman with an incredibly loud voice. Smith wondered whether she was actually aware of it. Emma didn't talk – she bellowed, and he'd developed a mild headache after only a few minutes of listening to her. He'd introduced himself and DC King and they were now sitting in Emma's friend's house in Badger Hill.

"How long have you and Jackie been friends?" he asked.

"Three years," Emma said. "We clicked during Fresher's Week, and we've been friends ever since."

"That accent isn't local, is it?"

"Newcastle," Emma said. "I couldn't wait to get away from the place. York is much quieter."

Smith wondered if she was aware that York had got a whole lot louder since she'd moved there.

"Can you talk us through your movements yesterday," he said.

"What?" Emma said.

"It helps us get an idea of the timescale involved," DC King said. "When did you last see Jackie?"

"We left the house at around eight yesterday morning," Emma said.

"You left together?" Smith said.

Emma nodded. "We usually do."

"Did you walk to campus?"

Another nod. "It's only a five-minute walk."

"Are you also studying law?" DC King said.

"Maths and Computer Science. I'm a bit of a geek."

"Did you see Jackie at all in between classes?" Smith said.

"No," Emma said. "The last time I saw her was when we got to the campus. That was about a quarter past eight."

"You told the officers first on the scene that you didn't come home last night," Smith said.

"I stayed over with a friend," Emma said.

"We're going to need the name of the friend," DC King said.

"What on earth for?"

"It's just routine," Smith told her. "Is it a boyfriend?"

"I don't have a boyfriend."

"So, it's just a friend?"

"Am I being accused of something?"

"Not at this stage," Smith said. "Did you ever hear Jackie talk about Professor Wild?"

"The name rings a bell."

"Do you know if he and Jackie were close?"

"What?"

"Did you ever get the impression that Jackie and Professor Wild were more than just student and professor?"

"Of course not."

"Are you sure?" Smith said.

"He's a law professor," Emma said. "And Jackie is a third-year student. What else is there to make of it? Besides, Jackie has a serious boyfriend. She's been seeing him for over a year."

"Do you have a name for us?" DC King said.

"Barry," Emma said. "Barry Gilbert."

"Is he also a student?" Smith said.

"He's a mechanic. Jackie's parents hate him."

"Do you have his contact details?"

"I don't have much to do with him," Emma said. "But he works at a garage on Monk Street so you shouldn't have too much problem finding him."

"Did you tell anybody that you would be spending the night at a friend's house?" Smith said.

"A few people," Emma said.

"We're going to need their contact details," DC King told her.

"I'm not really sure who I told."

"Then you'll need to think hard about it," Smith said. "It's possible that whoever killed Jackie knew she would be at home alone, so we need to talk to anyone who was aware of it."

"None of my friends would do something like this."

"You'd be surprised."

Smith's mobile phone started to ring. It was the ringtone for DI Smyth.

"I need to take this," Smith said. "Excuse me."

He left the house and took out his cigarettes. The phone went silent and then the opening bars of *Oliver's Army* sounded again. Smith lit a cigarette and answered it.

"Boss."

"Where are you?" DI Smyth said.

"Still busy with Jackie Grant's housemate. What's up?"

"Did you ask her about Professor Wild?"

"Of course," Smith said. "She didn't get the impression that Jackie was close to him. Why do you ask?"

"Because Bridge and DC King found out something interesting about Rebecca Stone. According to an ex-boyfriend, there was definitely something going on with Rebecca and Professor Wild."

"Sharon Atlee's boyfriend was convinced of it too, wasn't he?"

"He was," DI Smyth said. "And it's a link we need to explore further."

"I'll see what else I can find out. We've got the name of Jackie's boyfriend, and we'll be speaking to him later. Any news about Professor Wild's mobile phone?"

"Nothing yet. I'll see if I can speed things up a bit."

They ended the call and Smith finished his cigarette. He didn't go straight back inside the house. He thought about what DI Smyth had told him. If Professor Wild was in a relationship with the first two victims, what did it actually mean in terms of the investigation? Smith was convinced that the law professor was involved in the murders, but he still couldn't come up with a satisfactory explanation for it, especially if he was close to the victims. What possible reason could he have for wanting them dead?

Smith thought back to his time at university, and he recalled Professor Wild as something of a livewire. He was a bundle of energy and his passion for the law bordered on the obsessive. These memories of the man were at odds with everything that had happened in the past few days. Why would a man who holds the law in such high regard suddenly decide to disregard everything he once held dear? It was a paradox, and Smith hated paradoxes.

"Something happened," he voiced his thoughts. "Something happened very recently that caused you to become disillusioned with the law." Smith decided that this was definitely something to explore, and he didn't think he was going to get any answers from the friends of the victims. He went back inside the house and rejoined DC King and Emma Wilson in the living room.

"Sorry about that," he said. "Where were we?"

"Jackie and Professor Wild," DC King refreshed his memory.

"I'm sure I would have known if Jackie was seeing her professor," Emma said.

"Maybe not," Smith said. "Even though it's perfectly legal, surely a relationship like that would be frowned upon in the law department. There's a good chance they would have kept things discreet, especially if she had a boyfriend."

"Jackie was an open book," Emma said. "She couldn't keep secrets."

"You'd be surprised. We're going to need a list of Jackie's friends."

"She didn't have many," Emma said. "She was determined to focus on her studies. She got a bit behind at one stage, but she was keen to get back on track. She even cut back on the time she spent with Barry."

"Why did she get behind?" DC King said.

"Why do you think? Barry Gilbert."

"The relationship was serious then?" Smith said.

"Very."

"We'll definitely be speaking to Mr Gilbert."

"They actually broke up a month ago," Emma said.

"Do you know who ended the relationship?" DC King said.

"What does it matter?"

"It matters," Smith said.

"It was Jackie. With a bit of pressure from her parents. And I don't blame them."

"What do you mean?" DC King said.

"Jackie was acing the degree before Barry came along," Emma said. "She was always at the top of the class, and then her grades plummeted. She could have been a hotshot lawyer."

"Interesting," Smith said.

"Why is it interesting?"

Smith didn't reply.

"But they got back together?" he said instead.

"It happens," Emma said. "I did warn her against it."

"Why would you do that?" DC King said.

"Because I've been there, done that and got the T-Shirt. Relationships seldom work out when a couple have got back together after a break."

"You don't scare easily, do you?" Smith said.

"Excuse me?" Emma said.

"You've just come home to find your friend dead. She was murdered, and most people would be in a state of shock, but you seem to be taking it in your stride."

"I don't know what you mean."

"No," Smith said. "I don't imagine you do. I think we've covered everything. If you could get us that list of people we've spoken about, we'll leave you in peace."

CHAPTER TWENTY SIX

Smith was confused. He was also a bit annoyed. He'd decided to make a slight detour on the way back to the station and when he was directed to the hospital room where Professor Wild had spent the night, he was surprised to see PC Griffin sitting on a chair outside the door.

"What the hell are you doing here?" Smith didn't hold back.

"Orders, Sarge," PC Griffin said.

"Orders from where?"

"Superintendent Smyth insisted that someone stay with Professor Wild while he's here at the hospital."

"Since when did the Super have a say in what happens in a murder investigation?"

"Sarge?"

"Never mind," Smith said. "I just need a quick chat with him."

"That's not allowed Sarge."

Smith looked at the piggy-eyed PC, and he had a sudden urge to blacken one of those pinprick eyes. He decided against it.

"I'm going to speak to the professor, and there's fuck all you can do to stop me."

"I've been given orders that nobody is allowed in apart from the medical staff here."

"And what would happen if I went straight in?"

"I'd have to report it, Sarge. I'm just doing what I've been told to do."

Smith nodded. "We'll see about that."

He walked down the corridor and took out his phone. He called DI Smyth, and the call was answered immediately.

"Since when did we use up resources to babysit a man who is no more a flight risk than a one-armed bloke in a wheelchair?"

"I have no idea what you're talking about," DI Smyth said.

"Professor Wild. I'm at the hospital and PC Griffin is standing guard outside his room. What the hell is going on?"

"What are you doing at the hospital?"

"I just wanted to ask the prof a few questions. That's irrelevant."

"It's extremely relevant. The man is a suspect in a triple murder – you of all people ought to know that everything that involves him has to be done by the book."

"You still haven't answered my question."

"I wasn't aware that you'd asked one."

"Why is Griffin suddenly Professor Wild's bodyguard?" Smith said.

"I wasn't notified of it. Who authorised it?"

"Uncle Jeremy. What the fuck has this got to do with him?"

"Ah, that."

"Go on."

"It's probably because of the press conference," DI Smyth said. "I only got the bare minimum, but it looks like the press conference was all about expressing regret for making the mistake with Professor Wild, and the public were assured that he would receive fair treatment going forward."

"Are you even listening to yourself, boss?" Smith said. "You said it yourself - the man is a suspect in a triple murder, and we'll treat him accordingly. He's a dangerous man, and I'm not going to handle him with kid gloves because the general public might think York Police are being too harsh. Fuck that."

"I want you back here." DI Smyth said. "Right now."

"At least let me speak to one of the doctors first."

"Make it quick."

Smith ended the call and went to find someone who could help him. He was told by one of the people working in reception that Professor Wild was under the care of Dr Doreen Hill, and she was about to finish her shift. The receptionist told Smith that he would probably find her in her office, and he gave him directions. Smith thanked him and made his way there.

Dr Hill was a grey-haired woman with friendly eyes. Smith explained who he was and promised not to keep her for too long.

"I appreciate that you're about to head home," he said. "I just need to ask you a few questions about a patient who was admitted last night – Herman Wild."

"I'm in no rush," Dr Hill said. "Last night was relatively quiet and I'm still wide awake. Herman Wild, you say?"

"He was brought in complaining of chest pains," Smith said. "He'd been arrested, and he started to feel ill while in custody."

"That one is a strange one."

"How do you mean?"

"According to the paramedics who attended," Dr Hill said. "The patient told them he had a history of angina, but that's not what the ECG told us."

"I'm not following you."

"We did an ECG as soon as he was admitted. It's standard procedure."

"And there were no abnormalities with his heart?"

"Even a resting ECG can show up evidence of previous cardiac problems that may be related to angina," Dr Hill said. "And, as the patient told the paramedics that he was suffering an angina attack when he was brought in, we would expect to see ECG changes such as ST-segment depression and T-wave inversion, but there was no evidence of this."

"What does that mean?" Smith said.

"It means that either the patient defied all medical convention and suddenly developed a reversal of all the damage done to his heart, or he was misinformed about the angina."

"He had medication," Smith remembered. "Nitro something."

"Nitroglycerin," Dr Hill said. "Whether he had the medication or not is irrelevant – he didn't need it. I've treated many angina patients, and I can tell you that your prisoner isn't one of them."

Smith thanked her and left the office. He made his way back to Professor Wild's hospital room. After ignoring PC Griffin's protests, he pushed open the door and walked over to the man in the bed.

It had been nearly two decades since he'd last seen the professor of law, but Smith could still picture him in his mind's eye. And even the passing of twenty years couldn't change someone as drastically as this. The man staring up at him with frightened eyes was definitely not Professor Wild.

CHAPTER TWENTY SEVEN

"The professor has succeeded in making fools of us once more."
DI Smyth had just returned from an emergency meeting, and it was clear from his flushed face that it hadn't been pleasant.

"The man who was arrested following the search of Professor Wild's house is his older brother, Roger."

"He looks nothing like the professor," Smith said. "How did someone not twig?"

"I really don't know," DI Smyth said. "It appears that luck was on Professor Wild's side. Bridge was the arresting officer."

"I'd never met the bloke before the search of his house," Bridge said. "It's not my fault."

"Nobody is saying it is," DI Smyth said. "Professor Wild's arrival at the station also happened to coincide with a shift change in the custody suite. Sergeant Finch was relieved by Sergeant Plant, and he too had never met the professor."

"What about PC Griffin?" Bridge said. "He'd met the prof before, so why didn't he smell a rat when he was told to babysit the man at the hospital?"

"I asked him," Smith said. "And he never went inside the room."

"This is unbelievable," Whitton said. "You couldn't make stuff like this up."

"Has the real Professor Wild been picked up?" Smith asked.

"He's been apprehended, and he denies all knowledge of his brother's antics."

"Of course he does," Smith said. "We're going to be crucified when this gets out. We can't even arrest the right fucking suspect."

"Surely we can have the brother for wasting police time," DC Moore said. "That's something at least."

"Really?" Smith said. "All that will achieve is a load of paperwork for a paltry result. Professor Wild planned this – I know he did."

"We all know that to be true," DI Smyth said. "But we can't prove it."

"Surely there's something we can pin on the bastard," DC Moore said. "Professor Wild, I mean. And why would the brother even go along with it? Who in their right mind lets themselves get arrested for something they haven't done?"

"What did the brother say to you at the hospital?" Bridge asked Smith.

"He feigned confusion," Smith said. "He claimed not to know what was going on, but he was lying. He knew exactly what he was doing. He was the one who called the hack at the Daily Mail, so that proves he was well aware of everything that was happening."

"The arrest was carried out properly," Bridge said. "Herman Wild's name was clearly stated, so why did Roger Wild accept it? We must be able to charge him with more than just wasting police time."

"And how did the hospital not spot it?" DC King said. "Don't they have to get the details of their patients?"

"We won't dwell on that, Kerry," DI Smyth said. "What's done is done, and we need to move forward."

"We have bigger fish to fry," Smith said. "We'll nail the brother when we've got the bigger fish. Professor Wild is our priority, not his brother."

"I hate to put an even bigger dampener on things," DI Smyth said. "But I have more bad news. The tech team are finished with Professor Wild's mobile phone and there were no calls or WhatsApps to Jackie Grant yesterday. In fact, there's no correspondence between the two of them at all."

"How is that even possible?" DC Moore said. "Billie called the number, and she got Professor Wild's voicemail."

"He's got two phones, Harry," Smith said.

"Oh, right."

"And the phone he used to send the message and make the call is unaccounted for. We should have expected nothing less. A man like Professor Wild knows better than to leave such obvious evidence behind."

"This case is really starting to get on my nerves," Bridge said. "How do we stop a bloke like this?"

"By playing dirty," Smith said.

"We do this in accordance with the law," DI Smyth said.

"That's what we've been doing all along, boss," Smith said. "And how's that going for us? The man is making a mockery of the law. We need to play a move he won't be expecting us to make."

"What did you have in mind?"

"I'll think of something."

The room fell silent for a moment. The only sound was the deep sighs of the detectives around the table.

"We need a dirty tackle," DC Moore said eventually.

"A what?" Smith said.

"You keep saying that this is a game," DC Moore said. "And it's clear that playing by the rules isn't working, so we play a dirty tackle when the referee isn't looking. It worked for Vinnie Jones and the Crazy Gang back in the day."

"Never heard of them."

"Wimbledon," DC Moore explained. "In the late 80s they were notorious. They won the FA Cup, and some of the tactics they used were a bit unorthodox."

"You weren't even born in the late eighties," Bridge said.

"What's that got to do with anything?" DC Moore said. "I wasn't born in 1566, but I know about the great fire of London."

"1666," Whitton corrected.

"What?"

"The great fire of London was in 1666. I would have thought a Londoner would know that."

"That's enough," DI Smyth said. "Can we carry on?"

"I just think that using a tactic from the beautiful game might be a good play right now," DC Moore said.

"Football?" Smith guessed.

"What else, Sarge?"

"I've never seen the point of football," Smith said. "But you're on the right track. We're not going to catch Professor Wild by playing by the rules, so we need to do something drastic."

"Out of the question," DI Smyth said. "This is exactly the sort of thing that Professor Wild is waiting to exploit. We will beat him, and we will do that by sticking to the guidelines outlined in the law. This is not up for debate."

Smith got to his feet.

"I'm going home."

"You'll leave when I say you can leave," DI Smyth said. "We still have a lot to get through."

"I have a pile of boxes in my living room," Smith said. "And there might be something in there that can help us. I kept all my coursework from the law degree, and there was one particular seminar that I recall clearly. We discussed how feasible it is to get away with a crime and still operate within the bounds of the law. I've been putting it off, but I'm in the mood to sift through the boxes now."

"Do you need some help?" Whitton offered.

"I'll be better off doing it on my own," Smith said. "There is something in those boxes that's going to shed some light on what's been happening."

CHAPTER TWENTY EIGHT

The first thing Smith did was curse himself for not labelling the boxes. And when he opened the first one, he realised that this was going to be a mammoth task. The paperwork inside hadn't been put into any kind of order, and it dawned on him that he was probably going to have to go through the whole lot to find what he was looking for.

It was starting to get dark outside and Smith had to turn on the light inside the living room. The dogs had made themselves comfortable on the sofa and the snorts from the Bull Terrier and the Pug were somewhat distracting. Smith decided that he needed some music to inspire him. He selected a CD he hadn't listened to in a while – Thin Lizzy's *Live and Dangerous* and he turned up the volume. Soon afterwards, the guitars of *Jailbreak* filled the room and drowned out the snoring dogs.

Three boxes in, and Smith thought he'd got a lucky break. The paper was dated the sixth of March 2002, and the subject title was *Travesties of justice and flaws in the legal system*. After reading the handwritten first paragraph, Smith sighed. This wasn't what he was looking for. The paper focused on real-life cases, mostly in America where the justice system had failed.

The classic live album had reached the fourth track and Phil Lynott was singing about *Rosalie* and Smith had only finished with four of the boxes. He discarded the corporate law stuff and the theses and dissertations pertaining to financial law and focused only on the criminal law papers. It occurred to him that he couldn't recall writing some of it, and if it wasn't for his unmistakable scrawl on the pages he would have doubted whether he was even the author of a lot of it.

Six boxes down, and Smith needed a cigarette. A beer would probably make things more bearable too. He got one from the fridge, opened it and took a long drink straight from the bottle. He went outside and lit a cigarette. He could hear the music inside the house, and he closed his eyes when his favourite song on the album came on. It was a slow track, and Smith had never been a big fan of love songs but the long guitar solo in *Still in love with you* was one of the finest examples of fitting a solo to a song that Smith had ever heard.

If he'd hoped for some inspiration from the nicotine and the music, he was going to be disappointed. He still couldn't recall when the seminar he was interested in had taken place and it was annoying him. He knew that it had to have been some time towards the end of his degree, possibly not long before he decided to quit, but the exact timeline eluded him.

It came to him as he was getting another beer out of the fridge. *Don't Believe a Word* was blasting out of the speakers and for some bizarre reason it brought back a memory. A few of Professor Wild's students were discussing some aspect of the law or other in a pub close to the campus and the man himself happened to come in. He joined them at their table and the discussion continued.

The drinks flowed and somehow the conversation turned to topics that were definitely not on the curriculum for the law degree. Smith couldn't remember exactly what they spoke about, but one memory became absolutely clear. It was decided there in the pub that a special study group would be set up. The students invited were a select few and it would operate outside of university time. The seminar regarding getting away with murder and still acting in accordance with the law wasn't part of the syllabus – it was an extra-curricular thing, and Smith didn't think he would find any reference to it in any of the boxes in the living room.

The front door opened, and Whitton came into the house with Laura and Fran in tow. Smith turned down the music and glared at the boxes on the floor. It had been a pointless exercise and a waste of his time. He told Whitton all about it.

"None of the stuff we discussed in that seminar was documented, and I'm finding it hard to remember much of it."

"What about the other people in the group?" Whitton said. "Do you remember who they were?"

"There were three or four of us," Smith said. "But I've lost touch with all of them. Damn it, I really thought I'd get some answers from those boxes."

Laura came into the kitchen with something in her hands. She held up the trophy and grinned.

"This is so cool," she said. "There are loads of them in there."

"They were your great-grandfather's," Smith told her. "I never met him, but I heard all about him."

"What did he win them for?" Fran asked.

"Boxing."

"Awesome," Laura said. "My great-grandfather was a boxer."

"What's a great-grandfather?" Fran said.

"He was my grandfather," Smith said. "Which makes him Laura's great-grandfather."

"And when you have kids," Whitton said to Laura. "That'll make him their great-great-grandfather."

"Yuk." It was Fran. "Kids?"

Smith laughed.

"What's for tea?" Laura said.

"Steak and ale pie," Smith replied without thinking.

"It's a school night, Jason," Whitton reminded him.

"What's your point?"

"We can't take the girls to the pub on a weeknight," Whitton said. "They have school in the morning."

"I'll make sure they don't drink too much," Smith said. "Come on – it's still early, so we can be back before their bedtime."

"Please," Laura said. "I want to see Marge."

"Me too," Fran said.

"Looks like you've been outvoted," Smith said to Whitton. "We'll make it an early one. I can almost taste that pie."

CHAPTER TWENTY NINE

Smith was unaware that while he was getting ready to go out, a press conference was about to get underway. It was the second one in the space of a few hours, but the men and women in the bigger offices at York Police HQ had deemed it absolutely necessary. The debacle with Professor Wild had caused shockwaves far and wide and if ever there was a time where damage control was essential, now was that time.

It had been decided that someone from the investigative team should be present at the press conference and DI Smyth had drawn that particular short straw. Smith's name had come up and been discounted just as quickly. This was a delicate situation, and Smith was not known for his subtlety. DI Smyth knew that Smith wouldn't give a hoot anyway – if there was one thing he despised more than anything else it was press conferences.

PC Neil Walker nodded to DI Smyth and told him that it was almost time. The press liaison officer had suggested they keep it as brief as possible, and refrain from giving too much away. The focus needed to be on dispelling the rumours that York Police had dropped the ball in a spectacular manner, and the conduct of its officers was verging on the incompetent. PC Walker had also advised DI Smyth not to mention Professor Wild by name. This was extremely important. The last thing they needed was a defamation suit on top of everything else.

"He's got a contact at The Daily Mail," DI Smyth said. "He's been feeding them information as it happens. His brother used the telephone in the custody suite to call some of it in, for Pete's sake."

"We won't mention that," PC Walker said. "In fact, don't talk about the professor at all if you can help it."

"I feel that we have to give the public something pertaining to the investigation. Why else am I here?"

"Give them the usual spiel, sir. We are following up on a number of leads, we have a suspect in custody, and we are confident that we will be bringing the investigation to a satisfactory conclusion soon."

"That's a lie," DI Smyth said. "We all know that Professor Wild is involved in this, but we can't prove a thing. And he damn well knows it."

"It'll be fine. One more thing."

"Go on."

"Don't let Superintendent Smyth take the stage for too long."

"That's a given," DI Smyth said. "Wish me luck."

The large conference room was packed. DI Smyth recognised some of the faces but the majority of the people there were strangers to him. He took a seat next to his uncle and took a few deep breaths.

"Oliver," Superintendent Smyth said.

"Sir," DI Smyth said. "Has the press liaison officer briefed you?"

"Nobody in this building knows more about press conferences than me, Oliver."

"I appreciate that, sir," DI Smyth said. "But this one is going to be a tough one. We can't afford to make a single blunder. We're under the microscope like we've never been before."

"I am aware of that."

"Just be careful about what you say."

Superintendent Smyth wasn't allowed to make a comment on this. PC Walker's voice over the loudspeakers told them the press conference had started. After a brief introduction, the press liaison officer handed the floor over to Superintendent Smyth to give a short statement about the unfounded rumours in the press.

"In the interests of absolute transparency," he began. "I would like to reassure the men and women of this city that some of the things you may have read in the press have been blown out of proportion. There were some minor incidents where mistakes were made and protocol was not followed but those kinks have been swiftly ironed out, and the people responsible have been reprimanded. I can state categorically that it's business as normal in the halls of York Police. I'll now hand you over to the lead detective in the investigation. DI Smyth will give you an update on the progress thus far. Thank you."

DI Smyth was expecting a barrage of questions, but it didn't materialise. He was relieved, and he psyched himself up for what he was about to say. "Good evening. Thank you for coming. I'll take any questions you may have at the end, and I'll try to keep this brief. On Sunday, the body of a young woman was found in Heworth. I can tell you that she'd been strangled. On Tuesday, another young woman was found strangled and this morning a third victim was discovered. We believe the same perpetrator is responsible for all three murders. We have been working tirelessly – we're following up on a number of leads, and we have every confidence that we will bring the case to a swift conclusion. Any questions?"

"Is it true that you have a suspect in custody?" a man in the front row shouted.

"I can't comment on the details of that at this stage," DI Smyth said. "But I can confirm that we do indeed have a suspect in custody."

"The victims were all students," a woman's voice said. "Is that correct?"

"They were all studying law at the university," DI Smyth confirmed.

"Do the women at the university need to be concerned?" the same woman asked.

"No," DI Smyth said. "I don't see any reason to panic unnecessarily. All three murders took place off campus."

"Your suspect is a law professor, isn't he?" another woman said. "Edwina George, Daily Mail."

"As I said, I can't comment on that. If there's nothing else…"

"Will Professor Wild be pursuing an unlawful arrest case?" Edwina asked.

"I think we can wrap things up there," DI Smyth said. "A press release will be issued shortly. Thank you again for coming."

CHAPTER THIRTY

Smith savoured the taste of the Theakston beer. It really was one of life's pleasures and he never tired of it. He took another sip and looked around the pub. The Hog's Head was quiet – it was a Thursday evening in early December and fewer than half of the tables were occupied. This boded well – Smith was hungry, and he knew there wouldn't be much of a wait for the steak and ale pie he was looking forward to eating.

He'd left his mobile phone at home. He'd debated whether that was such a good idea but when the screen started to flash to tell him that the battery was almost dead, Smith reckoned it was a sign to tell him to forget about the investigation for a few hours.

"This is nice," he said to Whitton.

They were alone at the table. Laura and Fran had gone to see if Marge needed any help in the kitchen. The girls had become close to the elderly landlord of the pub, and she didn't mind having them around. And there was always the promise of ice cream after Laura and Fran had done a few jobs in the kitchen.

"I've been thinking," Whitton said.

"I always get a bit nervous when you say that," Smith said.

"You said that the elite group Professor Wild set up operated as an extra-curricular thing."

"It was all done off campus," Smith said.

"What if you went through the records from your time there to see if any of the names ring any bells."

"It's worth a try," Smith said.

"You have a strange memory, and I'm sure if you look through the records you'll recognise some of the people from back then."

"I'll give it some thought," Smith said, and quickly added, "tomorrow."

The girls came back. Marge wasn't far behind them.

"I'm going to have to put them on the payroll soon," she said.

"Isn't that slightly illegal?" Whitton said.

"Marge is kidding," Smith said. "I hope the girls haven't been getting in the way."

"Not at all. The food will be ten minutes. I'd better get back to the kitchen."

"Thanks, Marge," Smith said.

The waiter brought another round of drinks and Smith sank half of his beer in one go. The door to the pub opened and a man and a woman came in. The woman wasn't someone Smith knew but the man was very familiar. It was DC Moore, and he was dressed in a way Smith had never seen him dress before. The detective from London was wearing a pair of black jeans, a smart blue shirt, and a suit jacket.

"That looks serious," Smith said to Whitton.

"I wonder who she is," she said.

"Someone Harry wants to impress," Smith said. "He's seen us."

DC Moore seemed reluctant to come over at first. He hesitated for a moment and then he and the woman walked over to Smith's table.

"Harry," Smith said. "I don't often see you in here."

"We wanted somewhere quiet," DC Moore said.

"Are you going to introduce us?" Whitton said.

"What? Oh, this is Lorraine. Lorraine these are two of my work colleagues?"

"Detectives?"

It was one word, but it was enough for Smith to detect the southern accent.

"She's from Hendon," DC Moore said. "North London."

"Good to meet you," Smith said.

"Likewise," Lorraine said.

"You work at the hemp place, don't you?" Whitton said.

"Hemporium," Lorraine said. "It's not a dream job but I like it."

"We'll leave you in peace," DC Moore said.

He took Lorraine's arm and guided her away from the table. Smith thought he looked like he couldn't get away fast enough, and he noticed that DC Moore chose the table furthest away from theirs.

The food arrived and Smith took a moment to admire the pie on his plate before digging in.

"You really do take those pies too seriously," Whitton told him.

"Nonsense," Smith said. "When you have something as exquisite as one of Marge's steak and ale pies there is a ritual you need to follow to fully enjoy the moment."

"It's a pie, Dad," Laura said.

"When you're old enough I'll explain it to you," Smith said. "Life does not get much better than this."

He was halfway through the pie when the sound of Whitton's phone stopped him in his tracks.

"Don't answer it," he said, with a mouthful of pastry.

Whitton ignored him. She took out her phone and looked at the screen.

"Is it work?" Smith asked.

"It's my mum," Whitton said.

"Can I talk to her?" Laura asked.

"Let me see what she wants first," Whitton said.

She got up from the table and headed for the door.

She was gone for quite a while. Smith finished his pie and ordered another pint of Theakston. He kept one eye on Whitton, and he sensed from the expression on her face that something was wrong. Her face was full of concern and there was none of the animated hand gestures she often displayed when she was talking to her mother on the phone. Something was definitely wrong. She ended the call and returned to the table.

Whitton sat back down.

"Do you want to see if Marge needs any help in the kitchen?" she said to Laura and Fran.

"There might be some ice cream in it for you," Smith added.

The girls were out of their seats in a flash.

"What is it?" Smith said. "Are your parents alright?"

"It's my dad," Whitton said. "Mum's worried about him. He's not been eating much and he's losing weight like crazy. You know how much my dad loves his food."

"Has he seen a doctor?"

"He won't. He insists that he's fine, and it's just a bug that's going round."

"And you don't think it is?"

"He gets tired easily, and the weight loss is concerning. Of course, he puts it down to old age, but I think it's something more serious than that."

"You can't force him to see a doctor," Smith said.

Whitton nodded. "No, but you can."

"Me?"

"My mum thinks he'll listen to you."

"Why the hell would she think that?" Smith said. "I'm hardly a big fan of doctors myself."

"That's precisely why," Whitton said. "My dad knows how you feel about hospitals and doctors and if it comes from you, he'll be more inclined to listen."

"Your mother is a devious woman, Erica."

"Where do you think I get it from?" Whitton said. "Will you at least think about it?"

"I'll think about it," Smith found himself saying. "But I'm sure it's nothing to worry about."

Whitton's phone started to ring again and when Smith heard the sound of another mobile phone ringtone soon afterwards and realised that it was coming from DC Moore's table, he knew that once again, his plans for the evening were about to change.

CHAPTER THIRTY ONE

Smith and Whitton had a passenger in the car as they drove the short distance to Osbaldwick. A call had come in about a dead student in one of the houses there and DC Moore was now sitting in the back of Whitton's VW. The man from London had offered to take them in his car, but it didn't take Smith long to explain that he would rather walk than risk spinal damage by sitting in DC Moore's Subaru BRZ. Whitton had phoned Darren Lewis, and the teenage boy had come to pick up Laura and Fran in Smith's Sierra.

The dead student was Belinda James, and she was in her third year of a law degree at the university.

"Professor Wild is in custody, isn't he?" DC Moore said.

"I checked," Whitton said. "He's locked up in one of the holding cells."

"Which means he has another watertight alibi," Smith said. "But that means fuck all. How were things going with the lovely Lorraine, by the way, Harry?"

"I'd rather not talk about it, Sarge," DC Moore said.

"Fair enough. You look nice by the way."

"Sarge," DC Moore said. "Please don't say stuff like that – it makes me feel a bit strange."

It was clear when they reached the house where the student was killed that they'd arrived late for this particular party. The flashing lights of the ambulance always made Smith feel a bit depressed. There was nothing anyone could do for the poor woman inside the house now and once again, the ambulance was surplus to requirements.

Grant Webber's car was parked directly outside the house. Smith expected nothing less. He knew that the Head of Forensics would be hard at work inside. Two police cars with their lights on were parked further up the street and the uniformed officers were busy making sure that nobody came near the house. Police tape was already in place to tell anybody who happened to come along that the house was strictly off limits. It was like déjà vu – crime scenes rarely changed, and this time was no different.

Whitton parked close to the outer cordon and she, Smith and DC Moore got out of the car. After announcing their presence to the officer closest to the house they were allowed through, and they made a beeline for a man talking to someone on a mobile phone next to the ambulance. DI Smyth's body language and hand gestures told Smith that the conversation he was having was an animated one. He ended the call and rubbed his eyes.

"Problems, boss?" Smith said.

"It was that hack from the Daily Mail," DI Smyth explained. "Edwina something or other. I don't even know how she got my number."

"They have their ways," Smith said. "What did she want?"

"What do you think? A comment on how a woman can be killed when the person we suspect to be the killer is behind bars?"

"Don't let it get to you. What do we know?"

"The dead woman is Belinda James," DI Smyth said. "Twenty-two years old."

"Another law student?"

"Correct. The housemate has been away all week, and he noticed the smell as soon as he opened the front door."

Smith was suddenly wide awake. "She's been dead for some time?"

"It appears so. We won't have an accurate TOD until after the post-mortem, but the stench in there suggests at least a couple of days."

"Interesting."

"It certainly is," DI Smyth said. "It throws our professor's alibi clean out of the window."

Smith lit a cigarette and ignored the admonitory glare from DI Smyth. "It helps me think," he explained. "Where is the housemate now?"

"He's being looked after by the paramedics," DI Smyth said. "He's taking it badly, and he's being treated in the ambulance."

The ambulance wasn't a complete waste of time then.

"Did you manage to find anything in your boxes at home?" DI Smyth said.

"The stuff about that particular seminar wasn't documented," Smith said. "It wasn't part of the curriculum – a small group of us got together off campus to discuss topics not on the syllabus, and the notes from the seminar don't exist."

"Has anything come back to you about the seminar?"

"Unfortunately, not," Smith said. "But it might. Can I take a look inside?"

"It's not pleasant in there. That stench is enough to turn the stomach of someone with no sense of smell."

"I'll bear that in mind."

"You know the drill."

Smith did. He walked over to Webber's car and flicked his cigarette butt far into the distance. He opened the boot of the car and shook his head when it opened. Webber never locked the boot when he was busy at a crime scene and Smith was surprised that nothing had ever gone missing from the car.

After finding a SOC suit that looked like it was the right size, Smith squeezed himself into it and grabbed a pair of gloves from the packets Webber always carried with him. He also found some protective shoe covers. He would put these on when he entered the property.

PC Simon Miller was standing sentry outside the house. The light above the door shone down on his pasty face and Smith thought he looked a little green around the gills. He wasn't surprised – even with the front door closed the putrid odour of decaying human flesh was very apparent.

"You OK?" Smith asked him.

"Not really, Sarge," PC Miller said. "It makes you doubt the existence of a god, doesn't it?"

"You've lost me there, mate."

"Come on," PC Miller said. "Surely if there was some kind of higher being –
some entity that was responsible for the creation of everything on earth, he
or she would have made sure that a corpse smelled sweeter than this as it
made its way into the Kingdom of Heaven."

For some reason Smith started to laugh and it was highly inappropriate
under the circumstances. The smile was still on his face as he opened the
door to number 30 Hove Street and went inside.

CHAPTER THIRTY TWO

The stink inside really was offensive. It was a thick oppressive funk that felt like it had some substance to it. Smith had often thought that the foul gases that accompanied the decaying process were almost solid enough to touch, and this time was no different. He tried to push aside the physical aspect of the unpleasant reek and focused instead on the science behind it. He knew that the process began immediately after death. Once the heart has stopped beating the blood stops circulating and the cells are starved of oxygen. This results in the onset of the first stage of decomposition – the autolysis stage. The body's own enzymes, released from the dying cells start to break down tissues, resulting in rigor mortis. It is also at this time that the remaining blood begins to settle in the lowest parts of the body. Blood is heavy and with no internal pressure system to keep it flowing, it starts to pool, and livor mortis is the result.

There is hardly any smell at this stage. That occurs in the next stage when the bacterial gases in the intestines cause the body to swell. The cells in the blood begin to break down and sulphur is released. The next part of the process happens when the soft tissues in the body start to liquefy, and bodily fluids leak from the various orifices.

Smith guessed the temperature inside the house to be somewhere in the mid-twenties, and when he took into account the absence of insects at this time of year, it led him to speculate that Belinda James had been dead for at least three days, possibly four. If that was the case it meant she had been killed shortly after Rebecca Stone was murdered. He realised that he could be mistaken, but the time of death would be revealed soon enough anyway, so he didn't dwell on it.

"It stinks like nothing else on earth, doesn't it?"
Billie Jones was standing right in front of Smith.

"I've smelled worse," Smith said. "What do we know so far?"

"She's been dead for quite a while," Billie said.

"At least three days," Smith said.

"At least. Rigor and livor mortis are advanced, and she has the greenish-blue discoloration even on the parts of the skin where the blood is long gone."

"Was she strangled?"

Billie nodded. "No doubt about it. And we got lucky with the rope this time."

"He left it behind?" Smith said.

"The same hemp rope."

"How long?"

"Roughly two metres," Billie said.

"Why did he leave it behind with this one?"

"That's…"

"Up to me to determine," Smith finished her sentence. "I know – I was just thinking out loud."

"She had the same drawing on her stomach," Billie said. "With one small difference. The scales of justice weren't inverted."

"Interesting. How warm do you think it is in here?"

"Twenty-six degrees celsius."

"You seem pretty convinced," Smith said.

"A bloke by the name of Daniel Fahrenheit invented something really amazing over three hundred years ago."

"A thermometer," Smith said. "OK, I've had a few beers."

"And the central heating isn't on a timer," Billie added. "I checked. So, the temperature inside the house has been a balmy twenty-six degrees since she was killed. Do you want to have a look at her?"

"I don't think that will be necessary," Smith said. "I reckon you've given me an accurate enough picture. Did you find any evidence of forced entry? Any signs that a struggle took place."

"Nothing. It looks like a copy of the others – she knew her killer, and she probably invited him in with open arms."

"That's my department," Smith said.

"Touche, but I'm just translating what the forensic evidence tells me. Are you back for good?"

"What's that supposed to mean?" Smith said.

"I'd better get back to work. Do you need me to scratch your back before I go?"

"I'll be right, thanks."

Billie flashed him a smile and Smith was sure he caught a subtle wink before she turned around and walked down the hallway. He found himself staring at her backside as she went and he quickly averted his eyes.

"Damn you, Rupert Bridge," he said under his breath.

He went back outside and removed the SOC suit immediately. He wondered why someone hadn't designed more comfortable scene of crime attire. Surely, it wouldn't be hard to do.

Bridge had arrived on the scene, and he was talking to DI Smyth next to the DI's car. Smith joined them.

"She's been dead for a while," Smith told them. "At least three days. She was strangled but the drawing on her stomach is the right way round."

"What do you think that means?" Bridge asked.

"God knows," Smith said. "The rope that was used to kill her was left behind too."

"Hopefully Webber will be able to get something from it," DI Smyth said.

"If it's the same as the rope found in Professor Wild's house," Smith said.

"We'll have something to link him to at least one murder."

"They knew she would be home alone, didn't they?" Bridge said.

"Definitely," Smith said. "Which reinforces the theory that it's someone connected to the law department of the university."

"If she's been dead for as long as you suspect she has," DI Smyth said. "It means the fact that Professor Wild is in custody is irrelevant."

"It's extremely relevant, boss," Smith said.

"In what way?"

"I get the impression that Belinda was either the first or the second victim," Smith said. "But she was meant to be found much later. This was carefully planned. Whoever did this to her knew full well that her housemate would be away all week, and he would only be getting back today."

"Someone else could have raised the alarm before that," Bridge pointed out. "If it's been three days then surely someone would have started to miss her. What about the university?"

"I've got a horrible feeling that we're going to get an explanation for that very soon," Smith said.

He was about to be proved right. Billie Jones came outside and walked over to them.

"I thought you'd want to know," she said. "We found a mobile phone in the kitchen. It was unlocked and it didn't require a password or a fingerprint."

"And you found messages on there explaining Belinda's absence from the world," Smith said.

"How did you know that?"

"Because the plan was for her body to be discovered today," Smith said. "No sooner and no later."

"On Sunday afternoon she sent a message to someone not in her list of contacts," Billie said. "Judging by the content of the message it appears to be someone in the law department at the university. Belinda informed them that she had a family emergency to take care of, and she wouldn't be attending any classes for at least a week."

"Did she get a reply to the message?" Smith asked.

"Not until Monday morning. The person she sent the message to expressed sympathy and assured her that the university fully understood."

"Who was it?" Bridge asked.

"There's no name," Billie said. "But we should be able to find out who it was from the number."

"Were there any other messages?" Smith said.

"No messages," Billie said. "But shortly after the message to the university was sent a phone call was made. To none other than Rebecca Stone. She was in Belinda's contact list."

"The first victim?" DI Smyth said.

"Or so we thought," Billie said. "The call was answered."

"Belinda didn't make that call," Smith said. "Someone gained access to her phone, disabled all security measures, and called Rebecca Stone. I think we've got it all wrong – I think Belinda was our first victim."

CHAPTER THIRTY THREE

When Smith rolled over in bed the next morning and realised what time it was, he wondered if the clock had stopped. It was not yet six and he felt wide awake. It was still dark outside, and he knew that the sun wouldn't be up for at least another hour or so. He shifted the duvet to the side and got out of bed, careful not to wake Whitton, sleeping next to him. He used the bathroom and made his way downstairs.

He made some coffee and opened the back door. The icy blast of air that came into the kitchen told him it had probably dropped below freezing last night. He picked up his cigarettes and went outside. The city was strangely quiet, and it was somewhat eerie. Even at this time of the day, in the hour between night and day there was always something to break the silence, but now there were no car engines or house alarms to be heard.

It would soon be Christmas and Smith remembered what Chalmers had told him about the Christmas party. He wondered if it was going to go ahead as planned with everything else that was going on. Smith hoped it would be cancelled – he wasn't a big fan of work functions.

He was planning on interviewing Herman Wild today. He couldn't put it off any longer, and he had so many questions for the law professor. It was clear that Professor Wild was playing some kind of intricate game – the moves he'd played thus far had been all part of his endgame and Smith planned to find out more so he could formulate a counter move of his own. He wasn't intimidated by the mind of Professor Wild, but he knew he needed to be extremely careful.

He lit another cigarette, and his thoughts turned to DC Moore's suggestion of a dirty tackle. Smith had never seen this in practice in the game of football, but he understood the concept perfectly well. He also understood that for such an underhanded tactic to work against someone like Professor Wild, everything about it had to be perfect. He hadn't yet decided on the nature of the dirty tackle he was going to introduce to the game, but he was confident that something would occur to him.

By the time Smith went back inside, the coffee had gone cold. He emptied it down the sink and made another cup. The dogs were still nowhere to be seen, and Smith knew that they wouldn't surface until the sun came up, or the promise of food was on the cards. Smith sat down at the table and opened his phone. He had to use the fingerprint on the forefinger of his left hand to do so. He didn't know much about how his phone operated but he knew enough to be able to locate his *Settings* and then navigate to the *Lock Screen and Security Settings* menu. Smith's phone was a Samsung, and it was a couple of years old, but even with this older model in order to remove the security measures he was prompted to enter a password.

"Belinda James was forced to do this."

Smith didn't know where the next thought came from, but he knew he was right. Whitton happened to come into the kitchen a second before he voiced the thought.

"There were more than one of them."

"What on earth are you going on about?" Whitton said.

"I don't know about the others," Smith said. "But I think there were two people involved in the murder of Belinda James."

"Can I at least have a cup of coffee before I have to listen to your brain spouting forth its latest revelations?"

"Fair enough. I'll make it."

"Let's hear it then," Whitton said, five minutes later.

"Belinda's phone had no security measures in place," Smith said. "I don't know what phone she had, but I imagine someone her age will have had a pretty new model. I tried to disable my security measures, and even though my phone is relatively old it still asked me for a password to disable the fingerprint access thing."

Whitton sipped her coffee. "I'm still not following you. Where do you get the connection between that and the fact that there were more than one of them when she was killed?"

Smith got up and unplugged Whitton's phone from the charger on the wall. He held it in front of her face.

"Unlock it."

"What?" Whitton said.

"Say *make me.*"

"Have you lost your mind?"

"Just humour me," Smith said. "Say *make me.*"

Whitton sighed. "Make me."

Smith grabbed her hand, and Whitton automatically yanked it back.

"Unlock the phone," Smith said.

"No."

"Unlock the fucking phone."

Whitton observed her husband as though he was about to attack her.

Smith sat back down.

"Sorry," he said. "I got a bit carried away. But don't you see – I think there were two people there the day Belinda James was killed. One of them immobilised her while the other made his demands. They forced her to unlock her phone and then they killed her. I did wonder if they disabled the fingerprint access after she died but it would have been impossible because they would have needed her password too."

"I still think you're on the wrong track," Whitton said. "It could have still been a single killer. He murders Belinda and uses her fingerprint to unlock the phone. You know as well as I do that even the most modern phones can be unlocked with a print up to ten minutes after death."

"That's not what happened," Smith said. "The phone would have locked itself after a while and they couldn't let that happen. They needed access to it long after Belinda's heart had stopped beating."

"OK," Whitton said. "Let's say you're right. How does it actually help us?"

"Fingerprints. A phone screen is a perfect receptacle for prints."

"And you don't think they could have been wearing gloves?"

"Nope," Smith said. "They weren't. I just know that they weren't."

CHAPTER THIRTY FOUR

It took Smith longer than usual to find a parking space at the station. He'd half expected there to be some unwelcome guests when he got there but he wasn't prepared for the sheer number of reporters waiting to try their luck. He was pounced upon as soon as he got out of his car.

"Will you be releasing the professor this morning?" a man Smith knew to be a local reporter asked.

"Nope," Smith said and carried on his way.

"How did he kill her?" the same man shouted as he walked. "Some kind of magic trick?"

Smith didn't reply.

"How did he kill her?" A woman voiced the same question. "You must have something for us. How was it even possible? He was in police custody at the time."

Smith turned to face her. "You want to know how she died?"

"I'm on your side," the woman said. "I just want the truth."

"I very much doubt that," Smith said.

"Come on," she said. "Give me something I can use."

Smith leaned closer and whispered in her ear.

"He used a rope. It was Professor Plum in the library with the rope."

"Arsehole."

Smith grinned at her. "I could be wrong of course."

He went inside the station and stopped by the front desk.

"Anything new come in overnight?" he asked Baldwin.

"Just the usual crazies phoning in with irrelevant information," she said.

"That lot out there aren't helping matters."

"When did the press ever help matters?" Smith said.

"Professor Wild is demanding to know when we're going to get round to interviewing him."

"Is he now?" Smith said. "That's interesting."

"Will you be speaking to him this morning?"

"That was the plan," Smith said. "But now I'm not so sure it's a good idea."

"Don't you want to know what he has to say?"

"Of course I do, but the fact he's so keen to talk makes me suspicious."

"Aren't we obliged to interview a suspect at the earliest possible opportunity?" Baldwin said.

"That's the beauty of the law in this great country, Baldwin," Smith said. "There are many ways to interpret it, and *the earliest possible opportunity* can be translated many ways. Thanks for the heads-up."

Baldwin's facial expression told him that she had no idea what he was talking about, but Smith was used to that by now. He gave her a smile and headed for the canteen.

DI Smyth was alone on the table by the window, and he didn't look well at all. Smith wondered if he'd even slept. He got himself a coffee from the machine and joined him at the table.

"Everything OK, boss?"

"Nothing I can't handle," DI Smyth said. "I'm getting pressure from higher up. The powers that be want to know when we'll be interviewing the professor. The general consensus is they want a swift resolution to this. We're to charge Professor Wild or let him go. We can't keep him locked up indefinitely."

"He's involved in four murders," Smith reminded him. "We can keep him locked up until he proves otherwise."

"Therein lies the problem," DI Smyth said. "You of all people ought to know that the onus is not on the suspect to prove that. It is up to us to establish guilt and nothing we've uncovered so far has done that."

"We've got more than enough. He's involved."

"Everything we have is circumstantial, Smith," DI Smyth said. "Everything. We don't have a single concrete piece of evidence that ties the professor to any of the murders. And we haven't even got round to interviewing him. That does not look good for us."

"We'll interrogate him when we're good and ready."

"We need to do it sooner rather than later."

"I disagree," Smith said.

"I thought you were keen to get stuck in."

"That's exactly what he wants. He's been pressing for an interview, and that makes me smell a rat."

DI Smyth stood up and stared out of the window.

"I do believe it's going to snow later."

"Are you sure everything is alright, boss?" Smith said.

"It's not forecast, but those clouds are promising something. Here's where we stand. As I see it, we have until the end of today to either charge Professor Wild with something or let him go free."

"We're talking about four murders," Smith said. "It's as serious as it gets. We can hold him for the full three days."

"Not without the say-so of a magistrate. And as of right now we have nothing to offer a magistrate to justify it. Circumstantial evidence just won't wash – we need something solid, something that cannot be disputed."

"Then we find something like that," Smith said. "And if we can't we'll just have to get creative."

DI Smyth sat back down. "I'm not having this conversation again."

"I wasn't aware that I was repeating myself," Smith said.

"You're talking about playing dirty. We do this according to the guidelines set out in the law or we don't do it at all."

"I can be creative and still stay within the boundaries put in place by Lady Justice."

"And how do you plan to do that?"

"It's simple, boss," Smith said. "As Harry said, you just have to play the dirty tackle when the referee is looking the other way."

CHAPTER THIRTY FIVE

DI Smyth had reluctantly agreed to delay the interview with Professor Wild. They were well within their rights to do so, but time was running out before they would have to either charge the professor or release him. In the meantime, the team were put to work gathering together more pieces of the most complicated jigsaw puzzle any of them had ever come across. The clock was ticking, and they had until the sun went down to see if they could arrange the pieces into some semblance of order and get closer to seeing the full picture.

Smith had taken Whitton's advice, and he was sifting through the records of the admissions to the university during his stint there. He'd found the list relatively easily. As the people on it were no longer students at the university they weren't protected by the same privacy laws as current students, and the information Smith required was in the public domain. He hoped that some names would ring some bells, and he would be able to recall the people who were part of Professor Wild's elite study group.

He'd started the law degree in the September of 2000. He was eighteen years old. After scrolling down the list of admissions for that year and not recognising any of the names on it Smith decided to print it out. He did the same with the admissions for the 2001/2002 terms. He was convinced that the group was set up towards the end of his time there and calculated that it will have been sometime in 2002.

Smith realised that it was going to be much harder to conjure up a face from a name on a list than it was nowadays. There was no such thing as social media when Smith was studying at the university. Facebook was a few years away and Twitter only followed a couple of years after that. It would be another four years before Instagram was born.

Smith tried to remember if he'd submitted any photographs during the admissions process and he recalled that he had. He'd needed them for his student union ID, and he was certain that the faculty kept his ugly mug on file too. After getting through to three different people and being placed on hold for four minutes by one of them, Smith finally found someone who might be able to help him. He explained who he was and told the man what he needed. The line went quiet for a moment and Smith wondered if the admin clerk had hung up.

He hadn't but he might as well have.

"I'm afraid the university cannot give you access to our records without a warrant."

"I've already got the names of people who studied law there from 2000 to 2002 off the net," Smith informed him. "But I need the detailed files, complete with photographs."

"And I'll be more than happy to provide you with what you want," the man said. "When I see a warrant ordering me to do so."

He hung up before Smith had the chance to thank him for nothing. He needed a smoke, and for once his filthy habit turned out to be a blessing in disguise. As he passed by the front desk and heard Baldwin explaining on the phone that a lost dog wasn't a matter for the police, an idea started to form in Smith's head. He waited for Baldwin to finish with the distraught dog owner and explained his predicament with the university admissions. Baldwin listened and the six words she spoke next raised Smith's spirits no end.

I'll see what I can do.

The press contingent had moved off when Smith went outside and he was glad. He lit a cigarette and looked skyward. The clouds did look strange today, and the temperature had risen slightly. DI Smyth could be right – it did feel like there was snow on the way.

Whitton came out when he was halfway through the cigarette.

"Baldwin said I'd find you out here."

"I drew a blank with the admissions from my time at university," Smith told her. "But I've put Baldwin on it, and you know how she operates."

"Where *does* she get her information from?"

"I've never asked her," Smith said. "And I think it's better to keep it that way. Was there something you wanted to speak to me about?"

"I can't stop thinking about my dad. Mum sent me a WhatsApp this morning, and he's no better. If anything, he's getting worse."

"I'll talk to him," Smith said. "For what it's worth. That man is the most stubborn bastard I've ever met."

"They reckon that you marry your father, don't they? Not literally, but they say you go for someone like your father. The same is true about men being attracted to women who remind them of their mother."

"I must be the exception there," Smith said. "You're nothing like my mother, thank God."

He didn't feel like going straight back to work so he lit another cigarette.

"Do you really think this has all been about getting away with murder?" Whitton said.

"I do," Smith said. "And it goes much deeper than that. Plenty of people get away with murder, but very few get away with it by staying within the boundaries of the law. That takes some doing, and it requires serious planning and an encyclopaedic knowledge of the law."

"How are we going to beat this?"

"I can see only one way," Smith said. "But the DI has forbidden it."

"Is it worth it?"

"Is what worth it?"

"Breaking the rules," Whitton said. "Could you live with yourself afterwords?"

"I reckon I could."

"You don't know that. We're police officers, Jason. We've been appointed to uphold the law, and I know how much that means to you."

"The law has let us down in this instance, Erica. As much as I cannot see an innocent man go down for something he hasn't done, the reverse is the case. Professor Wild is as guilty as sin, and he's going to get away with it unless we do something drastic. I reckon my conscience will be squeaky clean afterwards. Anyway, I still haven't come up with a suitable plan."

"But you will," Whitton said. "I know you."

"I suppose I'll let you know when I've figured it out. Shall we go and do some work?"

CHAPTER THIRTY SIX

Smith needed a change of scenery. He found DC King and asked her what she was up to.

"I'm looking through the printouts of Belinda James's Facebook," she said.

"How did you manage to access her Facebook?" Smith said. "I thought we needed a whole load of court orders for that."

"Strictly speaking, what I'm doing is not exactly above board, but I'd say the time for worrying about legal nitty gritty has passed."

"I'm glad someone is on the same page as me," Smith said. "But how did you even gain access?"

"Her phone was unlocked, and there was no security on her Facebook on her phone. If we tried to get in from another device there probably would be, but we got lucky."

"Did you find anything?" Smith said.

"She used it a lot," DC King said. "Up to four hours a day on some days, but her activity ceased just before noon last Sunday."

"A corpse has no interest in social media."

"That's a bit morbid, Sarge."

"I'm in one of those moods," Smith said. "She was definitely killed on Sunday, wasn't she?"

DC King nodded. "She was. There isn't much to learn from her activity. She was an animal lover. There are a load of posts about animal shelters and rescue centres. She was a big fan of James Blunt."

"There's no accounting for taste. Did she interact much with her friends?"

"She didn't have many," DC King said. "Which is unusual for someone her age. I've only gone back a month or so, but in that time the person she interacted with most on Messenger was someone called Barry Gilbert."

"What do you know?" Smith said. "That's why I came to find you. Barry just happens to be Jackie Grant's boyfriend. He works at a garage on Monk Street, and I'm very keen to go and speak to the man."

"Do you suspect Barry to be involved, Sarge?" DC King asked. They were heading south on Tang Hall Lane.

"He was in a relationship with one of the victims," Smith said. "It's always the husband or the boyfriend, isn't it?"

"No," DC King said.

"It is in the movies. And now we know that he was friends with another victim too, so he's somewhere at the top of my list."

"Do you have a list?"

"It's always useful to have a list. I want you in the interview room with me when I interrogate the professor later."

"I don't think I'm the right person for the job, Sarge."

"I think you are," Smith said. "For you, Professor Wild is a blank page, and you'll be able to go in there without any preconceived opinions of the man. And I want you to be the one who asks the hard questions."

"I get to be *bad cop* for once?"

Smith smiled. "If you like."

"I don't think DI Smyth will go for it."

"You leave the DI to me. This place looks more like a chop-shop than a garage."

He stopped the car behind a vehicle that had definitely seen better days. All four wheels were gone, and the car was propped up on bricks. The bonnet had been removed and two of the doors were missing. DC King unfastened her seatbelt and placed her hand on the door handle. Smith stopped her. "Not so fast. I want to park somewhere else. I don't want to come out and find that my beloved Sierra has been stripped for parts."

He reversed and found a parking spot twenty metres away from the garage.

The reception area of the imaginatively named *Mike's Autos* consisted of a box-sized office behind a hatch at the front of the garage. Smith peered inside and saw a man engrossed in something on a mobile phone.

"Have you got a minute?"

The man looked up and sighed deeply. "Can I help you?"

Smith took out his ID and held it up. "We're looking for Barry Gilbert."

"Never heard of him."

"Are you sure?" Smith said.

"There's no Barry Gilbert here."

"I was under the impression that Barry worked here," Smith said. "Sorry to bother you. We'll just have a quick look around, seeing as we're here."

The man got to his feet and Smith was surprised to see that his head was at the same height as it had been when he was sitting down. This man couldn't be much more than four feet tall.

"Barry isn't in any trouble," Smith said. "We just need a quick word with him."

The midget sighed again. "Wait there."

Smith watched as he exited a door on the other side of the hatch and promptly slammed it behind him.

"I'll definitely give this place a go when my car needs a service," DC King said. "Do you think they're up to no good here?"

"Probably," Smith said. "But that's not our problem."

A man appeared from the side of the building and walked over to them. He placed a rollup cigarette in his mouth and lit it. He was tall with thick black hair and dark brown eyes.

"You were looking for me?" he said and smiled.

His teeth were straight and white, and he seemed self-assured. He was handsome in a swarthy Latino kind of way and Smith got the impression that he knew it. He introduced himself and DC King.

"Is this about Jackie?" Barry said.

"Is there somewhere we can talk that's more private?" Smith said.

"Do you mind if I eat my lunch while we talk?" Barry said. "We've got a lot on, and I don't want to be stuck here all night."

Smith couldn't place his accent, but he did know that it wasn't local. Barry removed a brown paper bag from his jacket pocket and took out a sandwich. "There's a bench over there." He pointed in the direction of where Smith had parked his car.

"I thought it was a wind up at first," Barry said.

He'd made himself comfortable on the bench and he was halfway through his second sandwich.

"Why would you think that?" Smith said.

He and DC King remained standing.

"You hear about it, don't you?" Barry said. "Murder I mean, but you don't expect someone to kill your girlfriend."

"How long were you and Jackie together?" DC King said.

"Over a year."

"It was serious then?" Smith said.

"It was. I loved her. We did break up for a while, but we got back together soon afterwards."

"Why did you break up?"

"Pressure from her parents. Look, I know what you probably think of me. A low-life mechanic with no future, but I wasn't the one holding Jackie back."

"I tend not to make assumptions," Smith said. "Can you elaborate?"

"I was behind Jackie a hundred percent. I knew she would go far. I also knew that she would probably leave me miles behind when that happened, but I accepted that. I was under no illusions that she would still want to date a grease monkey when she became a lawyer."

"But you still stayed with her?" DC King said.

"That's life, I suppose. I knew I wouldn't be able to compete with the people she would associate with in her new world - I'm not stupid."

"I can hear that," Smith said. "You're clearly an intelligent man."

"You're probably wondering why I'm working in a dump like this."

"I'm not," Smith said. "You must have your reasons."

"I do have my reasons. Would it surprise you to hear that I was actually accepted to Cambridge?"

"Nothing surprises me anymore," Smith said.

Barry started to laugh. "I'm pulling your chain. I left school with three GCSEs. Couldn't see the point in studying. What is it you want me to tell you? I was Jackie's boyfriend and now she's dead. That's all there is to it, unless you think I killed her."

Smith didn't think it was a question to bring up just yet.

"Where were you on Sunday?" he asked instead.

"Sunday?" Barry said. "What's Sunday got to do with anything? I thought Jackie was killed on Wednesday."

"Where were you on Sunday?" Smith asked once more.

"I can't remember."

"I'd prefer it if you could remember."

"Sunday?" Barry said. "I was probably at home."

"Probably?"

"I was. I went out with some mates on Saturday night – we ended up at a club and I didn't get home until gone three in the morning."

"Can anyone confirm this?" DC King said.

"I can give you the names of my mates."

"We're not interested in where you went on Saturday night," Smith said. "Is there anyone who can corroborate your story about where you were on Sunday?"

"I live by myself."

"Is that a no then?" Smith said.

"What is this?" Barry said. "Are you saying I had something to with what happened to Jackie? Because I can promise you I didn't. I was nowhere near her place on Wednesday afternoon."

"Have you made plans for this evening?" Smith said.

"What?" Barry said.

"You told us you didn't want to be stuck here all night," DC King said.

"It's Friday," Barry said. "Would you want to be stuck at work on a Friday night?"

"Fair enough," Smith said. "We'll let you get back to work. You were good friends with Belinda James, weren't you?"

Barry's eyes shifted downwards, and Smith knew that he'd touched a nerve.

"Belinda James," he said. "Can you tell us about your friendship with her?"

"Is that what this is all about?" Barry said. "Me and Belinda hooked up for a bit after Jackie dumped me. It was nothing serious, and it only lasted a couple of weeks."

"Are you sure?" Smith said.

"Of course, I'm sure."

"So, if we were to check your Facebook, we wouldn't find any recent correspondence between you and Belinda?"

"No."

"I'll ask you again," Smith said. "Are you sure?"

"I need to get back to work."

"In a minute. You're lying, Barry. You and Belinda engaged in long conversations on Facebook Messenger right up to the day she was killed."

He wasn't expecting Barry to do what he did next. He took out a mobile phone, tapped his finger on the back and swiped the screen.

"Have a look if you don't believe me."

He handed the phone to Smith.

"I'm not even friends with Belinda anymore. Jackie made me unfriend her."

"Kerry," Smith handed DC King the phone.

"Looks like he's telling the truth, Sarge," DC King said.

Barry grinned, revealing his white teeth. "Told you."

"And it also looks like he's deleted the message thread between himself and Belinda James," DC King added.

"That's bullshit," Barry said.

"It'll be easy enough to find out," Smith said. "Our tech team can do wonders these days."

"You can't take my phone," Barry said.

"We don't need to," Smith said. "Your reaction alone tells us that you're lying. We'll be in touch, Mr Gilbert."

CHAPTER THIRTY SEVEN

"Have you suddenly forgotten how to be a police detective?" It was the first thing DI Smyth asked Smith when he told him about the conversation with Barry Gilbert.

"He should have been hauled in and interviewed." DI Smyth added.

"Different rules apply with this one, boss," Smith said.

"The man should be in an interview room right now. You said he told you that he was nowhere near Jackie's house on Wednesday afternoon. How did he know that was when she was killed? That hasn't been released to the press yet."

"Perhaps he spoke to her," Smith said. "I don't know."

"Did I tell you that I had a haircut the other day?" DI Smyth said.

"If you did, it must have slipped my mind."

"I'll tell you what the hairdresser said, shall I? He suggested I consider using a subtle dye to hide the grey. He said it would take years off me. You're aging me, Smith – you're adding years I can't afford to have added on."

"Your hair looks perfectly fine to me, boss," Smith said. "The grey makes you look distinguished. Don't worry, I know what I'm doing."

"That's precisely what concerns me. Please tell me we're going to get in that interview room with Herman Wild soon."

"*We're* not," Smith said. "I decided it would be best if me and Kerry took him on."

"You *decided*, did you?"

"It makes sense. Kerry's sharp and Herman won't be expecting her. You have to trust me with this."

Smith's phone beeped to tell him he'd received a message. He looked at the screen and saw that it was from Baldwin. He swiped the screen and smiled when he saw what she wanted to tell him.

"I'll leave you to it," he said.

"Do I need to know what that message was all about?" DI Smyth said.

"Just something I asked Baldwin to do," Smith said. "We're on the right track here. We will crack this one."

He made his way to his office and booted up his laptop. The sky outside had turned an ominous greyish-brown and the clouds were moving quickly. Smith wasn't sure what this meant. He turned his attention to the laptop and opened up his emails. The most recent one was from Baldwin and when Smith clicked on the first attachment he shook his head. It was clear from the logo at the top that this had been downloaded directly from York University's database. It was the enrolment details of the students who had been accepted to study law there in 2000. Smith saw from the label on the attachment that this was the list from A-L.

"Where the hell do you get your information from?" he asked the screen. Everything he needed was here. The records included names, dates of birth and details about the qualifications achieved. There was a single photograph of every new student. A lot of the faces seemed familiar, but Smith expected them to be. He'd spent hours with most of the people in the file. Even though it was a long time ago, he still remembered them well. It was probably to his advantage that he hadn't met up with any of these people since he'd quit the degree, and the younger versions of what they would look like now would always be how he remembered them.

Halfway through the A-L records Smith's eyes fell on the face of a woman with short blond hair.

"Penny Fowler," he said.

It was a real blast from the past. He'd liked Penny and there had been a few sparks between them in that first year. Smith couldn't remember what had happened to prevent things going any further. It didn't matter – Penny

Fowler was one of the students in Professor Wild's elite group, Smith was certain of it.

He started to panic when he was scrolling down the list, and he'd reached the students with surnames starting with S. He remembered a lot of them, but he couldn't recall any of them as being members of the special group. He gasped when his own face stared back at him.

"Holy crap."

He looked like a schoolboy. The photograph was black and white, but it was still possible to see the flecks of blond. His eyes were bright and there were none of the lines and creases that he had now. He looked like a young man with hopes and dreams. And a whole lot yet to lose. It really was depressing looking at this younger version of himself, so he quickly moved on.

Two more faces made him look twice and a third glance told him he was on the right track. He wrote the names Peter Taylor and Neil Williams below Penny Fowler's name and decided that he had enough to go on for now. Or at least Baldwin did. He would put her special skills to use once more – it would be much quicker that way. He would speak to the people on his list when he got their details.

He needed some coffee. He left the office and went to the canteen to do something about his caffeine craving. Bridge was speaking to someone on his phone next to the coffee machine. Smith heard him say thank you to someone and then he hung up.

"That was Billie," Bridge said. "They managed to pull some prints from the screen of Belinda James's phone. Most of them were from Belinda but there are two that Forensics weren't able to identify."

"I knew it," Smith said. "Someone else sent that message to the university."

"Don't get too excited," Bridge said. "I said they weren't able to identify the other prints."

"I didn't expect them to. But it means I was right."

"I thought you were always right," Bridge said. "When are you planning on interviewing the prof?"

"I wish people would stop asking me that. It's getting irritating."

"I thought he would be your priority for today."

"He was supposed to be," Smith said. "Until I found out that he was asking when we were going to interview him. I want to let him sweat it out a bit longer in the holding cell. Do you know if he's changed his mind about legal representation?"

"Not as far as I'm aware," Bridge said. "Perhaps he's confident in his own abilities as a professor of law."

"I hope so, because that confidence could well be the beginning of his fall from grace."

CHAPTER THIRTY EIGHT

Smith was taking a break in his office when there was a knock on the door and Baldwin came in.

"I've got some info for you," she said.

"That was quick."

"There's good news and bad news," Baldwin said. "Of the names you gave me, one of them is dead and another is living in New Zealand. Peter Taylor died last year – heart attack."

"He was the same age as me," Smith said. "That's scary."

"And Neil Williams has been in Auckland since 2008," Baldwin said.

"Do I want to know how you got this information?"

"Easily. Facebook. It's the greatest detection tool ever invented. So that leaves Penny Fowler. Not only is she alive, she's still in the city. These are her details."

She handed Smith a sheet of paper.

He glanced at it. "She's a lawyer. Great."

"What did you expect, Sarge?" Baldwin said. "She was one of your elite group at university, so it's logical to assume she would follow that path."

"I was in that group," Smith said. "I joined the police instead."

"But you're a special case, Sarge."

"I don't know how to take that."

"Take it as a compliment," Baldwin said. "I hope it leads you somewhere."

"Me too," Smith said. "Thanks, Baldwin."

According to the details on the sheet of paper, Penny Fowler was a senior partner at a law firm that had their offices on Monkgate.

"Penny Fowler," Smith said out loud.

She was still Penny Fowler, so unless she'd retained her maiden name, she wasn't married. Smith wasn't sure why this interested him, and he focused on something else. He took out his phone and keyed in the number on the page. The call was answered by a man with a deep voice.

"Lloyd, Lloyd and Jenkins."

"Good afternoon," Smith said. "I'm calling from York Police, and I was hoping to speak to Penny Fowler."

"What is it regarding?"

"Miss Fowler's name has come up in the course of an investigation," Smith said. "Would it be possible to make an appointment with her?"

"Penny's on leave. She isn't due back at work until Monday."

"No problem," Smith said. "I'll call back then. Thank you."

He had no intention of doing that. Baldwin had also managed to get Penny's address. She had a house just east of Heworth on Stockton Lane and Smith recalled that the properties in that part of town weren't cheap. Penny Fowler had obviously done well from practicing law. After checking the time, Smith decided that he had time to go and pay her a visit. He grabbed his phone and car keys and left the office.

Number 17 Stockton Lane was an attractive, face brick property with an enormous driveway. The house was a double story detached place, and Smith reckoned you wouldn't get much change from a million if you wanted to buy it. There was a green 4x4 in the driveway and there was plenty of room for Smith to park next to it. He got out of his car and felt a solitary snowflake kiss his cheek. More snow started to fall, and Smith found himself turning to face the sky. The light snow felt good on his face.

"What on earth are you doing?"

Penny Fowler hadn't changed much. She had a few more lines at the corners of her eyes and she'd put on a bit of weight, but Smith was taken back twenty years. Penny still had mousy blond hair, cut into a bob, and her green eyes were bright. Smith wiped the snow from his face and smiled at her.

"Jason?"

"Penny," Smith said. "How are you?"

The snow was falling harder now.

"Do you want to come inside?" Penny asked. "Or would you prefer to stay here and play in the snow for a bit longer?"

"I reckon inside would be better," Smith said.

Penny opened the door and looked behind her.

"Jason Smith. Who would have thought it?"

She led him down a wide hallway and asked him to take a seat in a room that had a kitchen at one end and a huge dining area at the other. French doors looked out onto the garden at the back. The lawn was already covered in a thin blanket of snow.

"Can I get you something to drink?" Penny said.

"Coffee would be great," Smith said.

Penny switched on an expensive looking machine and came and sat down opposite him.

"I'm sorry to turn up unannounced," Smith said. "But I was hoping you might be able to help me."

"How did you find me?"

"I called your work," Smith said. "And they said you were off until Monday."

"How did you know where I lived?"

"From the electoral roll."

"I very much doubt that. This house is still in my ex-husband's name. The deeds haven't yet been transferred."

"I have a highly advanced search engine," Smith said. "I call her Victoria."

Penny made the coffee and handed Smith a cup. It smelled delicious and it tasted even better. This was not cheap instant coffee.

"How have you been?" Smith said. "Apart from the nasty divorce of course."

"How do you know it was nasty?"

"You're living in your ex-husband's house," Smith said. "Which probably means you nailed him in the divorce. And that leads me to believe he deserved it. Plus, you've reverted back to your maiden name."

"You're still as sharp as ever," Penny said. "And you're correct. My ex is a bastard of the first degree. He left me for a woman not long out of school. But he made the mistake of marrying a lawyer in the first place. How about you? I know you're a police detective – what else can you tell me?"

"I'm married," Smith said. "To another police detective."

Penny smiled. "That must be interesting."

"It is. We have three girls. Two of them adopted. It's a long story."

"I imagine it is. Are you here about Professor Wild?"

Smith nodded. "Is it that obvious?"

"Why else? Are you hungry?"

"As a matter of fact, I am," Smith said.

"I have some quiche in the fridge. It's not exactly winter fare, but who cares?"

She sliced the quiche, placed two plates on the table, and told Smith to help himself.

He took a slice and left it untouched on the plate. "This is a long shot, but I was hoping that you remembered the study group we were part of."

"Professor Wild's dream team," Penny said.

"I don't recall it being called that."

"It wasn't but that's what it boiled down to, wasn't it? We were fooling ourselves."

"What do you mean?"

"Putting the world to rights. It's refreshing to be young and naïve, isn't it? Of course, we knew nothing then of how the real world works. You haven't touched your quiche."

Smith obliged and took a bite. It tasted odd – there was too much pepper.

"I've been trying to remember one of the topics we discussed," he said. "All I know is it was about how a person can get away with murder. Legally."

"That was one of Professor Wild's more fanciful ideas," Penny said.

"Can you remember any of the details?"

"I can do better," Penny said.

She got up and left the room without further explanation.

Smith forced down the rest of the slice of quiche while he waited. Penny came back and placed a file on the table.

"It's all in there."

"You made notes?" Smith said.

"I always made notes," Penny said. "I still do. It's a running joke with my colleagues."

"Can I get a copy of this?"

"You can keep it. I have no need for it. Do you believe that Professor Wild is putting his theories into practice?"

"I'm afraid I can't discuss that," Smith said.

"I'm bound by lawyer client privilege remember."

Smith laughed. "You're not my lawyer, and I'm not your client."

"No," Penny said. "You were once much more than that. Sorry, I'm reminiscing. But nothing you tell me will go any further. You trusted me once."

"My trusting days are long gone," Smith said.

He picked up the file.

"Don't be a stranger, Jason," Penny said.

"Thanks for the coffee and the quiche," Smith said. "And this of course."

He held up the file.

"I hope there's something in there that will help."

"So do I," Smith said. "I really hope so."

CHAPTER THIRTY NINE

Smith decided not to go straight back to the station. He parked his car as close as possible to the university campus and got out. As he started to walk away, he caught a glimpse of the file Penny Fowler had given him on the back seat. He unlocked the car, took out the file and locked it in the boot. He didn't really know why he did it, but he sensed that the contents of the file were important, and he didn't want to risk losing it.

The snow had stopped falling and the clouds had moved off, letting the sun shine down on the university campus. There were very few people around – it was mid-afternoon, and Smith assumed that the students were making plans for the weekend ahead. He headed straight for the buildings that housed the department of law.

His first stop was the admissions office. The door was closed but he could hear voices within. He knocked but the conversation inside didn't stop. Smith placed his ear to the door, and he was sure he could hear people laughing. It sounded like a man and a woman. He knocked again and the voices became quiet. Soon afterwards the door opened, and Rachel Bright's face appeared in the gap. The head of admissions didn't look happy to see him.

"Can I help you?"

"I hope you can," Smith said. "Can I come in and have a word?"

"Now isn't a good time," Rachel said.

"It won't take long," Smith said. "I just need to ask you a few more questions."

"Meet me in the canteen in five minutes. I have a few things to tie up here first."

"No worries."

"Do you know where it is?"

"I'm sure I'll find it. Five minutes, you say?"

Rachel nodded and closed the door again. Smith could hear her voice through the door. He walked away and stopped. There was a huge fake plant against the wall further down the corridor. Smith stepped behind it and pretended to be looking at something on his phone. He heard the sound of the door opening and he glanced in the direction of the admissions office. The man who exited the office didn't see Smith behind the plant, but Smith got a full view of him. It was the cleaner. The man who'd introduced himself as Doug looked left and right and walked straight past Smith without noticing him.

Soon afterwards the door to the admissions office opened again and Rachel Bright emerged. She too passed him by without casting him a glance. Smith was instantly alert. The voices he'd heard inside the office were definitely amiable ones and the cleaner and the admissions woman seemed to be sharing a joke. It contradicted what Doug had told them earlier. He'd definitely made out as if Rachel Bright wasn't any friend of his. Smith didn't know what to make of it.

After finding someone to direct him to the canteen he walked through the corridors and found it without getting lost. Only a few of the tables were occupied. A couple of men were busy ignoring each other at the table closest to the food counter. Both of them were more interested in the screens of their phones. A young woman was reading a book at the table next to them. She glanced at Smith when he came in and she smiled. Smith smiled back. Rachel Bright was sitting close to the door. There were two cups of coffee on the table in front of her and Smith took this to be a positive sign. He joined her at the table.

"I won't take up too much of your time."

"Take all the time you like," Rachel said. "Classes have been suspended for the rest of the term."

"There isn't much of the term left anyway, is there?"

"What is it you want to talk to me about?" Rachel said.

Smith picked up the coffee and took a sip. It tasted terrible.

"I wanted to ask you about the dead women."

"I don't know if I can help you there."

"You're the head of admissions," Smith said. "You're privy to all sorts of information."

Rachel opened her mouth to say something, but Smith beat her to it.

"I appreciate you're bound by university rules regulating the details of the students here. And I'm not asking you to break those rules, but there's nothing stopping you from giving me some basics."

"Go on."

"From what I've gathered so far," Smith said. "The women who were murdered were exceptionally bright. The very fact that they'd come this far suggests they'd applied themselves and they were determined to succeed. Can you comment on that?"

"Your assumptions are correct," Rachel said.

"Can you elaborate?" Smith said.

"No."

"I'm asking for your help here," Smith said. "And I'm being honest with you when I tell you that we still have no idea why these women were targeted. Help me, please."

Rachel looked around the canteen. The two men were gone. The young woman had put down her book and Smith noticed that she was looking in their direction. She shifted her gaze when she realised that the head of admissions was looking straight at her.

"I can get the details of the dead women," Smith said. "I can come back with a warrant and force you to divulge everything."

"I was under the impression that you already had a list of the students."

"Names are all very well," Smith said. "But I want more. I want to know about the pecking order in the law department. Which of the students are barely scraping by, and which ones are rising stars? I imagine if I was privy to that information, it would become apparent that the dead women are in the latter category."

"When you return with your warrant," Rachel said. "I'm sure you'll get all the answers you seek. I have to go."

She stood up. "I really can't help you."

"Just one more thing," Smith said.

"Do detectives actually say that in real life?"

"Just me," Smith said. "I'm trying to come up with a better line. Do you have a card?"

"A card?"

"Something with your details on it," Smith said. "Your phone number and email address. It would save us both a lot of time if we didn't have to communicate face to face in the future."

Rachel slipped her hand inside her jacket pocket, took out a business card and handed it to Smith. It was laminated – he'd hoped it would be.

She placed it on the table in front of him. "Office hours only, please."

"Of course," Smith said. "That goes without saying. Thank you for your time."

He waited for her to leave the canteen and took out the small plastic evidence bag he'd brought along with him. Carefully, he picked the business card up by the edge and slipped it inside the bag. He sealed it and put it into his pocket.

"Can I have a word?"

Smith looked up. Standing there, was the woman who had been reading the book. She sat down without being invited. She put the book down on the table and Smith saw from the cover that it was a collection of short stories by someone called Ring Lardner. He'd never heard of him.

"You're here because of the dead students, aren't you?"

The woman introduced herself as Holly Brown.

"Did you know any of them?" Smith said.

"I knew all of them," Holly said. "I knew them well."

"Are you studying law?"

Holly nodded. "I'm in my third year, and I'm scared."

"I don't think you have anything to worry about."

"I think I have everything to worry about," Holly said. "I'm the only one left."

"I'm not sure I understand."

"There were five of us in Professor Wild's Wednesday night study group," Holly said. "And now it's just me."

CHAPTER FORTY

"Tell me more about this group."

Smith had suggested they go somewhere away from the university campus, and Holly Brown had been happy to oblige. They were sitting in a pub called the Hawthorne. Smith didn't know it existed. Both of them had cokes in front of them and both drinks remained untouched.

"I received an email," Holly said. "Just before the beginning of the new academic year. It was August or early September."

"This year?" Smith said.

"That's right. I was invited to join an exclusive group of students in an extra-curricular study group."

"Did the invitation come from Professor Wild?"

"It did. He'd selected a handful of students to participate."

"Were you made aware of the other people who would make up this group?" Smith said.

Holly nodded. "That's the main reason I accepted. I knew all of them. We were all fiercely competitive and I thought it would be interesting, not to mention a good thing to have on my CV."

"I imagine it would," Smith said. "Are you saying that Professor Wild only chose the top students?"

"Jackie and Rebecca were always ahead of most of us," Holly said. "But we weren't far behind. We're talking top five percent here."

"I know exactly what you mean."

This was an understatement. He'd been there, done that and got more than one T-Shirt.

"What did you discuss in these study groups?" he asked.

"All sorts. At first it was real-life cases where Professor Wild believed the outcome to be wrong. It was mostly trials from America."

"Why does that not surprise me? Do you have an idea why the people in the group were killed?"

"I have no idea," Holly said.

"Were the study groups kept secret?"

"We were encouraged not to talk about what was discussed there, but I don't think they were a secret."

Smith was feeling animated. This was possibly the first concrete lead they'd had in the investigation. Four women who were personally invited to join an elite study group were now dead. It was definitely significant, and the only thing missing was the motivation behind their murders. He was confident that that would become apparent very soon. He decided to ask Holly if she had any theories.

"Can you think of any reason why four members of that group were murdered?"

"What do you think?" she said. "If I knew that, I would have taken it straight to the police. I'm in danger, aren't I?"

"We don't know that," Smith said, even though he knew that she had a very valid point.

He made a mental note to speak to DI Smyth about it as soon as he got the chance.

His gaze shifted to the bar counter at the back of the room.

"Can I get you a drink?"

"I've got one thanks," Holly said.

"I mean a *drink*," Smith said. "I see they stock my favourite beer."

"Aren't you on duty?"

"Does that bother you?"

Holly smiled for the first time. She had a nice smile – it was a genuine smile that made her eyes shine.

"I'll take that as a yes then," Smith said. "What will it be?"

He went to the bar and returned with a pint of lager and a Theakston for himself. He took a sip and turned to face Holly.

"Tell me some more about the study group."

"Some of the discussions got heated," Holly said. "Every one of us was passionate about the law, and I suppose that's why Professor Wild chose us."

"I thought he selected you based on your grades."

"That too, but there were a few other students who could have been picked because of that, but we were the only ones."

Smith debated whether to tell her about the similar group he was a part of two decades ago. He decided that it wouldn't do any harm.

"I studied law here."

"You did a law degree before you joined the police?" Holly said.

"Sort of. I dropped out before I was due to graduate. And I was also part of one of Professor Wild's elite study groups."

"You're kidding me?"

"It was twenty years ago," Smith said. "And I remember thoroughly enjoying it, even though some of the topics for discussion were rather unorthodox."

"We've also analysed some pretty bizarre cases."

"I'm not talking about real-life cases," Smith said. "I'm referring to hypothetical ones. Hypotheses that bordered on the insane."

Holly picked up her lager and took a long drink. "Has Professor Wild really been here that long?"

"I idolised the man," Smith said. "He was the one who spurred me on."

"He has that sort of personality. He's an enigmatic presence. You think he's behind the murders, don't you?"

"I can't comment on that."

"You don't have to," Holly said. "I can read the undertones. I'm in danger, aren't I?"

Smith drained half of his pint in one go and nodded.

"I think you are."

He sighed deeply.

"Is this where you tell me that resources won't stretch to police protection?"

"You're sharp. And yes, my boss isn't going to go for it."

"So, I just have to hope and pray that I'm not the next victim? Although I'm the only one left. All the other women are dead."

Something occurred to Smith, and he cursed himself for not thinking about it earlier.

"All of you were selected for your legal brains," he said. "Why are there no men in the group? Surely the women in the class haven't got the monopoly on intellect?"

"Of course not," Holly said. "In fact, I was surprised that some of the men weren't chosen too."

"I'm not," Smith said. "Come on, drink up."

"Where are we going?"

"I'm going to organise your police protection."

"I thought you thought that wasn't possible."

"There are many ways to skin a cat," Smith said. "You're not a cat person, are you?"

"I prefer dogs," Holly said.

"Then you and me are going to get along just fine."

CHAPTER FORTY ONE

"Have you lost your mind?"

DI Smyth's eyes were fixed on Smith's and there was a concerned expression in them.

"Do you want to arrange police protection for her?" Smith said.

"Based on a hunch? The answer would be a resounding no."

"It's more than a hunch, boss," Smith said. "Holly Brown is the only remaining member of a group of students, hand selected by Professor Wild. Only women were picked and that's because they're generally easier targets. Holly is in grave danger."

"Has she received any threats?" DI Smyth said. "Has she had any impression that somebody has been watching her?"

"That's not how this killer operates. She's on the list and unless we do something drastic, her name is going to be added to a more macabre list very soon. Could you live with yourself if that happened?"

"Don't you dare use the guilt trip thing with me," DI Smyth said.

"She's in danger, and I'm not going to sit back and wait for a phone call confirming that I was right. I knew you wouldn't agree to police protection, so I've offered you an alternative solution."

DI Smyth didn't say anything for a while. He ran his hand through his hair and narrowed his eyes.

"There must be another way."

"If you can think of one, I'm all ears."

"You're talking about arresting an innocent woman. Not only is it immoral – it's illegal."

"Not if she plays her part," Smith said. "She's already agreed to it. She gets to enjoy the finest hospitality York Police has to offer, and she's safe to boot."

"I've heard some harebrained ideas come out of your mouth before, Smith," DI Smyth said. "But this has to be the outright winner. You want to lock up a young woman for the weekend – a woman who has never broken the law in her life. She's a law student, for Pete's sake."

"And her life is in danger. She gets the protection she needs, and we get to give her that without putting a dent in the budget. At least promise me you'll give it some thought."

"You've left me no choice," DI Smyth said. "If the press get wind of this, I'll be right behind you in the dole queue."

"Don't be so negative," Smith said. "It'll be fine."

"Where is she now?" DI Smyth said. "Where is our innocent prisoner?"

"I asked her to wait in my office."

"What are you planning on arresting her for by the way?"

"I hadn't thought that far ahead."

"For God's sake, Smith. I can actually hear the grey hairs spouting from my scalp. Do you know what I want engraved on my tombstone?"

"You're getting morbid now, boss."

"*Here lies Oliver James Smyth – Damn you, Smith.*"

Smith grinned. "Oliver James? OJ?"

"Don't you dare."

"Wouldn't dream of it," Smith said. "You won't regret it."

He got up from the chair and headed for the door.

"I wasn't aware that..."

Smith wasn't listening. He was already halfway down the corridor, on his way to his own office.

"Sorry to keep you waiting," he said to Holly Brown.

"What's going to happen now?" she asked.

"I don't know yet," Smith said. "I thought I could arrange for you to be arrested and arraigned for the weekend, but I didn't consider the consequences of that. You could risk getting a record and it could affect your future."

"I'd say that's a small price to pay," Holly said. "There's a strong possibility I won't have a future anyway if we don't do this."

"Give me a few hours to think about it," Smith said. "I'm sure I'll figure something out. You're welcome to stay here in the meantime. There's a canteen upstairs that offers decent coffee."

"I'll see if I can come up with something too. Perhaps there's a way we can do this and avoid any repercussions."

"Give me your phone number," Smith said.

"Do you have a card?" Holly asked.

Smith took one out and gave it to her. She tapped his number into her phone, Smith's phone started to ring and then went silent.

"You've got my number," she said and handed the card back.

"I have to go," Smith said. "If anyone asks what you're doing here, tell them you're doing some research for me."

"Do you think they'll believe me?"

"They'll believe you," Smith said. "Don't leave the station."

He was planning on paying Grant Webber a visit. Rachel Bright's business card was still in a forensic bag in his pocket, and he needed to see if Forensics could match the fingerprints she'd left on the laminated card to anything that they'd uncovered in the investigation. It was a long shot, but Smith knew from experience that long shots sometimes hit the target.

He was just about to leave when DI Smyth's voice stopped him in his tracks.

"Where do you think you're going?"

Smith turned around. "I just need to check something at the New Forensics Building, boss."

"Is your phone not working?"

"It's not that kind of check," Smith said.

"I'm listening."

"It's more of a gut feeling at this stage, boss."

"Marvellous," DI Smyth said. "Another one of Smith's hunches. Have you forgotten the small matter of a prime suspect who is waiting to be interviewed?"

"Of course not," Smith said. "Me and Kerry will interrogate the professor as soon as I get back. I won't be long."

CHAPTER FORTY TWO

It was a ten-minute drive across the city to the New Forensics Building but Smith made it in half that time. He parked as close as he could get to the ugly building. It really was a blot on the landscape and there had been some very unhappy residents when the neo-modern structure was completed more than ten years ago. The construction work wasn't cheap, and nobody really knew where the funding had come from. It was a mystery, and Smith didn't think he would ever find out who actually paid for it. Even though the place was over a decade old it was still referred to as the New Forensics Building and he reckoned it always would be.

He greeted the friendly man manning the desk on the ground floor and made his way up to the lab where Webber usually worked, not bothering to explain the nature of his visit to the man. He wasn't pressed for it. Smith's presence in the building was nothing unusual.

He found Webber in his office. The Head of Forensics wasn't doing much at all and Smith presumed he was on a break.

"Am I interrupting anything?" he asked.

"If it's possible to interrupt nothing," Webber said. "Then I can answer in the affirmative."

"You're in one of those moods," Smith said.

"I'm stating a fact. Is taking a break from doing nothing, actually the opposite? Is it really a contradiction in terms? It's a philosophical quandary, isn't it?"

"I'll take your word for it. I need you to analyse some prints."

"The correct way of phrasing it would be somewhere along the lines of: *would you be so kind as to take a look at some prints for me, that's if you're not busy with anything else of course*?"

"Is Billie around?" Smith said.

"Relax," Webber said. "What have you got?"

Smith took out the forensics bag with the business card inside.

"Come on then," Webber said.

Billie Jones and Pete Richards weren't at their usual stations in the lab and Smith asked Webber about it.

"I let them get off early. We've all been working flat out since the start of the week, and they need a break."

"Lucky for some," Smith said.

"Let's have a look at your prints then."

"How long is it going to take to compare them to anything you've recovered during the course of the investigation?" Smith said.

Webber raised an eyebrow.

"I'm not being pedantic," Smith said. "The DI is breathing down my neck to get on with interviewing the professor."

"If they're on file," Webber said. "I can get the results in less than twenty minutes."

"I'll stick around then," Smith decided. "Did you know the DI's middle name was James?"

"Why would I know something like that?"

"OJ Smyth," Smith said. "It has a certain ring to it, don't you think?"

Webber didn't offer a comment.

He donned a pair of gloves and removed the business card from the plastic bag.

"Rachel Bright?"

"She's the head of admissions for the law department at the university," Smith explained.

"Is she a suspect?"

"Everyone's a suspect until we decide otherwise."

"I suppose there's a certain logic in that. This wasn't obtained in the proper manner, was it?"

"Who cares?" Smith said. "I stopped giving a shit about doing things by the book when Professor Wild made it perfectly clear how he was going to play the game."

"You know whatever we find can't be put into evidence?"

"Not right now," Smith said. "But if we get a result there are plenty of ways to put it into evidence later. You let me worry about that."

He watched Webber get to work. It took no longer than five minutes for his well practiced hands to dust the surface of the business card, front and back and gently tap the card to remove any excess powder. Then he photographed both sides and applied a length of adhesive tape to lift any prints that may be present. The tape was then attached to a lift card and photographed once more.

"There are some real beauties here," Webber said. "Fuming won't be necessary."

He walked across the room to a desk with a laptop on it. The photographs were sent directly to the laptop and Webber promptly got to work tapping away on the keypad.

"Are you going to the Christmas party tomorrow?" Smith asked him as he worked.

"It's not tomorrow," Webber said.

"Chalmers said it was next Saturday."

"Indeed, it is."

"That's tomorrow," Smith said.

"Tomorrow is *this* Saturday," Webber explained. "The Saturday after that is *next* Saturday."

"That makes no sense whatsoever. Surely *next* Saturday can only be translated as the next Saturday, which in this instance is tomorrow."

"It's a Yorkshire thing," Webber said. "I thought you'd spent half your life here."

"Some things I'll never understand," Smith said. "Do we have a result?"

"We do," Webber said. "And I'm going to disappoint you. The prints from your admissions lady have not come up during the course of the investigation."

"Are you sure?"

Webber's expression answered the question beautifully.

"OK," Smith said. "One more thing."

"You really need to come up with something more original than that," Webber told him.

"Can you check something else for me?"

Smith handed him one of his own cards.

"I assume your prints will be all over this?" Webber said.

"No doubt, but they're in the system. I won't ask you for anything else."

Webber repeated the procedure with the card. After eliminating Smith's fingerprints Webber nodded his head slowly.

"We have a match."

"I was actually hoping we wouldn't," Smith said.

"A thumbprint on your business card matches the thumbprint we pulled from one of the wine glasses at the scene of Jackie Grant's murder. Who is it?"

"A young woman I was planning on arresting for fuck all," Smith said. "This case gets more and more bizarre by the minute."

CHAPTER FORTY THREE

Smith's first port of call when he got back was DI Smyth's office. He told the DI what he'd discovered at the New Forensics Building.

"Holly's print was on one of the wine glasses at Jackie Grant's place. I don't know what to make of it."

"It doesn't necessarily mean that Holly was the one who killed her," DI Smyth pointed out.

"Why didn't she mention it?" Smith said. "Why didn't she tell me that she was at Jackie's house that day?"

"Did you ask her?"

"What?" Smith said. "No, I didn't ask her."

"How did you even get Miss Brown's prints?"

"I wanted her phone number," Smith said. "And she asked me for a card so she could phone me. Hold on..."

"Here we go."

"I think I've been played."

"It won't be the first time."

"No," Smith said. "I'm such an idiot. It was all planned. Fuck it."

"Are you going to explain what on earth is going on?"

"Holly approached me," Smith said. "She was the one who volunteered the information about the extra-curricular study group. She asked me for a card and then she gave it back to me. Everything about it was too convenient."

"What does it mean in terms of the investigation though?"

"I have no idea."

"If you're right," DI Smyth said. "It means that Holly is somehow involved. You need to tread carefully with her, and I would suggest you rethink your plan to arrest her for nothing."

"I disagree, boss."

"I thought you might say that."

"Hear me out," Smith said. "If Holly is a part of this it means she and Professor Wild have been working together."

"How does that help us?"

"Where is the prof now?"

"You know where he is," DI Smyth said. "He's waiting patiently in the holding cells for you to get off your backside."

"Exactly. And that's why It's even more vital that we arrest Holly for something. And we make damn sure Professor Wild is aware of it."

"This could come back to bite you,"

"I know what I'm doing," Smith said. "I have a cunning plan."

"That's not your line either."

"I'll come up with a more original one," Smith said. "I'm just going out for a quick smoke and hopefully I'll come up with something we can arrest Holly Brown for, then I think it's time to see what Professor Wild has to say."

Smith went outside and lit a cigarette. The snowfall earlier was a distant memory and there was nothing on the ground to even suggest it had happened. The nicotine was doing nothing to help make any sense out of the mass of information inside his head. He was dealing with an intricate plan, of that there was little doubt, but he still couldn't come up with a satisfactory counterplan. What was the endgame in this? What did Professor Wild hope to achieve? The motivation behind the murders was still eluding Smith and he hated it when that happened.

He lit another cigarette from the end of the first one and thought about how he was going to handle Holly Brown's arrest. It didn't take him long to come up with a plan in that regard. He smoked the cigarette quickly and went back inside the station to break the news to her.

"You can't do this," she said.

Smith had found her sitting behind the desk inside his office.

"My hands are tied," Smith lied. "I've discussed it with my boss, and if we arrest you without reasonable grounds, not only would we be looking at an internal investigation, both of us could lose our jobs. I can't risk it."

"I've already said I'll cooperate," Holly said. "I'll do whatever you want me to do – I'll sign documents admitting to my part in it, so I won't be able to cause trouble for you afterwards."

"It's too risky."

"You're just going to let me loose?" Holly said. "Four of my friends are dead, and I'm the last one on the list. My life is in danger, and you know it. You can trust me."

"I trust you," Smith lied. "But I still can't take the risk."

Holly shot up from the chair so quickly that Smith took a step back. She took a couple of steps towards him.

"Are you familiar with Section 89(1) of the Police Act 1996?" she said.

"Don't do this, Holly," Smith warned.

"According to Section 89(1), the severity of the sentence depends on the level of harm caused and the culpability of the accused is also taken into account."

"This is a really stupid idea," Smith said. "Think of your future. You could…"

He didn't get the chance to finish the sentence. Holly was surprisingly quick. Her right fist connected with Smith's lip, and he was knocked backwards. He put his hand to his lip and wiped some blood away. He could feel it starting to swell already, and he could taste more blood in his mouth.

"Will that work for you?" Holly said.

"That wasn't the brightest thing to do," Smith said.

"Assaulting a police officer is a serious offence," Holly said with a smile on her face. "You now have grounds for arrest."

"You realise that if I do that," Smith said. "Your career in law is over."

"Not necessarily," Holly said. "I mentioned Section 89(1) specifically because in it, it is stipulated that for an assault on a police officer charge to work, the officer in question must qualify for the execution of duty clause. And I'll quote: the officer must be acting within the scope of their duties for the offence to be made out. I could be wrong but what you're occupied with right now isn't exactly acting within the scope of your duties, is it?"

"What are you suggesting?" Smith said.

His lip felt like it had swollen to twice its size.

"You lock me up while you examine your options. I just punched you in the face. You should see your lip. When the case is examined after the weekend, it will become clear that there are no charges to face. Case closed. I'm sorry, by the way."

Smith looked at her. There was something in her eyes he didn't like. He wasn't sure if she really was unstable or whether it was a part of the act, he was certain she was playing. He rubbed his lip again.

"I walked into a door. Holly Brown – you're free to go."

CHAPTER FORTY FOUR

"What happened to your face?" DC King asked.

"Don't ask," Smith said. "Are you ready to go up against the professor?"

"I've thought about nothing else all day. He's going to try to trick us, isn't he?"

"No doubt about it, but we'll be ready for him. Come on then."

Professor Wild was still adamant that he didn't require the services of a lawyer. He was escorted to one of the interview rooms and told to wait for Smith and DC King. They came in five minutes later. Smith didn't greet Professor Wild. He turned on the recording device and stated the usual stuff for the record.

"You haven't aged well, Jason," Professor Wild said. "And I would get that lip seen to if I were you."

"As of yet," Smith said. "You haven't been charged with anything. I would like to ask you if you wish to reconsider the option of legal representation."

"Why would I reconsider if I haven't been charged with anything?"

"Professor Wild," DC King said. "You're a professor of law at the university – is that correct?"

"It is."

"How long have you worked at the university?"

"Twenty-four years and seven months. I was offered the tenure of professor twenty-one years ago."

"That's impressive," DC King said. "You must have taught half of the lawyers in the city."

"More than that," Professor Wild said. "Is there a point to this?"

"My colleague is merely establishing some background information," Smith said.

"How have you been?" Professor Wild asked. "I've been following your career closely. You really have been in the wars, haven't you?'

"Let's talk about the current students," DC King said. "How many people on average do you teach each year?"

"Somewhere in the region of a hundred," Professor Wild said.

"And I imagine there are some rising stars amongst them."

"There always will be. Ask your colleague. He was one of them, once upon a time. I really was disappointed in you, Jason. Although I imagine you had your reasons."

"We're not here to talk about my colleague," DC King said.

"This all feels somewhat rehearsed," Professor Wild said. "Too rehearsed, although I could be wrong."

"Professor Wild," DC King said. "Let's move on to the events of the past week. Belinda James, Rebecca Stone, Sharon Atlee and Jackie Grant – do those names mean anything to you?"

Smith had suggested she list the names of the victims in the order they were killed, not the order their bodies were discovered.

"Of course they mean something to me," Professor Wild said. "They were all students of mine."

"And they're all dead," Smith said.

"Also correct."

"How do you feel about their murders?" DC King said.

"How do you think I feel? Someone killed them – it's tragic."

"Do you associate with any of your students outside of the university?" DC King said.

"Sometimes. Ask Detective Smith. We often shared a drink or two, didn't we?"

"Did you socialise with any of the dead women after hours?" Smith said.

"You phrased the question in such a morbid way," Professor Wild said. "But yes, I did see them outside of class."

"All of them?" Smith said.

"On occasion, yes."

"You told us that you received a message from Sharon Atlee asking you to come to her house on the day she was killed," DC King said. "Is that correct?"

"Yes and no," Professor Wild said.

"Yes, and no?" DC King said.

"Yes, I did receive a message from her, but no, I didn't yet know it was the day she would be killed. You need to work on the phrasing of your questions too."

"What was the reason she asked you to come round?"

"She didn't give one."

"Weren't you curious?" Smith said. "Didn't you want to know why one of your students wanted you to make a house call?"

"I imagined the reason would become apparent when I got there."

"Do you make a habit of visiting your students at home?" DC King said.

"Not at all."

"Can you explain why you confessed to killing Rebecca Stone and Sharon Atlee?" Smith said.

"I don't recall doing that," Professor Wild said.

"I thought you might say that. You told the duty sergeant that you couldn't take it any longer and you owned up to their murders."

"There is no way I would express myself in that manner. And why would I confess to two murders I didn't commit?"

"You had an alibi for the murder of Rebecca Stone anyway," DC King said.

"Then that makes your claim about my confession even more ridiculous, doesn't it?"

"Moving on to the murder of Jackie Grant," DC King said. "Jackie received a text message just before she was killed. The sender of the message asked if she was home and shortly afterwards, she received a phone call from the same number. When we called the number, we got your voicemail."

"I don't think so," Professor Wild said.

"It was your voice on the voicemail, Professor Wild."

"Please, call me Herman."

"Can you explain about the voicemail?" Smith said.

"There is no correspondence between me and Jackie Grant," Professor Wild said. "You have my phone if you want to check."

"You have two phones," Smith said and instantly regretted it.

"Prove it."

"Why did we find a length of rope in your living room?" DC King said. "It was a very unusual rope and there aren't many places where you can get it."

"Hemp," Professor Wild said. "I bought it at a place on James Street. Hemporium, if I remember."

"How much did you buy?" Smith said.

"Fifteen metres."

"We found only five metres at your house," DC King said. "What happened to the other ten metres?"

"I used it to hang some garden ornaments," Professor Wild said. "It's durable rope and it stands up to the elements well. I would have thought your forensics officers would have checked that."

"Let's talk about the search of your house," DC King said. "What was your brother doing there?"

"Roger has a key. I really didn't know he would be there at the same time you decided to raid the place."

"We didn't raid the place," Smith said. "Why would your brother claim to be you and let himself get arrested?"

"You'll have to ask him that."

"You had no idea he would do that?"

"Was that a question?"

"Were you or were you not aware that your brother was going to pretend to be you when the search was carried out?" Smith said. "And that was a question."

"Roger isn't well," Professor Wild said. "He becomes somewhat delusional when he forgets to take his tablets."

"What's wrong with him?" DC King said.

"He has a number of mental issues."

"Speaking of tablets," Smith said. "You suffer from angina, don't you?"

"My lifestyle isn't what you would call healthy," Professor Wild said. "I've tried to do something about it, and I haven't suffered an angina attack for a long time."

"What was Roger doing with your pills?" DC King said. "He faked an angina attack and claimed he wasn't allowed access to the pills."

"He also neglected to mention to the duty sergeant that he had an underlying health condition," Smith said.

"That's because he doesn't," Professor Wild. "Why would he lie to the duty officer?"

"I think you and your brother planned all of it, Herman," Smith said.

"Prove it."

"Not yet," Smith said. "There's nothing wrong with your brother, is there?"

"I can give you the details of mental health care professionals who will beg to differ," Professor Wild said.

"What are you hoping to achieve, Herman?" Smith said. "What's the point of this experiment of yours? What is your endgame?"

"Experiment?" Professor Wild repeated. "Endgame? I have no idea what you're talking about. I don't imagine you'll have forgotten anything about your life before you made the decision you did. You'll still have a good grasp of the law, and it's that part that's really baffling. You arrested an innocent man because you didn't even check to see who he was. You fabricated a confession, and you subsequently arrested another man based on nothing more than a couple of circumstantial coincidences. I really expected more from you. Is this how you normally operate, because if it is, God help the people of this city."

Smith decided that now was the time to bring up the extra-curricular study groups. He cursed himself for not looking through the file that Penny Fowler had given him. It was possible it might have given him some ammunition.

"Can you remember the study group you set up twenty years ago?" he said.

"Of course," Professor Wild said. "I recall it being rather memorable. We discussed some interesting theories, didn't we?"

"We certainly did. Did you continue with the groups?"

"For a few years," Professor Wild said. "They petered off after a while. You know how these things go."

"So, you haven't done anything similar recently?" DC King said.

"Not for many years."

"Are you sure?"

"An exceptional memory is a basic requirement for a professor of law – of course, I'm sure."

"Your memory is clearly not what it used to be," Smith said. "Because we know about the study group you personally invited a select few students to join very recently. All of them women. Does that ring any bells?"

"I'm sure I would have remembered it."

"There were five members," Smith said. "I say *were*, because four of them are now dead – all of them were murdered this week. Does that jog your memory a bit more?"

"No," Professor Wild said. "It does not."

"You're lying," DC King said. "We know for a fact that all of the dead women attended an outside study group."

"Prove it."

Professor Wild looked at Smith and he realised two things at the same time. Holly Brown was definitely involved in this, and she was going to deny any knowledge of any extra-curricular study group. Smith couldn't prove a damn thing.

CHAPTER FORTY FIVE

Smith decided to take a short break for the sole reason that he was running out of questions to ask, and he needed some time to come up with some. He also needed to take a look at the file that was still locked in the boot of his car. He went to fetch it, and he smoked a cigarette while he was in the car park. He'd expected Herman Wild to be slippery, but he hadn't been prepared for what transpired in the interview room.

He retrieved the file and slammed the boot closed. His phone started to ring inside his pocket. The ringtone told him it was Grant Webber. Thomas Dolby was lamenting about being blinded with science and Smith wondered what the Head of Forensics was calling about this late in the day.

"Webber," he answered it.

"I have something for you," Webber said.

"Something that's going to make me smile?"

"Your student," Webber said. "The one who drank wine with Jackie Grant."

"Holly Brown," Smith said. "She's been released."

"That was a bit hasty."

"She wanted me to keep her here for the weekend," Smith said. "She even punched me in the face to force an assault on a police officer charge, but I thought it was best to let her go. What's the problem?"

"The prints on your business card have come up in the investigation."

"We already know that," Smith said. "She was the one who drank wine with Jackie Grant. I think she'll have a perfectly good explanation for it, and I haven't got time for crap like that. What else has she been involved in?"

"I've only just got around to analysing the phone found at the scene of Belinda James's murder. Holly Brown's prints were on the screen of that phone, Smith."

"Fuck it."

"If I were you, I would try to locate Miss Brown at the earliest possible opportunity."

"Thanks for stating the obvious, Webber."

He ended the call and slammed his hand on the roof of his car. He'd been such an idiot. Holly Brown had volunteered to be locked up, and he'd sent her on her way, and now he knew she was definitely involved in at least one of the murders.

He turned to head back to the entrance of the station and stopped in his tracks.

"Hold on."

Something felt wrong and it didn't take Smith long to realise what it was. Holly had given him her fingerprints on a plate. She'd asked for a business card when she could have just got his phone number verbally. She did that for a reason, and when Smith thought about it, he knew that it was just another part of the game she and Professor Wild were playing with the professor pulling the strings. She'd appeared at the table in the canteen of the university immediately after Rachel Bright had left, and it was quite possible she'd seen what Smith did with the business card the head of admissions had given him. Smith wasn't sure what to do with this information, but he knew instinctively that bringing Holly Brown in right now wasn't the right thing to do. He needed more time to think. He wanted to read what was in the file Penny Fowler had given him and he wanted to do that now. Professor Wild and Holly Brown were just going to have to wait.

Smith opened the file and started from the beginning. Penny had typed out her notes, and it made Smith smile. The date at the top of the first page was the 20th of May. Smith remembered that this was shortly before his Gran's death and therefore it was not long before he gave up on practising law and joined the police.

Penny had arranged the notes as though they were describing some kind of scientific experiment, and Smith decided that it was exactly what it had been. It was a hypothetical experiment, and Penny had labelled it at the top. *The legal possibilities of evading prosecution in a homicide.*

Step one dealt with something Smith hated with a passion. Misdirection, or sleight of hand was a concept he'd come across many times, and he despised it more than anything else. The first stages of the discussion group came back to him as he read.

"It is entirely possible to get away with murder," he read. "The first step is to understand detection techniques absolutely."

Smith couldn't believe that Professor Wild had even dreamt up this topic. It really was a bizarre proposition.

"Seeds of doubt," Smith read on the second page. "Contradictory evidence and shadow of doubt."

This section interested him. Penny's notes went on to talk about forensic evidence and alibi. It was clear that Professor Wild had put forward the proposition that when a piece of evidence is contradicted by another piece of evidence, seeds of doubt will be sown and the investigation into the crime will become muddied. Smith decided that this was exactly what had happened during the course of the present investigation.

Specifics were discussed and some of them were so close to the events of the past week that Smith couldn't ignore them. It was imperative for fingerprints at a crime scene to be explained. Forensic evidence also had to be justified. Smith thought about the length of rope found in Herman Wild's house and Holly Brown's prints on the wine glass and the phone of one of the victims. Professor Wild had explained about the rope and Smith knew for a fact that Holly would somehow explain the prints too.

"Legal requirements and the responsibility of law enforcement," Smith read.

This was more complicated than Smith remembered. Penny's notes went on to examine the legal nitty gritty that formed a part of any serious investigation. There were protocols to adhere to, and every piece of evidence needed to be handled correctly. Smith hadn't thought about this for a very long time, and the more he read the more he realised that there had been plenty of cases where he hadn't followed the rules, and it was a miracle that some of his cases even led to a conviction. This instance was no different. In fact, most of the evidence they had, hadn't been handled properly.

"The element of surprise."

This was documented towards the end. Smith carried on reading about how important this aspect was. They'd discussed dropping a bombshell at precisely the right time. The investigation had been riddled with bombshells, and he wondered if there were more to come. Did Professor Wild still have some aces up his sleeve? It was possible that he was far from finished.

Everything in the twenty-year-old case notes was relevant to the case they were working on, and Smith knew he had to share it with the rest of the team. They would put their heads together and see if they could come up with a possible next move. If they could predict what Professor Wild had up his sleeve next, they would be able to come up with a counter move he wouldn't be expecting. But first, Smith needed to reconvene the interview with the man. There was still a whole load of questions to ask.

CHAPTER FORTY SIX

Smith started the recording device again and stated the time. It was past six and the sun wouldn't be back for another thirteen or fourteen hours.

"When we left off last time," he said. "We were discussing a study group for a select few elite students."

"And I recall that I asked you to prove the existence of such a group," Professor Wild said.

"You did, yes. But I'd like to talk about a different study group you brought up. The extra-curricular group I was a part of almost twenty years ago."

"Is this relevant," Professor Wild said. "Or is it merely nostalgia on your part?"

"A bit of both," Smith said. "Humour me, please."

"If you insist."

"Can you remember what was discussed in some of those sessions?"

"Of course."

"One particular topic stayed in my head for a very long time," Smith said. "You asked us to consider if it was possible to carry out a murder and get away with it. The details are somewhat hazy, but I think it was something along the lines of the legal possibilities of evading prosecution in a homicide."

A broad smile spread across Professor Wild's face.

"Would you care to share the joke?" DC King said.

"I'll allow DS Smith that honour," Professor Wild said. "Jason, you cannot possibly think a professor of law is using the amateurish findings of a group of law students to carry out a series of perfect murders. Twenty years after the discussions. Please tell me that this isn't a serious line of enquiry."

"Do you remember that particular discussion?" Smith said.

"I've already told you I remember it."

"There were various stages," Smith said. "We discussed misdirection and diversion tactics. Then there were detection methods and ways to exploit them using contradictory forensic evidence and seeds of doubt. If we were to go back through the events of this investigation, we would find striking similarities between the topics discussed in those study groups and the events of the past week. And I know what you're going to say – from an evidence perspective it's useless, and it's circumstantial at best, but you have to agree that it is worth looking into."

"I'm a professor of law suspected of multiple murder," Professor Wild said. "It's not my place to agree nor disagree. I believe the onus is still on you and your people to establish guilt, unless that has changed in the short time I've been wrongly incarcerated."

"I suggest we go back to the beginning," DC King said. "There are still a number of loose ends that are bothering me."

"Is she always this serious?" Professor Wild asked Smith.

"She has a good point," Smith said. "And a few things are bugging me too. Belinda James was killed first, wasn't she?"

"You tell me."

"She was," Smith said. "She was killed sometime on Sunday, possible only a few hours before Rebecca Stone was brutally murdered. We also have reason to believe that there was more than one perpetrator involved in Belinda's murder, and we have evidence that supports this."

"What evidence?"

"As you've quite rightly pointed out," DC King said. "You're a professor of law accused of murder, and the onus is on us to establish guilt. We're not required to discuss the evidence with you."

"Let's just say," Smith said. "The evidence is irrefutable, and it proves that there was more than one person involved in Belinda's death. We've already established that you have an alibi for Sunday from ten in the morning until three that afternoon, but we're not particularly concerned about that."

"Rebecca Stone," DC King said. "We initially believed that she was the first victim because she was found first, but we now know that it was intentional."

"An element of misdirection never goes amiss, does it?" Smith said. "Throw a bit of confusion into the mix to make life harder for the investigative team. But once you move past the subtle sleight of hand, a picture starts to form – a picture that is now extremely clear. Sharon Atlee. She sent you a message on Tuesday afternoon to ask you to come round to her house. We've touched on that, but you still haven't told us why she wanted to see you."

"It was nothing important."

"Are you in the habit of making house calls to your students for nothing important?" DC King said.

"What did she want, Herman?" Smith said.

"It's not relevant to the investigation."

"It's extremely relevant," DC King said. "Shortly after you claim to have left Miss Atlee's house, she was murdered."

Professor Wild rubbed his eyes, and Smith sensed that for the first time since the start of the interview, some cracks were beginning to appear. He decided to try and chip away at them a bit more.

"Do you know Sharon's boyfriend?"

"I can't say I do," Professor Wild said.

"He claims to know you," DC King said. "In fact, he knows quite a bit about you."

"You were sleeping with Sharon, weren't you?" Smith said.

Professor Wild looked him in the eyes. "Are you going to arrest me for sleeping with one of my students?"

"No," Smith said. "You're already under arrest for something more serious. Were you and Sharon in a relationship?"

"I wouldn't call it a relationship," Professor Wild said. "We had some fun, that's all."

"Is that what you were doing there on Tuesday," DC King said. "Having some fun?"

"Sharon was anxious, and she asked me to pop round because I believe she wanted someone to talk to."

"What was she anxious about?" Smith said.

"She was experiencing doubts about her abilities," Professor Wild elaborated. "I assured her that she had no need to question her capabilities and when I left, she seemed upbeat. My words seemed to have had the desired effect."

"And you achieved that in the space of half an hour?" DC King said.

"Wisdom is something that comes with age. You'll understand when you get a bit older."

"Let's move on to Jackie Grant," Smith said. "We have a very brief timescale to look at in Miss Grant's murder. Shortly before she was killed, she received a message from a number we've as yet been unable to trace. There was a missed call from the same number shortly after the message arrived. When we called the number, we got your voicemail. You deny all knowledge of this, and once again it has no real evidence value. It would be possible for someone to acquire a phone, mimic your voice on the voicemail message, and claim that it's you, but we can't prove it was actually you who sent the message and made the call. But we have something better than that. We know that Jackie enjoyed a glass of wine with someone shortly before she was killed and we now know exactly who the other person was."

"Well done," Professor Wild said. "Haul them in and book them."

"That's on the list of things to do this evening," Smith said.

"The net is closing in around you, Professor Wild," DC King said. "I have to give you credit – you orchestrated every step of this plan beautifully, and if it wasn't for the one element you overlooked you probably would have succeeded in proving that it is very possible to get away with murder."

"In any murder investigation, without exception," Smith said. "The perpetrator, or perpetrators in this instance will neglect to consider something that will later point in their direction."

"You have a hundred percent clear-up rate," Professor Wild said.

"I have an exceptional team," Smith said. "Don't feel bad. You almost did it. You were close to proving that there really are legal ways to evade prosecution in a homicide, but you're a professor of law – you're not a killer, and that's why you dropped the ball. You'll probably make the headlines after this, so at least that's something."

"I've never been one to chase fame and fortune."

"I want to ask you about the drawings on their stomachs," Smith said.

"I'm afraid I have no idea what you're talking about," Professor Wild said.

"The scales of justice," DC King said. "The symbol of Lady Justice. Was that your idea?"

"I'm still not following you."

"The drawing was found on all four victims," Smith said. "Can you explain why the image was inverted in the first three but not on the body of Belinda James?"

"I thought you'd established that Belinda was the first victim. You really need to pay more attention to the details."

DC King took out an A4 sized photograph. She put it on the table in front of Professor Wild.

"Is this supposed to mean something to me?" he said.

"I imagine so," Smith tapped his finger on the photo. "That is the symbol of everything you hold dear. Or at least I thought you held the law in high regard."

"There is nothing more sacred than the law."

"Then why turn it on its arse like that?" Smith stabbed at the photo again. "The drawings on the stomachs of the victims suggest an absolute lack of respect for the law."

"I suppose it depends on how you choose to interpret it," Professor Wild said.

"What happened, Herman?" Smith said. "What caused this sudden change in you?"

Professor Wild shrugged his shoulders.

"Are you starting to feel the pressure?" Smith said. "Trying to keep up with the brilliant young minds must take its toll. Is that what it is? Are you afraid you'll wake up one morning and find you've lost your touch? Is this some kind of twisted midlife crisis?"

"Brilliant. I'll make sure to pass on your theory to my good friend Edwina. I'm sure The Daily Mail would kill to print something like that."

"Something definitely happened," Smith said. "Something recent. We will figure out what it is, Herman."

"Right," Professor Wild said.

He got to his feet.

"Please sit down," DC King said.

"I've had enough of this place. The tape is still running, so I suggest you put it on record exactly what it is you plan to do next. I've been placed under arrest for four murders that you have no concrete proof I was involved in. You've admitted that I had an alibi for two of those murders, and the evidence you have against me for the other two is all circumstantial. The ball is in your court now. Think very carefully before you make your next move."

Smith nodded. "Interview concluded, 18:29."

"I presume I'm free to go?" Professor Wild said.

Smith looked at DC King. She didn't give anything away.

"You're free to go," Smith said to Professor Wild. "Don't leave town."

"I'll inform the duty sergeant," DC King said and left the interview room.

"You won't win this game, Jason," Professor Wild said.

"I wasn't aware that we were playing a game," Smith said.

"Don't be so naïve. There's no tape running – it's just you and I here now, so you don't have to pretend anymore."

"No pretending then," Smith said. "Nothing you tell me now can be used against you. Why? Something has to be motivating you – tell me what that is."

"Once in a lifetime you're going to come face to face with a crime where the motive will elude you. Accept it – that's just the way it is."

CHAPTER FORTY SEVEN

Smith needed a drink. The interview with Professor Wild had drained him and he wanted to top himself back up again with a pint or six of Theakston. Herman Wild had all but admitted to his involvement in the four recent murders, but Smith had nothing left to throw at him. There was a chance that Holly Brown might crack under pressure – Smith debated whether to have her picked up, but something stopped him from doing that. He knew she was another part of Professor Wild's scheme, and he suspected that she would come up with a perfectly reasonable explanation as to why her prints were on the wine glass in Jackie Grant's kitchen and on the mobile phone found at Belinda James's house.

Smith went inside his house and heard Whitton's voice coming from the kitchen. Smith wondered if they had visitors but when he walked down the hallway, he realised that his wife was talking to someone on the phone. He grabbed a beer from the fridge and sat down at the table. Whitton was talking to her mother – that was quite clear, and they were talking about her dad again.

"I'll ask him," she said before she said goodbye and ended the call.

"Ask me what?" Smith said.

"If you'll have a chat with my dad," Whitton said.

"He's not going to listen to me. The man is more stubborn than I am, and I'm really not in the mood."

"Please, Jason," Whitton said. "My mum is really worried about him, and she thinks he'll listen to you."

"We don't even know that there's anything wrong with him."

"It's getting worse. He's hardly eating at all now, and it's obvious that he's in pain. Please, give him a call and suggest a drink."

"It's been a hell of a day, and I was looking forward to forgetting about it with the help of as many beers as I can manage."

"Then you can kill two birds with one stone," Whitton said. "Ask my dad to meet you for a few beers

"Now?" Smith said.

"Something is terribly wrong with my father, and he needs to see a doctor."

"If he's not eating," Smith said. "He's hardly going to be in the mood for a few beers."

"Please, Jason."

Smith drained the beer in his glass. "OK, I'll make you a deal. You know how uncomfortable me and your dad get when we're talking on the phone. I'm going to have a quick shower, and you can sort out the rest. Hog's Head – half seven."

* * *

Smith had to admit that Harold Whitton did look a bit peaky. Whitton's dad was already there when Smith went inside the Hog's Head. He was sitting alone at a table close to the bar. An untouched pint of bitter was on the table in front of him. Smith had known Harold for a long time, and he'd always been extremely fit for his age. He was strong and he had the constitution of an ox. Smith couldn't remember him ever getting sick but the man sitting in the Hog's Head looked quite ill. His face was gaunt, and it was clear that he'd lost a bit of weight.

Smith got a pint of Theakston from the bar and joined him at the table. "Harold."

"Evening, son," Harold said.

"Have you been waiting long?"

"Just got here."

He picked up his beer and took a sip. Smith took a much bigger drink from his glass.

"What brought this on?" Harold said. "I just got told by Jane to be here at half-seven, but she didn't elaborate, and I know better than to ask her to." Smith had thought a lot in the back of the taxi on the way there, about how he was going to bring up the subject of Harold's ill health and he decided not to come straight out with it. He would work up to it.

"I needed a beer," he said. "And there's something you might be able to help me with."

"If it's got anything to do with DIY," Harold said. "You're barking up the wrong tree. My strength isn't what it used to be."

"It's not DIY," Smith said. "You know a bit about football, don't you?"

"I've been following the Minstermen since I was in short pants, for all the good that's done me. You're not a big fan of football, are you?"

"I can't see the point of it," Smith said. "I don't know what the fuss is all about. It's a bunch of grown men in shorts kicking a ball around."

"You're Australian, so I won't hold that against you."

"One of my DCs is from London," Smith said. "Wimbledon to be more precise and he mentioned something about the team from the late 80s."

"The Crazy Gang," Harold said and smiled.

He drained half the beer in his glass.

"I've never heard of them," Smith said.

"Vinnie Jones, Dennis Wise, Dave Beasant and the other mad buggers. I've never been keen on the London teams, but this crowd really were entertaining. They rocked the football world. They even lifted the FA cup, if I remember rightly."

"My DC mentioned something about them not quite playing by the rules."

"You could say that. That was back in the good old days when you didn't have all your divas and poofter millionaires falling over when they were so much as sneezed on. And the referees made the calls. A ref and his linesmen would be the only eyes on the pitch – they didn't have all their fancy camera stuff back then. You'd expect to take a few knocks when the ref wasn't watching, especially when you went up against Wimbledon. Why the sudden interest in football?"

"I'll get us another round in," Smith said.

He ordered the beer and was about to take it back to the table when his phone started to ring in his pocket. The ringtone told him it was Whitton.

"I still haven't got round to bringing it up," Smith answered it. "I'm working up to it."

"That's not why I'm calling," Whitton said. "We've got another dead woman. The DI doesn't expect you to attend, but I thought you'd want to know that it's Holly Brown."

"Fuck," Smith said under his breath. "Thanks for letting me know. I'll see you later."

He wasn't expecting this. He couldn't have anticipated it in a million years, and he had a sinking feeling that the person responsible for killing Holly was someone they hadn't yet considered during the course of the investigation. He drained a full pint of beer, ordered another one and took them to the table.

CHAPTER FORTY EIGHT

"She hasn't been dead long."

Grant Webber and Billie Jones were working in the kitchen of the house that Holly Brown shared with two other students. One of them, a second-year Physics student had come home to find her lying, face down on the floor next to the cooker. Early indications suggested that she was strangled.

"She's still warm," Webber said. "And it's not exactly tropical in here. I'd say were looking at an hour, two tops."

"It's exactly the same as the others," Billie crouched down next to the body. "No sign of forced entry and no indication that Holly put up any kind of fight. It's almost as though these women knew what was about to happen to them."

"Ridiculous," Webber said.

"I'm just thinking out loud. Help me to turn her over."

Webber bent down next to her.

"We're going to touch you now," Billie spoke the words to the corpse on the floor.

"That's enough of that," Webber said. "On three."

He took hold of Holly's legs while Billie grabbed her shoulders.

"Three," Webber said."

The welts on the neck were identical to the ones found on the first four victims.

"There are some fibres here," Billie said.

She opened up a small plastic evidence bag and carefully removed the strands of rope with some tweezers. She dropped them inside the bag, sealed it, and labelled it.

Holly was dressed in a pair of jeans and a long-sleeved T-Shirt. Webber rolled up the bottom of the T-Shirt to reveal her stomach.

"No drawing," Billie noticed.

She shifted the T-Shirt right up to her neck but there was no artwork on her skin.

"Perhaps they drew it on her back," Webber said.

It didn't take long to check. There was nothing drawn on the skin of Holly Brown's back either.

"What do you think it means?" Billie asked.

"Absolutely nothing," Webber said. "Nothing that concerns us anyway. Are you going to be at the Christmas party next week?"

"I already have a date."

"I wasn't asking you out on a date – I was merely making conversation."

"I'll be going with Rupert, yes."

"I shall be alone," Webber said. "And I'm perfectly happy about that."

"If you say so."

"Smith isn't going to solve this one," Webber said.

"Is everything alright?" Billie asked. "You're acting a bit strange."

"I have no doubt about his capabilities as a police detective. Smith has the finest detective mind I've ever encountered, but all the signs are indicating that he's going to meet his match with this investigation."

"I disagree."

"You're entitled to disagree," Webber said. "I'm merely pointing out how it's going to be."

"Would you care to bet on it?"

"I'm not a gambling man."

"Chicken," Billie said. "And I'm not talking about money."

"What did you have in mind?"

"If I'm right, and Smith does crack this case you have to bring a date to the Christmas party."

Webber raised an eyebrow. "And if you're wrong?"

"That's up to you."

"Let me think about it. Can you carry on here? I want to have a word with DI Smyth."

He left her to it. He walked down the hallway and exited the house. He removed his gloves and facemask as soon as he was outside. He made his way over to DI Smyth and DS Bridge.

"It's very similar to the others, with one obvious difference."

"Was she strangled?" Bridge said.

"It looks like it," Webber said. "But there was no drawing on her skin. We checked front and back and they didn't draw on her."

"They were interrupted," DI Smyth said.

"That's why I came straight out. Her skin was still warm and it's cold inside the kitchen. I think the housemate came home while the killer was still in the house."

"We've got a door-to-door underway," DI Smyth said.

"If I were you," Webber said. "I would focus on the houses at the back of the property."

"What's back there?" Bridge said.

"The back door leads out onto a small patch of grass. There's a fence at the bottom but anyone with two working legs would be able to get over it. There's a service road running the length of the back of the houses and there are properties on the other side of that road."

"I'll make the officers involved in the door-to-door aware of it," DI Smyth said. "Do we know anything else?"

"Billie seems to think she was expecting it."

"You can't be serious?" Bridge said.

"I don't buy it either," Webber said. "But the fact that there is nothing to indicate that any of the victims put up any kind of resistance is puzzling. Will Smith be joining us?"

"I told Whitton to inform him it wouldn't be necessary," DI Smyth said. "I want to see if Harry and Kerry have managed to get any sense out of the housemate. She was in a state of deep shock when we arrived and I asked the paramedics to give her a once over, but it's possible she saw or heard something that can help us."

"She missed the killer by minutes," Webber said.

"That doesn't tie in with the others," Bridge said. "The first four victims were killed when the murderer knew they would be alone in the house – what makes this one different?"

"Do I ask your opinion on hyperspectral imaging and its benefits in determining chemical changes in fingerprints?"

"What?" Bridge said.

"Precisely. I must get back to work now."

CHAPTER FORTY NINE

"Is everything alright?"

Harold Whitton took a drink from the fresh pint of beer.

"You look a bit flabbergasted," he said.

"It's nothing that can't wait," Smith said.

He wasn't going to burden Harold with the details of the most puzzling murder investigation he'd ever worked on.

"Tell me some more about the Crazy Gang. My colleague mentioned something called a dirty tackle."

"How long have you got?" Harold said.

"Perhaps give me the short version."

"There isn't one. Now, you've got a dirty tackle and a dirty tackle."

Smith didn't think this made any sense whatsoever, but he didn't tell Whitton's dad this.

"The dirty tackle has always been a big part of the gentleman's game," Harold said. "I know it sounds like a contradiction in terms, but there is a certain finesse to it when it's done properly. Take those Wimbledon blokes for example. They took it to another level, and it caused some waves. Not only did they make it look good, they weren't discreet. I remember one occasion where Vinnie Jones took out the legs of a bloke on the opposing side smack bang in front of the referee. Not only that, once he'd picked the poor bastard off the ground, he shook the hand of the ref as he accepted his red card and walked off the pitch to a standing ovation. Those were the days."

"What's the other kind of dirty tackle?" Smith said.

"The sneaky one," Harold told him. "I'm not a great fan of that one. That's the one where the perpetrator makes damn sure nobody is paying him any attention when he moves in for the kill. He might deck a bloke who is nowhere near the ball for example, or he could dole out a subtle elbow to the ribs when nobody's looking."

"What's the purpose of that?" Smith said.

"Power games mostly. Or it could be an act of desperation."

"A last resort?" Smith said.

"Aye," Harold said. "Something like that. Why the sudden interest in football?"

"It's just something that I've been considering."

"Are you thinking of pulling off a dirty tackle yourself?"

"I reckon I am, but I'm worried that it might come back to bite me on the arse if I don't do it properly."

"There's a strong possibility of that if you don't take everything into consideration. You have to make sure that you're going to get away with it. And it needs to be something your opponent will never suspect in a million years. Plus, the best dirty tackles work when the people on your own side are not expecting it either. That way, you don't have to worry about one of them giving the game away before you've had the chance to put it into action. Is that why you invited me here tonight – to pick my brains about the dirty tackle."

"No," Smith said without thinking. "That's not the main reason we're here." Harold stood up. "Hold that thought, son. I need to make room for some more beer. The old bladder isn't what it once was."

Smith wasn't sure how he was going to broach the topic of Harold's health. Discussing football in a pub was all very well – it was something that men in Yorkshire had talked about for years, even if Smith couldn't care less about it, but asking his father-in-law to go and get himself checked over by a doctor was a different kettle of fish altogether.

Harold returned with two pints of beer. He put them on the table and sat back down.

"Out with it."

"This wasn't my idea," Smith said.

"I might be old," Harold said. "But I'm not daft, and I know it wasn't your idea. In all the time I've known you, you haven't once invited me out for a few beers. The women have been conspiring."

"Who are we to argue?"

"Spit it out, son."

"Erica is worried about you," Smith said. "She's been on the phone to Jane and they're both worried."

"I'm a big boy now."

Smith nodded. "Jane says you haven't been eating, and you're losing weight. I can see that's true. Perhaps it wouldn't be such a bad idea to go to see a doctor."

"Waste of time."

"You know me, Harold," Smith said. "You know how I feel about doctors and hospitals, but what harm can it do to go and get a professional opinion?"

"I appreciate your concern, son," Harold said. "But I'll deal with this in my own way, and I'll ask you to respect that."

"Help me here. I'm caught between a rock and a hard place. Erica asked me to talk to you, but it looks like you've made up your mind."

"Aye. I have."

"But what if it is something serious?" Smith said. "Or what if it's something that's not serious now but could be if you leave it too long?"

"I'd quite like to talk about something else now," Harold said.

"I promised Erica, I'd get you to go and see a doctor."

"And you tried," Harold said. "You can't do any more than that."

Smith didn't know what else to say. The two men remained quiet for a moment. Smith finished half of the beer in his glass, merely for something to do to break the awkward silence. He stole a glance at Harold. Whitton's father really did look unwell, and Smith couldn't leave it.

"You're a stubborn old fool."

Smith wasn't prepared for what Harold did next. A grin spread on his face, and he began to laugh. He raised his beer in a toast and Smith found himself toasting him back.

"Please reconsider," Smith said. "Just make an appointment with a doctor. What harm can it do? What have you got to lose?"

Harold's smile faded and he sighed deeply.

"It's too late."

"What are you talking about?" Smith said.

"I've already been to see a doctor," Harold told him. "Two weeks ago. I've known something was wrong for a while now and I needed it confirmed."

"Go on."

"I'll tell Jane and Erica in my own time," Harold said. "I don't want you blurting it out."

"You have my word."

"It's prostrate cancer."

Smith definitely wasn't expecting this.

"Prostate cancer can be fixed, Harold," he said. "You can get treatment for it."

"It's spread," Harold said. "The doctor called it Stage 4 or something. Apparently, it's no longer only in the prostrate – it's gone to the lymph nodes and there's a high risk of it spreading to the liver. There's bugger all they can do about it."

"There has to be," Smith said. "What about chemotherapy and radiotherapy?"

"That was explained to me as well. And I've made up my mind. If I leave it to run its course and take only painkillers, I'm probably looking at three to four months, and if I give the treatment a go, I'll be lucky to double that. It's not worth it, son."

Smith nodded and took a drink of beer. It didn't taste as good as it had earlier.

"You have to tell your family, Harold," Smith said. "This is not something you can keep from them. You're going to need their support."

"That's precisely the main reason I haven't broken the news yet," Harold said. "I love my Jane to the moon and back, but her idea of support isn't the same as mine. I'll be monitored twenty-four-seven – she'll scrutinise everything I eat, and I won't be left alone for a second. I'll tell them. I'll tell them when I'm good and ready and I'll ask you to respect that."

"I'm sorry, Harold."

"I've had a good life. I've passed my three score and ten, and I'd say I've done alright. It's time I was off. From the pub, I mean – I'm not quite ready to shuffle off this mortal coil just yet."

"Do you need a lift?" Smith asked. "Do you need me to call a taxi for you?"

"I've got the car. I'm probably a bit over the limit, but I'd say the time to fret over stuff like has passed, wouldn't you?"

"I'll see you soon."

"Aye," Harold said. "Good luck with your dirty tackle."

Smith watched him go. As much as he tried to hold his head high, it was clear that he was a man with the weight of the world on his shoulders. Smith had planned on getting a steak and ale pie while he was here, but he no longer had an appetite.

CHAPTER FIFTY

Harold Whitton's revelation was weighing heavily on Smith's mind as he sat at the table in the kitchen the next morning. He hated keeping secrets from Whitton, but Harold had made him promise. Smith decided he would give Harold a week to break the news to his family and then he would give him an ultimatum. Either he tells Jane and Whitton about his illness or Smith tells them. He hoped that would never become necessary – he was praying that Harold would speak up before then.

Whitton had pounced on him the moment he came home last night. She'd wanted to know if her father was going to see a doctor. Smith told her that he'd tried his best, but he wasn't sure if Harold had really listened. This wasn't too far from the truth and Smith reckoned he could live with the little white lie for a bit.

He needed to turn his focus back to the investigation anyway.

"What do we know about the murder of Holly Brown?" he asked Whitton.

"I didn't get much when I spoke to the DI," she said. "But it looks like the killer was interrupted before he could draw on her stomach. And Billie Jones thinks she was half-expecting the murder."

"That's ridiculous," Smith said.

"That's what I think."

"What made Billie suspect that?"

"You'll have to ask her," Whitton said.

"What do the girls have planned for today?" Smith said.

"Nothing," Whitton replied. "Absolutely nothing at all. And that was a direct quote from Laura."

"That kid is getting weirder the older she gets."

"She didn't ask for the DNA she was given. Are you ready to go?"

* * *

Smith wasn't looking forward to the morning briefing and when he saw that Grant Webber and Billie Jones had also been invited, he knew that it was going to be a long, drawn-out affair. DI Smyth began by outlining the details of the murder of Holly Brown. Holly had been found, face down on the kitchen floor by one of her housemates at just before seven yesterday evening. Tanya Richards was planning on spending the evening with some friends at a pub, but she'd started to feel ill and returned home early. The other housemate had already gone home for the holidays.

Early indications suggested that Holly was strangled with something – possibly a thick rope and the forensics team hadn't found the rope at the scene. There was nothing to indicate that any kind of struggle took place and there was no evidence of forced entry to the property. Holly didn't have a drawing on her stomach.

"Initial thoughts?" DI Smyth said.

"She knew her killer," Smith said. "He or she was interrupted before they could draw the scales of justice on her stomach, and they were also aware that Holly would be alone in the house."

"If the housemate hadn't been feeling sick, we probably would've had a carbon copy of the others," Bridge said.

"Did we get anything from the door-to-door?" Smith said. "If the housemate did interrupt the killer, it's safe to say that they exited the house out the back."

"We spoke to most of the neighbours in the houses on the opposite side of the access road to Holly's house," DI Smyth said. "Nothing of interest yet."

"I must admit that this one came as a surprise," Smith said.

"You spoke to her, didn't you, Sarge?" DC Moore said.

"She was here with us yesterday," Smith said. "She was the one who gave me a fat lip, and I never expected to be discussing her murder now."

"You need to tell us everything that was discussed," DI Smyth said.

"Are you implying that this is somehow my fault?"

"Is it?"

"What the hell is that supposed to mean?"

"Tell us what you and Holly discussed. From the beginning."

"She was the one who approached me," Smith said. "In the canteen at the university. She was keeping an eye on me and the admissions woman and when I'd finished talking to Rachel Bright she came over to my table and sat down. She claimed to have been a part of the study group the other dead women were in and she told me she was scared."

"With good reason, it turns out," Bridge said.

"I believed her at first," Smith said. "She sounded genuine, but the more I got talking to her the more I started having my suspicions. When I told her I needed her phone number she asked me for a business card. She put my number into her phone and gave me the card back. I'd just tricked Rachel Bright into giving me her prints on one of her cards and I'm sure Holly saw me do it. She wanted me to have her prints because she knew I would check them and find a match to the wine glass in Jackie Grant's house and Belinda James's mobile phone. I thought she was part of Professor Wild's plan."

"She asked for police protection, didn't she?" DC Moore said.

"She was convinced that she was in danger," Smith said. "And that's when I came up with the genius idea to arrest her for something so we could keep her safe in the holding cells for the weekend."

"But you let her go instead," DI Smyth said.

"You were consulted, boss," Smith said. "And you told me it was a terrible idea. This isn't my fault."

"I'm not following this," DC Moore said. "If Holly was working with Professor Wild, why did she end up as the next victim?"

"When the professor was safely tucked up in an interview room, to boot," Whitton said. "If that's the case it means there's a player in the game we haven't even considered yet."

Smith turned to look at Billie Jones. "You mentioned something about getting the feeling that Holly knew this was going to happen to her. What made you think that?"

"We already know that she was scared, Sarge," DC Moore said. "She told you herself."

"Yes, but Billie didn't know about that," Smith said.

"I don't know what it was exactly," Billie said. "There was something about the whole scene that felt wrong. Strangling someone with a length of rope is not easy, and it's not a quick method to dispatch someone. I know for a fact that if someone tried to do that to me, I would do everything I could to make it as difficult as possible for them. I would kick and scream and scratch with everything I had inside me. There would be evidence of that struggle, but we found nothing in the kitchen where Holly was killed, nothing at all."

"How do you explain that?" DC King said.

"Webber," Smith said. "Do you have any theories? How is it possible for someone to strangle a woman in a relatively confined space without leaving anything to tell us that was what happened?"

Webber shook his head in reply.

"This was someone she knew," Smith said.

"We established that from the get-go," DC Moore said.

"And there were two of them."

"It still doesn't explain the lack of evidence."

"She knew the person who was in the kitchen with her," Smith said. "She knew them, and she didn't see them as a threat. She felt completely safe with them, and her guard was down."

"It still doesn't explain…"

"Shut up, Harry," Smith said. "There was only one person inside the kitchen with Holly."

"But you just said there were two," Bridge reminded him.

Smith held up his hands. "There was only one of them. Holly felt safe with them. They posed no threat whatsoever. But then..."

"Enter the accomplice," DC King said.

Smith grinned like an idiot.

"Holly didn't know there was someone else there," Smith said. "They creep up behind her and bam! The rope is around her neck, and she's paralysed with shock."

CHAPTER FIFTY ONE

The briefing concluded three hours later and nothing had been achieved. Everyone on the team was feeling exhausted and demoralised. It really was the most puzzling case any of them had ever worked on. Five women were dead – all of them were law students and all of them were rising stars. The volume of evidence was extraordinary, but none of it was getting them any closer to a logical conclusion.

Smith was still dwelling on the lack of motive. He knew that Professor Wild lay at the heart of the murders, but his motivation was proving to be elusive and there was nothing that frustrated Smith more. Why was a respected academic killing off his students? What did he possibly stand to get out of it?

"We've missed something," Smith told DC King in the canteen.

"We always miss something," she said.

"This is something important. Look at the heap of evidence we have. There are more clues in this investigation that I've ever seen before, but we haven't been able to decipher them properly."

"We've gone through everything," DC King said. "We've gone over it again and again and we always end up back at the beginning. We know that Professor Wild is in this up to his neck, and we can't prove a damn thing. How did he manage to pull that off?"

"Meticulous planning," Smith said. "By not leaving anything to chance."

"Is he going to get away with it?"

"Not if I can help it. We need to look into his accomplices. He's not doing this alone – that part is obvious, so who is helping him?"

"You thought Holly Brown was a likely accomplice, Sarge," DC King said. "And now she's dead."

"Which means she was on the list all along. The study group is bugging the hell out of me."

"Do you think it even existed?"

"If Holly Brown was telling the truth," Smith said. "There were five of them in that group and now all of them are dead. The only person who knows whether it's fact or fiction is the man we're trying to nail to the wall. He's succeeded in eliminating evidence as he goes along."

"He's removing witnesses."

"That's precisely what he's doing, Kerry," Smith said. "But he isn't doing it by himself. I need a smoke."

He was stopped by DCI Chamers before he got outside.

"Afternoon, boss," Smith said.

"We need to talk," Chalmers said.

Smith followed him out and lit a cigarette as he walked.

"We're being monitored," Chalmers said and lit his own cigarette.

"Monitored?" Smith repeated.

"Smoke breaks. It was discussed in a management meeting. Some anti-smoking dickhead came up with some claptrap about how many man hours are being lost due to unauthorised smoke breaks."

"And?"

"And," Chalmers said. "I'm giving you a heads-up. Pretty soon, we're going to be caught on camera every time we come out here for a smoke break."

Smith turned around and looked at the CCTV camera over the entrance to the station.

"I thought we always were."

"That thing." Chalmers pointed to the camera. "Hasn't worked in donkey's years, but they're talking about doing something to rectify that."

"Haven't top brass got more important stuff to worry about than fixing a camera to spy on sneaky cigarette breaks?" he said.

"You know the score. Speaking of which, what's the score with you and the professor?"

"Right now," Smith said. "I reckon he's one-nil up, going into the break."

Chalmers laughed. "Since when did you talk like you knew more than fuck all about football?"

"I've been learning," Smith said. "What are your thoughts on the concept of the dirty tackle?"

"It all depends on when you want to play it."

"When would you suggest playing it?"

"When you've explored all the avenues and you've come to nothing but dead ends. Is there something I need to be aware of?"

"I'm just considering some underhand tactics, boss," Smith said. "Because playing by the rules isn't working for us right now."

"Be careful," Chalmers warned.

"You know me."

"That's what I'm worried about. Let me give you some advice."

"I'm all ears," Smith said.

"When you're planning on deploying a dirty tackle, you have to take a number of things into consideration."

"Make sure the referee is looking the other way?" Smith guessed.

"That's the obvious one. For a dirty tackle to be effective you need to time it right. Not only do you have to make sure the ref is otherwise engaged, you need to catch your opponent off guard too. And you need to be mindful of what particular dirty tackle will be the most effective."

"Match it to the circumstances?"

"Right. Are you planning on doing something illegal, Smith?"

"I wouldn't dream of it," Smith said. "It's all hypothetical at the moment anyway. I'm still learning the ins and outs of your beautiful game. Are you sure that CCTV camera has never worked?"

"Not since I started smoking out here," Chalmers said.

"What's the point of it then?"

"It offers the illusion of surveillance. For what it's worth. We're supposed to be the force of law and order in this city, and we can't even afford to have an operational camera on the premises. Haven't you got some work to do?"

"Actually, I have," Smith said. "I appreciate the chat. I'll give your suggestions some serious thought."

"I wasn't aware that I'd made any suggestions."

"Thanks, boss," Smith said.

He grinned and threw his cigarette butt into the distance.

CHAPTER FIFTY TWO

Smith was on his way to the New Forensics Building for the second time in as many days. He'd left Penny Fowler's file with Bridge and DC Moore and asked them to read through it. It was possible they would spot something that Smith had missed. He'd been informed that Whitton and DC King were busy speaking to Holly Brown's housemate. When DI Smyth had attempted to talk to Tanya Richards in the ambulance last night she'd recoiled as though the DI was going to attack her, and they'd subsequently learned that Tanya wasn't comfortable in the presence of men. The reason was explained to Smith, but he'd instantly forgotten what it was. It was decided that it would be better for two female officers to speak to Tanya anyway.

The chat with Chalmers had given Smith an idea of sorts. He wasn't sure if it was going to work and he didn't know if he would come out of the end of it with his career intact. It was also possible he would face criminal charges if what he was planning ever saw the light of day, but desperate times called for desperate measure and Smith had never felt so desperate during an investigation and he was willing to try anything. Playing by the rules wasn't going to crack this case.

He was told by the amiable man on the reception desk that Grant Webber wasn't in, but Billie Jones was up in the lab. Smith thought this boded well, and he headed upstairs feeling positive. He opened the door and went inside the lab where the majority of the forensic work was carried out. Billie Jones was examining something under a microscope at a desk on the far side of the room. Smith walked over to her. Billie was dressed in a pair of tight black jeans and Smith found his eyes drawn to her backside as she bent over the microscope. Once again, he offered Bridge a silent curse for constantly referring to Billie's arse.

"Did you want something?" Billie asked without turning around. "Or are you merely here to admire the view?'

Smith felt his face heating up and he hoped the blush wasn't too obvious.

"I was actually looking to catch Webber," he lied. "But you'll do."

"Bullshit," Billie said. "Simon will have informed you that Webber isn't here as soon as you came in."

She turned to face him.

Smith held up his hands. "Busted. Have you finished with the rope you found at the scene of the first murder?"

"Belinda James?"

"That's the one. She was killed first but she was only found much later. Hers was the only murder where the rope was left behind."

"Why are you interested in the rope?" Billie asked.

"Have you finished with it or not?"

Billie turned her attention back to the microscope.

"What are you looking at?" Smith said.

"We pulled some fibres from Holly Brown's neck," Billie said. "I wanted to confirm that the same kind of rope was used to strangle her."

"And?"

"It's hemp. And the welts on her neck were identical to the others. Can I ask you a question?'

"Shoot."

"It's about Webber."

"What about him?" Smith said.

"Why is he still single? I understand that he's getting on a bit, and his personality is an acquired taste but he's not a bad looking bloke, and his heart is in the right place."

"He has his reasons," Smith said.

"That's obvious," Billie said. "I'm asking you what they are."

"Webber's life was shattered a few years ago," Smith said. "We had a DI – Bryony Brownhill was her name, and she too was an acquired taste. We clashed heads early on – she was a bit overbearing, but she soon came to understand the dynamic of the team and she mellowed a bit, and I grew to like her. Webber hooked up with her. In hindsight, it was actually a match made in heaven, and it was clear that they loved each other dearly."

"She was the one who was killed on duty."

Smith nodded. "It was towards the end of a pretty nasty case. We had a psychopath who killed people and used their blood to paint with. DI Brownhill was lured to a house and attacked. When we found her, she didn't have a drop of blood left in her body."

"Jesus," Billie said. "That must have been awful."

"We were all devastated," Smith said. "It was something that just didn't happen and it took a long time to get over it, but Webber took it the worst of all. He and DI Brownhill were planning on getting married. Theirs was supposed to be a happy ever after thing."

"I knew something terrible had happened," Billie said. "But I didn't know the details."

"Don't discuss this conversation with him."

"Of course. And that's why he stays single?"

"I suppose he's afraid of getting his heart smashed to pieces again. About that rope."

Billie switched off the microscope and focused her attention on Smith. "Why are you so interested in the rope?"

"I need it," Smith said. "And I'd prefer it if you didn't ask me why?"

"It's already been logged into evidence."

"Are you anticipating having to re-examine it?"

"I don't think so."

"Then it won't matter if I take it with me."

"You're going to have to sign for it."

"I'd prefer not to do that," Smith said.

"No signature, no rope."

Billie folded her arms to emphasise that this wasn't up for debate.

Smith nodded and walked towards the door.

He turned back around. "Help me out here."

Billie walked up to him. "Why should I do that?"

"Because a cold-blooded killer is going to get away with it if you don't."

"The question is, are you going to get away with it?"

"I really don't know," Smith said. "But I'm running out of ideas. Professor Wild has kicked my arse every step of the way, and I don't think I'm going to beat him any other way."

"Kiss me," Billie said.

"What the hell?"

"You want your rope," Billie said. "Kiss me."

"I'm a married man, Billie," Smith said.

"I'm not asking you to run away with me. Kiss me and you get your rope – no questions asked."

"Why?"

"I've always wondered what it would feel like. Well?"

Smith sighed and took a step towards her. He leaned in and gave her a peck on the cheek. Billie didn't let him off that easily. She took hold of his cheeks and planted a kiss on his mouth. Her lips opened and Smith could taste mint on her breath. Billie pulled him closer, and Smith felt her tongue on his. He closed his eyes and gave in.

The embrace lasted quite some time. Smith broke it off first.

"What the hell was that?"

Billie smiled at him. "Not bad."

"We shouldn't have done that."

"Relax," Billie said. "It'll be our little secret. Let's go and get that rope, shall we?"

CHAPTER FIFTY THREE

Smith's next port of call was the hospital. He hadn't pre-warned Kenny Bean about his visit, but he knew the Head of Pathology wouldn't expect him to. He found him in his office and walked in without knocking.

"Kenny," he said. "Have you got a minute?"

"I was about to head home," Dr Bean said. "It's Saturday and I was planning on making the most of what's left of it."

"I need to take a look at the bodies of the five dead women."

"I believe there are dedicated porn sites for that kind of thing."

"Christ, Kenny," Smith said. "That's beyond sick."

"I cut up dead bodies for a living," Dr Bean said. "What's your point?"

"Can I have a quick look at the bodies?"

"Be my guest," Dr Bean got up from his desk. "Sarah will assist you."

"I don't need any assistance," Smith said. "Thanks, Kenny."

"I don't believe I did anything."

"I appreciate it," Smith said. "Will you be going to the Christmas thing next weekend?"

"I imagine I will. I didn't think work do's were your cup of tea."

"People can change. Thanks again.'

Smith left the hospital thirty minutes later. He smoked a cigarette before he got into his car. He was halfway through it when his phone started to ring, and the ringtone told him it was a call he needed to take. He let it go to voicemail and soon afterwards the phone beeped to tell him he'd received a message. He would listen to it later, even though he had a rough idea of what it would consist of.

He got into the car and drove away from the car park. He drove slowly – he needed to think, and the drive wasn't a long one. This was the part of the plan that he had no real control over, and it was making him nervous. He slowed down even further and the honk of a car horn behind him told him the driver in the car behind wasn't happy about it.

Smith increased the speed, and his thoughts turned to what had happened at the New Forensics Building. He really hadn't expected Billie Jones to kiss him, and he wasn't sure what to do about it. Smith would never do anything to hurt Whitton – he'd already made that mistake, and he wasn't planning on repeating it. Plus, Billie was in a relationship with one of his best friends, and if it ever came out that they'd kissed life would become extremely unpleasant. He hoped that Billie Jones had been serious when she told him it would be their little secret.

Smith parked his car around the corner from Professor Wild's house. He got out and made sure it was locked, boot and all. He walked along the path until the three-bedroom property came into view. He stopped and took in the front of the house. Three feet above the door was a CCTV camera. Smith had expected nothing less. After making a short phone call he made his way across the road to number 45 Newton Street. There was a small black car parked in the driveway and Smith knew the professor was home.

He rang the bell, and the door opened shortly afterwards. Professor Wild was dressed casually in a pair of jeans and a sweatshirt with the logo of an American university on it. He looked past Smith and scanned the road on either side.

"You're alone."

"Can I come in?" Smith said.

"I assume this is an unauthorised house call."

"Can we please talk inside?" Smith said. "It shouldn't take long."

Professor Wild opened the door wider and stepped to the side. Smith took this as an invitation, and he went into the house. Professor Wild took another look outside and closed the door behind them.

He suggested they talk in the kitchen.

"It's the only room in the house where I'm allowed to smoke," he explained.

"I thought you lived alone," Smith said.

"It's good to have self-imposed regulations," Professor Wild said. "Don't you think? Can I offer you something to drink? Coffee, or perhaps something stronger, as you're clearly not on duty."

"No thanks."

"Are you concerned that I may be about to poison you?"

"Not at all. This is an unauthorised visit, and nothing you say will be admissible as evidence."

He placed his phone on the table.

"I'm not covertly recording the conversation," he added. "And I'm not wearing a wiretap. You can check if you want."

"That won't be necessary. As this isn't an authorised visit, the wiretap evidence would be inadmissible anyway. What do you want, Jason?'

"I want some answers. Can I use your bathroom before we begin?"

Professor Wild started to laugh. "You can't possibly expect me to fall for that one."

"I need a piss."

"And while you're out of sight some piece of damning evidence will mysteriously appear, shortly followed by an unexpected raid on my property."

"I'm tired of playing games, Herman," Smith said. "Can I use your bathroom or not? You can come with me if you like."

"I'll do that."

He escorted Smith upstairs and indicated which room was the bathroom. Smith was relieved when he didn't go as far as to join him inside. He closed the door, but he didn't lock it. He wanted Professor Wild to be able to walk in at any minute. He didn't need the toilet, but he waited a minute, flushed the toilet, and washed his hands anyway. After a quick glance in the medicine cabinet, he opened the door to find Professor Wild still standing there.

"That was quick."

"I'm blessed with a strong steady flow," Smith said.

"I'm glad you felt the need to share that with me. Shall we go back downstairs?"

Smith nodded. He knew that Professor Wild would probably go through the bathroom with a fine-toothed comb as soon as he'd gone.

Smith glanced at the calendar on the fridge and sat back down at the table. The calendar was completely blank. There were no appointments on it whatsoever.

"You're still hunting for your motive, aren't you?" Professor Wild asked.

"Is it that obvious?" Smith said.

"You were one of the most promising students I'd ever taught, and very few students who came after you even came close. I know you had your own reasons for throwing it all away, but I never expected you to join the police."

"It seemed like the right thing to do at the time," Smith said. "Why, Herman? Tell me why you did this, and I'll be on my way."

"And what will you do with that information? You have nothing linking me to any of the murders."

"Everything I have links you to the murders, Herman," Smith argued.

"But none of it will make a blind bit of difference, will it? You can't prove a thing – I'm not going to confess, so what are you hoping to achieve here?"

"Peace of mind," Smith said. "Is that too much to ask for?"

"I think it's time you left now," Professor Wild said. "Before I phone your bosses and make them aware of what you're up to."

"What *am* I up to?" Smith said.

"Nothing productive. I have a question for you before you go if I may."

"Go ahead," Smith said.

"In what world did you ever expect to beat me? You're either delusional or you're making another feeble attempt to outsmart me."

"I'm neither," Smith said. "I'm just a bloke who believes in justice, nothing more, nothing less. I'll leave you to enjoy the rest of your weekend."

"Crusaders always end up disappointed in the end," Professor Wild said. "When you're fighting for something that you realise isn't actually worth fighting for, disappointment is the only possible outcome."

"A bloke can live in hope, can't he?"

Professor Wild shook his head. "A delusional optimist. It's possibly the worst combination there is. Prepare yourself for a mountain of disappointment, Jason. Our paths won't cross again."

Smith got up from the chair. "No worries. I'll see myself out."

He picked up his phone and left the kitchen. Professor Wild didn't follow him.

CHAPTER FIFTY FOUR

"Just about everything that was in that file has happened this week," Bridge said.

The team were discussing Penny Fowler's notes in the afternoon briefing.

"It's as if the prof used the notes as a how-to guide to committing the perfect murder," DC Moore added.

"How does it help us?' DI Smyth said. "Unless there's a section in there about how the police can stop someone who commits the perfect murder, those documents are about as much use as the rest of the evidence we've gathered during the course of this cursed investigation."

Smith came in at this point.

"Is everything OK, boss?"

"Where the hell have you been?" DI Smyth said.

"I believe they call it intelligence gathering."

"I'm not in the mood for jokes."

"I'm not in a particularly jovial frame of mind either," Smith said. "What have I missed?"

"Not much," DC Moore said. "We were just talking about the file about getting away with murder, and even though it's pretty damning it's not going to help us. This professor has thought of everything. How do you catch someone like that?"

"We'll get him," Smith said.

"I wish I shared your confidence, Sarge. I'm knackered."

"We're all exhausted, Harry," DI Smyth said. "But we have to keep going."

"Nope," Smith said. "I disagree."

"Do you have a better idea?" DI Smyth said.

"I have a much better idea," Smith said. "We all take the rest of the weekend off."

"Have you lost your mind?"

"Quite possibly," Smith said. "But we're not going to make any progress with this investigation if we burn ourselves out."

"I will not authorise time off when the women at that university are in danger."

"The danger has passed, boss," Smith said. "You'll have to trust me on that."

"Is there something you're not telling the rest of us?"

"Probably," Smith said. "But I haven't quite figured it out yet. I'll see you on Monday."

He left the small conference room, leaving a wide-eyed bunch of detectives in his wake.

"He might have a point," DC King said. "What else is there to discuss?"

"We have to keep going," DI Smyth said. "There must be something we've missed along the way – there usually is."

"If there is," Bridge said. "It'll still be there on Monday. I'm on the same page as Smith with this one. We keep on at this and we risk going backwards. All of us are in desperate need of a break."

"I agree," Whitton said. "We'll come back to this with fresh heads after the weekend."

"I think so too," DC Moore agreed.

"I wasn't aware that we were operating under a democracy," DI Smyth said. "But it seems to me that the masses have spoken. Monday it is then."

He got up and went the same way Smith had gone.

"Smith is up to something," Bridge said. "I know when he's got something planned and I can sense it now."

"I think so too," DC King said.

"Where did he disappear to earlier?" DC Moore said.

"I gave up trying to understand my husband a very long time ago," Whitton joined in. "It's a pointless exercise."

"He's definitely up to something," Bridge said. "Seeing as we've got the weekend off, I say we make the most of it. I'll going to see what the forensic officer with the finest arse in York is up to this evening."

"Bridge," Whitton said. "Stop it. It's starting to get quite disturbing."

Bridge shrugged his shoulders and left the room.

"I can't just switch off," DC King said. "I know Smith has a valid point, but I'm not going to be able to enjoy the weekend when Professor Wild is free."

"I can," DC Moore said. "Enjoy it. I'm going to catch up on some sleep."

"Let's get out of here," Whitton said. "Before the DI changes his mind."

She stopped by the front desk for a quick chat with Baldwin and left the station. Smith was standing by his car smoking a cigarette. He was talking to someone on his mobile phone. He looked like he was concentrating hard on whatever the person on the other end of the line was saying. Whitton waited for him to end the call and walked over to him.

"That looked serious."

"Technology," Smith said. "It was Barry Stone, Bridge's mate, and he might as well have been speaking Swahili."

"What did Barry want?"

"He's helping me out with something."

"Is it related to the investigation?"

"Sort of," Smith said.

"What are you up to?"

"Nothing."

"You're up to something," Whitton said. "I know you too well."

"It's better if you don't know at this stage."

"You're planning on doing something stupid again, aren't you?"

"You make it sound like it's a regular thing."

"That's because it is."

"Don't stress," Smith said. "I know what I'm doing. What do you feel like doing later?"

"I hadn't thought about it."

"We could go out somewhere."

"I'm not in the mood for the Hog's Head."

"We could go somewhere else," Smith said.

"Sounds good. There's a new Indian place in Rowntree Park that's had rave reviews."

"Indian?"

"You can order something mild," Whitton said. "I'm in the mood for a curry that will burn the skin off my tongue."

"You're not pregnant, are you?"

"No, I'm not pregnant. Where did that come from?"

"God knows," Smith said. "Indian it is then."

CHAPTER FIFTY FIVE

Smith wasn't too fond of hot food but when he and Whitton went through the doors of The New Raj on River Street the aroma of garlic and spices caused him to reconsider. The smells coming from the kitchen were truly mouthwatering and he was instantly hungry.

They were shown to a table for two, the waiter placed a couple of menus in front of them and took their drinks order. The New Raj didn't stock Theakston, so Smith chose an Indian beer he'd never heard of. He was feeling adventurous.

Lucy and Darren had been more than happy to look after Laura and Fran and the two girls were equally content. Smith knew that they would probably be glued to the television until they fell asleep. There was no school tomorrow, and they didn't have to get up for anything.

"This place is nice," Smith said.

It was just after seven and the restaurant was already busy. The clientele was a mixed bunch, with couples, families with children, and groups of young men and women – students probably. The student dormitories were only a stone's throw away across the river, and Smith imagined that this was a popular place for them.

The waiter returned with two bottles of Kingfisher beer. He poured it into two glasses, and he took too long about it for Smith's liking. He was thirsty and he had no interest in the waiter's explanation that there was a certain method in pouring this particular beer. Smith would offer to pour his own when he ordered the second round.

"What do you feel like eating?" Whitton said. "I'm tempted by the lamb vindaloo. With naans and the works."

"That's a hot dish, isn't it?" Smith said.

"You don't come to an Indian restaurant and order something that doesn't hurt a little bit."

"I do," Smith said. "I don't see any steak and ale pies. I'm kidding. I like the look of the butter chicken."

The restaurant was filling up with customers, and the noise level was increasing. Even so, Smith could still hear the sound of his mobile phone ringing in his jacket pocket. It wasn't a ringtone he'd assigned to anyone at work, so he decided that it was safe to take the call.

"I'm going outside for a quick smoke," he told Whitton.

"Who's calling?"

Smith looked at the screen of the phone. "Barry. I won't be long."

It was freezing when Smith went outside. The air was crisp, and Smith knew the temperatures would drop below zero tonight. He answered the phone and lit a cigarette at the same time.

"I'm not interrupting you, am I?" Barry Stone said.

"I'm at the new Indian Place on River Street," Smith said. "I was just outside having a cigarette. Is there a problem?"

"Everything's set. I thought about it, and I think it's better if we meet up in person tomorrow."

"I agree. It probably won't come to it, but the fainter the trail we leave behind, the better."

"I feel like I'm in a spy film when you say stuff like that."

"Are you having second thoughts?" Smith said. "Because there's still time to back out."

"Do you want me to?"

"No," Smith said. "If this is going to work, I need your help."

"Then I'm still in. I've had a look at the system and it's nothing special. Are you absolutely sure there isn't an alarm?"

"Not absolutely," Smith said. "But I didn't see any key panels or loudspeakers. It's possible there's a silent alarm, but by the time it's activated and anyone comes to investigate, I'll be long gone."

"This must be really important to you," Barry said. "You're risking a hell of a lot here."

"It's the only way," Smith said. "I'll speak to you tomorrow."

He finished his cigarette and went back inside the restaurant. He was glad of the warmth – he was starting to lose the feeling in his fingers. There were two more beers on the table and Smith was relieved to see that they had already been poured.

"What did Barry want?" Whitton asked.

"Nothing important. Have you ordered yet?"

Whitton nodded. "Lamb Vindaloo and that girly chicken thing you wanted."

"Food shouldn't hurt, my dear," Smith said. "And anyone who thinks it should needs help."

It didn't take long for the food to arrive and when Smith saw the size of the portions he wondered if he was going to be able to eat it all. He took a bite of the chicken and smiled. It really was tasty.

"How's the sheep on steroids?" he asked Whitton.

"Hot as hell," she said. "Just how it's supposed to be."

They ate in silence and Smith's thoughts turned to the investigation. He was confident that Professor Wild would finally lose the game tomorrow. He wouldn't be able to argue his way out of it when Smith had played the move he was planning. But Smith still wasn't satisfied. There were still a number of unanswered questions, and he knew that Professor Wild wouldn't be the one to answer them. He was still wondering about the other people involved. It was clear that Professor Wild wasn't working alone – Smith had his suspicions about who might be helping him, but he wasn't absolutely certain of it.

"Are you still with us?"

Whitton's voice woke Smith from his reverie, and he realised he'd raised his fork to his lips and left it suspended in mid air. The sauce from the chicken was dripping onto the plate.

"You were miles away there," Whitton said.

"I was thinking about the guitar solo from *Comfortably Numb*," Smith lied. "I reckon I'm going to crack it tomorrow."

"I worry about you sometimes."

"There's no need."

"I've been wondering about Professor Wild's accomplices."

"I think I might have figured that out," Smith said.

"Go on."

"I'm not completely sure yet, but I reckon I'm on the right track."

"I'm actually pig sick of this investigation."

"We all are," Smith said. "But it will be over soon, and then we'll be wishing for another juicy murder case to get our teeth into."

"You're definitely not right in the head."

"You're sweating," Smith said. "Food should not do that to a person."

"It's good for the pores. That was the best vindaloo I've ever tasted."

"This butter chicken has beaten me. I'm admitting defeat. This has been nice."

"Even though you can't get your mind off the investigation?"

"How do you know that?" Smith said.

"Because I know you inside out," Whitton said. "And whatever it is you have planned, you need to know that I'm behind you a hundred percent."

"Do you mean that?"

Whitton raised her glass of beer. "I mean it."

Smith lifted his own glass. "You don't know how much it means to hear you say that."

CHAPTER FIFTY SIX

Smith woke late the next morning, and he felt well rested. The clock next to the bed told him it was half-nine and Whitton wasn't in the bed next to him. He got dressed, used the bathroom, and went downstairs. He could hear Whitton's voice in the kitchen – it sounded like she was on the phone to her mother again. Smith wondered if Harold had broken the news about his cancer yet, but the tone of the conversation didn't fill him with hope. Whitton was laughing and it was clear that she and her mum were sharing a joke.

Smith made some coffee and opened the back door for the two dogs who were begging to go out. He followed them and lit a cigarette. It was bitterly cold, and Smith wondered if winter had arrived early. The snow that had fallen earlier in the week suggested that it had. He smoked the cigarette quickly and went back inside the house.

Whitton had finished talking to her mum and she had a grave expression on her face.

"What is it?" Smith said.

"Your phone rang earlier," Whitton said. "And I saw that it was Barry Stone, so I answered it."

"OK," Smith said slowly.

"Why are you meeting him later?"

"It's just something we're working on," Smith said. "Nothing for you to worry about."

"You know you can tell me," Whitton said.

"I know, but the less you know about this, the better for everybody."

"Do you know what you're doing?"

"I reckon I do. I've got this."

"That's good enough for me."

"Have I told you I love you recently?" Smith said.

Whitton started to laugh. "You don't need to. What time are you meeting Barry?"

"Eleven," Smith said. "Which is in precisely an hour. I suppose I should get a shower and get ready."

* * *

Smith got out of his car and walked round to the boot. He unlocked it, took out the bag and stuffed it inside his jacket. He looked around him. The Sunday morning streets were quiet. The bitter temperatures were keeping people indoors, and Smith hoped that the weather wasn't going to stop Herman Wild from breaking a habit of a lifetime. For the plan to work, it was essential that the professor maintained his weekly routine of a meal in the Meaty Pig.

Footsteps behind him made Smith turn around. It was Barry Stone. Bridge's IT friend was walking quickly with his hands in his pockets.

"All set?" he said.

"Explain to me again how this is supposed to work," Smith said.

Barry took out something that resembled a small handheld radio and handed it to Smith.

"This is a Wi-Fi jammer. The cameras we're dealing with are cheap DIY jobs and they rely on a Wi-Fi signal to record. What this does is emit signals the same frequency as the cameras – roughly 2.4GHz or 5 GHz. They work by overpowering the legit signals and effectively rendering the cameras useless during the time they're being jammed."

"I understood about half of that," Smith said.

"There is a downside," Barry said. "Your man will no doubt have the CCTV linked to a mobile device and there will be an activation alert when the Wi-Fi goes down. It'll notify him that the cameras are offline. It's possible there'll have been Wi-Fi problems in the past and he won't be too suspicious, but you need to be in and out quickly."

"That's what I'm hoping to do," Smith said.

"How exactly are you planning on getting in?"

"You don't have to worry about that. Are you positive that this thing will work?"

Smith held out the Wi-Fi jammer.

"It'll work. Just make sure you activate the jammer before you're picked up by the camera on the front."

Smith took a few deep breaths in quick succession.

"What about the other problem? He's got me on camera paying him a visit yesterday. I can't let it be known that I came to the house without authorisation."

"Already sorted," Barry said. "I carried out a man-in-the-middle attack last night."

"I have no idea what you're talking about."

"It's basically a cyber attack where all I have to do is intercept the comms between the cameras and the receivers, which in this case are the mobile devices linked to the CCTV. Think of it as a kind of eavesdropping."

"How did you manage to do that?" Smith said.

"Easily. I got into his email account and forced a reply to a fake mail from the CCTV system operator. Your man thought he was updating the functions, but he was actually giving me complete control of the system."

"I imagine that isn't strictly legal?" Smith said.

"What do you think?" Barry said. "But trying to prove it is another thing altogether. I still don't understand why you even need the jammer. I can control the system from the comfort of my living room. I can delete any footage you need erasing."

"I have my reasons," Smith said.

He'd thought hard about this. It was risky, but he believed the only way for this to work was if Professor Wild knew what was happening. Smith wanted him to be fully aware of what he was doing and he also wanted him to think that the CCTV footage would prove it. In an hours' time he would get a notification on his phone telling him that someone was outside his house. He would see Smith on the doorstep, holding up the jammer to the camera and soon afterwards the footage would stop, and Professor Wild would be notified that his cameras were offline. The Meaty Pig was a ten-minute drive from the house on Newton Street and that would give Smith more than enough time.

"I'll give you a shout when I see him," Barry said. "The Meaty Pig, you say?"

"It's in Murton," Smith said. "Have a bite to eat while you're there. You could do with a bit of meat on your bones – you've lost far too much weight."

CHAPTER FIFTY SEVEN

"I was under the impression that all operations were suspended until tomorrow."

DI Smyth didn't sound happy at all.

"We need to search Professor Wild's house again, boss," Smith said.

"On what grounds?"

"Call it a hunch. I've got a feeling we're going to find something this time."

"You want me to obtain a search warrant on a Sunday based on a hunch?"

"Trust me," Smith said. "This will be worth it. You know people – I know you know people. We need that warrant within the hour."

"And what happens if I don't manage to get the warrant in that time?"

"Then the plan goes tits-up," Smith said. "I will explain everything to you when this is all over, but you have to trust me."

"Did I tell you that I think I'm developing an ulcer?" DI Smyth said. "And it's all your fault."

"Are we going to get that warrant?"

"You'd better be right about this," DI Smyth said. "Because if it comes to nothing, I'm going to make damn sure you take the fall for it."

"I'm right," Smith said.

Barry Stone's message arrived forty-five minutes later. Smith smiled when he read it. It was precise and if anyone else were to read it, there would be nothing about it that could implicate either man in anything illegal. *In position.*

Smith crossed the road and turned onto Newton Street. There was nobody around, but Smith tried to walk as if he belonged there. He didn't want to arouse any suspicion from any nosy neighbours in the area. He stopped outside number 45, opened the gate, and walked up to the front door. He gazed up at the CCTV camera and held up the Wi-Fi jammer. He was tempted to offer Professor Wild the middle finger, but he didn't think this was the time for reckless arrogance. After holding the jamming device up for long enough he took out the key and inserted it into the lock. When he was here yesterday there was a bunch of keys hanging on a hook behind the door. Smith had hoped it was a spare set, as he'd seen an identical bunch of keys on the kitchen table. He'd swiped the keys on his way out of the house yesterday and he also hoped that Professor Wild hadn't noticed that they were gone.

The key turned in the lock, Smith opened the door, went inside, and closed the door behind him. He still didn't know if the house was alarmed and he half expected the blare of a siren to fill the house at any time. He walked towards the kitchen and opened the microwave. He took out the evidence bag and carefully removed the length of rope. He placed it inside and closed the microwave door. The glass on the front was tinted and it was impossible to see what was inside. There was no way to see the rope on the tray. The rope that had been used to strangle the last breath out of Belinda James was now tainted with the DNA of Sharon Atlee and Jackie Grant, and there were strands of hair from Rebecca Stone and Holly Brown entwined in its fibres.

Smith had to get out now. There was no wailing alarm as he made his way back towards the front door. He replaced the keys on the hook and opened the door a crack. The street was still deserted. He closed the door and heard the satisfying click of the Yale lock. He walked down the path and closed the gate behind him. When he was sure he was out of sight of the camera on the front of the house he disabled the Wi-Fi jammer. He removed the gloves he'd been wearing as he walked and deposited them in a bin on the corner of the street. Then he walked back to where he'd parked his car to wait.

* * *

Professor Herman Wild arrived home almost exactly the same time as the first police car arrived on the scene. The car was blocking the driveway, so the professor had to park on the street. Two more cars pulled up shortly afterwards and Smith's Ford Sierra brought up the rear. He'd ignored all the rules and smoked three cigarettes in quick succession inside the car while he waited. It was the longest wait of his life and time seemed to slow down for the duration.

He got out and walked over to DI Smyth.

"Is this going to aggravate my ulcer?" DI Smyth said.

"I hope not," Smith said. "I've heard that they can be very painful. I assume we've got our warrant then?"

"You owe me, Smith. And this had better be worth it."

"He's not a happy bloke, is he?" Smith nodded to the commotion outside number 45.

Herman Wild was arguing with one of the uniformed officers and he looked like he was about to resort to violence. The mild-mannered professor of law was furious.

"Let's get this done before things gets out of hand," DI Smyth said. "I think it would be better if you took no part in it."

"I agree," Smith said. "Make sure he accompanies you throughout the search, and don't start in the kitchen."

"I've heard that people have actually died from ulcers," DI Smyth said.

"Stop whining," Smith said. "Let me know what you find."

He walked away and took out his phone. He tapped out a short message to Barry Stone and lit a cigarette. The wind had picked up and the icy breeze that blew down the street crept into Smith's clothes, but he didn't care. He felt great. He'd had a brief internal debate with himself about whether his actions were justified – it hadn't lasted long, and when it was over he'd come to the conclusion that everything he'd done was for the greater good and he would do it all again if he had to. All he had to do now was wait and see what happened.

He walked back towards number 45 and watched as DI Smyth produced the search warrant. Smith couldn't hear what was being said but he could translate the hand gestures and facial expressions. Herman Wild was definitely not a happy man. Smith's phone beeped and when he swiped the screen, he saw that Barry Stone had sent him a message consisting of nothing but a thumbs up. Everything was going exactly how Smith had hoped it would.

He'd only managed to smoke one more cigarette before the front door of the house opened and Grant Webber emerged. The Head of Forensics was holding an evidence bag in his hand, Smith couldn't see what was inside it, but he had a good idea. DI Smyth came out shortly afterwards with Herman Wild. The professor was escorted to one of the waiting police cars, helped inside and shortly afterwards the car pulled away from the kerb.

Smith caught DI Smyth's eye, and the DI gave him a subtle nod. Smith was sure that he was grinning, and he wondered if his ulcer was getting better.

CHAPTER FIFTY EIGHT

"His lawyer is talking some bull about us planting evidence," DI Smyth said. It was two days since Professor Wild had been arrested for the murders of five women, and he'd surprised Smith when he'd requested the assistance of a legal representative. It boded well – it meant that the professor was rattled, and Smith hoped to exploit that.

"He's desperate," Smith said. "Clutching at straws."

"Professor Wild is adamant that he can prove it," DI Smyth said.

"Let him try. I'm not worried about it. Where is the lawyer now?"

"Still in consultation with his client. Are you going to enlighten me on exactly what it is you did to ensure that we got an arrest?"

"All in good time, boss," Smith said. "We've got more than enough to charge him, but I want more than that. I want his accomplices."

"How are you planning on doing that?"

"I think I know who they are," Smith said. "I just need something to confirm it. Can you do me a favour?"

"I believe you've run out of favours."

"Just one more," Smith said. "And I won't ask again."

"Go on."

Smith told him. DI Smyth thought about it for a moment and reluctantly agreed.

The two nights in the holding cells had taken their toll on Herman Wild. The professor looked like he hadn't slept at all in that time. The dark rings under his bloodshot eyes made him look ten years older than his fifty-seven. The woman sitting next to him in the interview room was a dour-faced lawyer called Norma Glenn. She'd acted defensively from the moment she introduced herself, and Smith got the impression that she was very confident in her abilities as a lawyer. That suited him just fine. Professor

Wild had shown an absolute disregard for the law from the onset – he'd demonstrated a flagrant lack of respect for the very thing that Smith held dear, and it was time to reset the balance.

Smith sat down opposite the two silent law experts. DC King sat next to him.

"Herman," he said to Professor Wild. "I trust you're being treated well."

"Everything you have to say to my client needs to be said on record," Norma informed him.

"No worries," Smith said and started the recording device. "It's Tuesday 7th December. The time is 12:21. Present DS Smith, DC King, Herman Wild and Professor Wild's legal representative Norma Glenn. Herman, is it OK if I call you Herman?"

"It's my name," Professor Wild said.

"That's correct," Smith said. "And I imagine that after this your tenure at the university will be cancelled and you will no longer be a professor."

"I will always be a professor."

"Detective Sergeant," Norma said. "Could we get started?"

"I digress," Smith said. "Herman, you've denied any involvement in the crimes you're accused of throughout, is that right?"

"Why would I admit to crimes I didn't commit?" Herman said.

"Why indeed? Although I seem to recall you doing just that not so long ago."

"We've already been over this," Norma said. "My client denies that, and you have no evidence to prove otherwise."

"Herman," Smith said. "I'll get straight to the point. During a search of your property, a length of rope was discovered in the microwave in your kitchen. It's a very unusual rope, and there are very few suppliers of it in the city."

"You planted it there," Herman said. "I know you did."

"We'll come back to that," DC King said.

"As I said," Smith said. "The rope in question is a 14mm rope made from hemp. You've admitted to purchasing fifteen metres of an identical rope last month. Do you deny that now?"

"Of course not," Herman said.

"Good," Smith said. "Because we have CCTV footage showing you buying it. Why hide it in the microwave? That was rather sloppy."

"You're not going to get away with this."

"I have no idea what you're talking about."

"Could you please get to the point?" Norma said.

"That's what I'm trying to do," Smith said. "But your client keeps interrupting me. Herman, the rope has been examined, and I can tell you it's not looking good for you."

Herman got to his feet. "This is a farce. An absolute farce."

"Please sit down," DC King said.

Norma Glenn nodded to Herman to do as she'd asked.

"The rope was examined," Smith said. "And we found traces of DNA and strands of hair from all five victims."

"Nonsense," Herman said. "I've never seen that rope before, and I certainly did not hide it in my microwave. What kind of an idiot does something like that?"

"You tell me?" Smith said. "Belinda James, Rebecca Stone, Sharon Atlee, Jackie Grant and Holly Brown. Five young women brutally murdered. Five rising stars with their whole lives ahead of them. All of them were strangled, and all of them can be linked to that rope. Can you explain that?"

"You're not going to get away with this," Herman said. "I know you planted that rope."

"Prove it." Smith couldn't help himself.

"Your career is over, Jason. I suggest your forensics team take a look at the footage from my CCTV cameras."

"Our tech team already have," DC King said. "In fact, it was one of the first things we did. What is it you're referring to exactly?"

Herman Wild was smiling for the first time since the interview started. "Let me think," he said. "If I recall it was around five-thirty on Saturday. DS Smith called round to my house. The visit was unauthorised, and I would imagine his superiors would be interested to hear about it."

"I don't remember going to your house," Smith said.

"You don't have to," Herman said. "The CCTV doesn't lie. And on Sunday, you paid another visit to my house. I wasn't home and in hindsight, I ought to have considered the fact that you would check out my weekly routines. I eat out at The Meaty Pig every Sunday, and you were aware of this."

"Could we please concentrate on the matter at hand," Smith said.

"Please," Herman said. "This is a real farce."

Smith winced and raised a hand to his head.

"Are you getting another migraine, Sarge?" DC King said.

Smith shook his head. "Let's carry on."

"Not only do I have proof that you were outside my house around noon on Sunday," Herman said. "I have footage of you holding something up to the camera over my front door. Shortly after that the Wi-Fi signal went down and it was reactivated five minutes later. You entered my property, planted the evidence and left. Soon afterwards you arrived mob-handed and raided my house. Coincidence?"

"That's quite an imagination you have there, Herman," Smith said. "And I hate to be the one to burst your bubble, but none of it is true. Firstly, why would I break into your house when I knew there were cameras there?"

"You did something to them," Herman said. "I know you did, but you were too stupid to carry it out properly."

"And how did I get in?" Smith added. "According to the report, there was no sign of a break in at your property. Perhaps you left your door unlocked – is that what you're saying?"

"I never leave the house without locking the door."

"There you go then," Smith said. "Can we stop wasting time and carry on?"

"You were caught on camera, Jason," Herman said.

"Kerry," Smith said to DC King. "Could you do the honours please."

DC King picked up her laptop and switched it on.

"What is this?" Norma Glenn said.

"It takes a while to warm up," DC King said.

"Our tech team sifted through your client's CCTV footage," Smith explained. "And they found nothing to corroborate what Mr Wild has just accused me of. It's clear that he doesn't believe me, so I'm going to show him."

"Here we go," DC King said.

She clicked the keypad and slid the laptop across the table to Herman and his lawyer.

"For the record," Smith said. "Could you state what you're looking at."

"This is outrageous," Herman said.

"Could you please be a bit more descriptive."

"You were there," Herman said. "How?"

"Mrs Glenn," Smith said. "Perhaps you could explain what it is you're looking at. Your client appears to be at a loss for words."

"This is the outside view of number 45 Newton Street," Norma said.

"What time is it on the footage?" Smith said.

"17:20."

"He must have arrived later," Herman said. "He was definitely there."

"There is nothing on there to show that I was anywhere near your house on Saturday, or Sunday when you say I broke into the property," Smith said.

"In fact, the first time I went there was on Sunday, shortly before you were arrested."

"Bullshit," Herman said. "Bring up the footage from Sunday. I got a notification on my phone to tell me that someone had activated the sensor on the camera. It was you – I saw you with my own eyes. You were looking straight at me, you bastard."

"Professor Wild," Norma said. "Please."

"Soon after that," Herman said. "I was informed that the camera was offline. You did something to the Wi-Fi, didn't you?"

"I really have no idea what you're talking about," Smith said. "And there is nothing on that footage that reinforces your theory."

"It's not a theory. You did something to the Wi-Fi, and you broke into my house and planted the rope."

"The CCTV footage doesn't lie, Herman," Smith said. "You've just said it yourself, and if I was planning on doing something like that, why would I allow myself to be filmed outside the house?"

"You're lying."

"Professor Wild," DC King said calmly. "What you're suggesting is not only extremely far-fetched it has been disproved by the CCTV footage. I appreciate the predicament you're in, but can we please have no more of your time-wasting tactics, moving forward."

Smith rubbed his eyes and winced. He looked across the table at Professor Wild.

"Damn migraines."

"I've never had one," Professor Wild said.

"Never?" Smith said.

"I'm blessed with a healthy head."

"I suggest we take a short break there," DC King said.

"I'm not going to argue with that," Smith said. "I've got some painkillers in my desk. Interview with Herman Wild paused, 12:49."

CHAPTER FIFTY NINE

Smith didn't have a migraine. His head had never felt clearer. He made his way to DI Smyth's office and went in without knocking.

"Have they been picked up?"

"Are you absolutely sure about this?" DI Smyth said.

"I am. I had my suspicions and it's starting to make sense. The pills in Professor Wild's bathroom cabinet are the same ones I take for my migraines. He's just told me that he's never had a migraine in his life so why would he have a box of sumitriptan in his medicine cabinet? I think Rachel Bright and he are more than friends. She stays over at his place sometimes, and she keeps a stash of her migraine pills there."

"It's flimsy evidence at best," DI Smyth said. "And where does the cleaner come into the equation?"

"The sumitriptan is flimsy," Smith said. "On its own, but the CCTV footage isn't. Professor Wild dropped the ball there. The camera footage shows the admissions woman and the cleaner arriving at number 45 Newton Street numerous times in the past few weeks. What reason would they have to be there, and why were they there together?"

"It's still not proof that they were actually involved in the murders," DI Smyth said.

"No, and that's where we need to get creative."

"Are you suggesting a three-way trade-off?"

"Something like that. We interview all three of them concurrently, and we drop a few false hints along the way. One of them is bound to crack if they think the others are talking. It's worked in the past."

"Can I suggest a slight change of plan?"

"I'm listening."

"I want you and Kerry to interrogate the cleaner," DI Smyth said.

"Good call," Smith said. "I think he's the one likely to crack first. Are you going to handle the professor?"

"I am. I'll take Whitton in there with me, and Bridge and Harry can interview the admissions woman. Do you think this is going to work?"

"It's the only way I can think of to get a confession of sorts," Smith said. "And I'm still missing my motive. I get the feeling that the professor isn't going to give it to me, but I might get lucky with the cleaner."

"We have officers on standby," DI Smyth said. "I can have them picked up within the hour."

Smith went upstairs to the canteen and got himself a strong cup of coffee from the machine. He took it to his usual table and sat down. The sky outside was an incredible shade of blue and Smith wondered what that meant in terms of the weather. As he gazed out across the tops of the buildings to the east, he found himself smiling. The investigation wasn't over, but it felt like the end was in sight. Smith was confident that they would have enough to charge Professor Wild, Rachel Bright and Doug, the cleaner before the day was over.

Whitton came in with Bridge and DC King. They joined Smith at his table.

"Has the DI briefed you on the plan?" Smith said.

"He has," Bridge said. "Who would have thought it? A professor, an admin woman and a cleaner. It sounds like the start of a bad joke."

"Are you sure about their involvement?" DC King said.

"The migraine pills got me thinking," Smith said. "Why would a man who has never suffered a migraine in his life keep those specific tablets? And when I saw the CCTV footage, I knew I was right. What plausible reason would an admissions woman and a cleaner have to visit a university professor after hours?"

"It's possible he'll argue it away," Whitton pointed out.

"I'm expecting him to," Smith said. "But I don't care. We have the rope and we're going to get Rachel Bright and the cleaner to admit everything. Where's Harry?"

"He's around somewhere," Bridge said. "What can you tell me about Rachel Bright. The DI wants me and Harry to take her on."

"She's not stupid," Smith said. "But there is something you might be able to use to touch a nerve or two. I get the impression that she's full of resentment. She couldn't cut it as a lawyer and that's why she took the job she did. She'll be reminded of what she could have been every single day, and I think it will rattle her if you keep bringing that up."

"I'm sitting in with the DI in the interview with Professor Wild," Whitton said. "Any tips there?"

"Work on the assumption that the other two have already told us everything," Smith said. "Herman won't believe you, of course, but make references to indisputable evidence and don't elaborate. It's possible he'll take the change of personnel to mean that I've been sidelined and that'll work in our favour. If he thinks I've been substituted at halftime he'll probably be more confident, and his guard will be down."

"Can you please ease off with the football references," Bridge said. "It doesn't suit you."

"I've learned a thing or two about your beautiful game," Smith said. "And I have to admit that some of the tactics used can be beneficial in a murder investigation."

"Are you going to let us in on your dirty tackle?" DC King said.

"I reckoned you'd have all figured it out by now," Smith said. "Me and you are going to interview the cleaner, and I've got a strong suspicion that he'll be the easiest to break. Doug and the admissions woman are a bit more than work colleagues if you know what I mean."

"You can't be serious," Bridge said.

"I heard them. Our friend Doug wasn't telling us the truth when he referred to the admissions lady as a dragon. I heard them in her office, and it didn't sound like they were sworn enemies. We will crack this one. Before the end of the day, we'll have all three of them – I can feel it in my bones."

CHAPTER SIXTY

"We did it, boss," Smith said.

It was six in the evening, and he was sitting next to DI Smyth in his office.

"I thought I'd seen everything," DI Smyth said. "But that was what can only be described as a *menage a trois* of the most bizarre kind. And I know for a fact that you've never encountered a motive like theirs."

"Three different motives," Smith corrected. "And, no I've never seen anything like it."

The interviews were carried out in stages over the course of four hours. It was agreed that they would take regular breaks to confer with one another and the tactic had paid off. As expected, it was the cleaner who had broken down first. Douglas Clough had lasted thirty minutes before the cracks started to show, and Smith had no problem chipping away at them until the cleaner crumbled. Doug was deeply in love with Rachel Bright. He was so smitten that he would do anything she wanted him to. He admitted that he was reluctant to go through with the first murder, and he almost didn't play the part he'd agreed to play with Belinda James, but he carried it out and afterwards he was caught between a rock and a hard place. Either he did what Rachel told him to do or face the consequences of Belinda's murder. Douglas Clough had no choice.

The university cleaner told Smith and DC King everything, and Smith felt sick at the end of it. He was accustomed to death and murder but listening to Douglas Clough was extremely unpleasant. Five young women had their lives cut short for nothing. Douglas explained that Professor Wild played no part in the murders themselves, but he was the one who told them how to do it. Rachel Bright would act as the decoy. The head of admissions would gain entry to the victim's houses and lull them into a false sense of security. Rachel was well known at the university, and she was also well liked. None of the women would have suspected a thing. Douglas would strike when they were least expecting it. He was a strong man, and it didn't take long to overpower the women with the rope.

Rachel Bright's reasoning was more twisted than the cleaner's. Not only was she resentful of the bright young students with their rosy futures and their youth, she was madly in love with Professor Wild. It was common knowledge on campus that the professor had more than a professor-student relationship with some of his female students, and this was Rachel's main motivation. She dreamed of a life with Professor Wild – she would often spend time at his house, and she could picture a future together. Killing the students wasn't difficult for her. Douglas did the dirty work, and she merely played the part of the dupe.

It took Bridge and DC Moore a lot longer to get Rachel to break but when she did finally crack, she cracked in a spectacular manner. She broke down in tears and what followed was an account of each of the murders in vivid detail. Rachel outlined the instructions that Professor Wild had given out during the times they met at his house.

Belinda James was killed first. The twenty-two-year-old student was strangled on Sunday morning. She shared a house with another student, but he was away at the time of the murder and would only be returning to the city in a few days. Douglas and Rachel were aware of this. The cleaner had overheard Belinda talking about it in the canteen at the university. Smith recalled something that he'd told him. People paid him no attention, and they weren't aware that he was privy to all kinds of information.

Professor Wild had spent the night with Belinda the day before the murder and something she told him caught his attention. Belinda was friends with Holly Brown and Holly had helped Belinda to set up her new phone. Her fingerprints would be all over the phone, and they could use this to their advantage. It paid off. Forensics did indeed find Holly's prints on the phone but the explanation for them being there was an innocent one.

Rebecca Stone was the next victim. Rebecca had also engaged in a sexual relationship with Professor Wild, and he knew her routine inside out. After killing Belinda, Douglas Gough was ordered to carry out another murder soon afterwards and Rebecca's life was snuffed out just hours after Belinda drew her last breath. It was this murder where Professor Wild came up with the idea of inverting the drawing on the victim's stomachs. Rachel told Bridge and DC Moore that he thought it was a nice touch, and it would throw a bit of confusion into the mix. She also explained that had the detectives working on the investigation been more on the ball they would have realised that the drawings were created by a left-handed person. Rachel was the artist, and she was left-handed.

Bridge and DC Moore were forced to listen as the head of admissions went on to describe the brutal killing of Sharon Atlee, Jackie Grant and Holly Brown. The extent of the homework Professor Wild had done beforehand was staggering. He'd left nothing out and he'd convinced his accomplices that they would get away with it. He'd even gone as far as to plant a wine glass with Holly Brown's fingerprints on it in Jackie Grant's kitchen to further confuse the forensics officers.

When questioned about Professor Wild's reasoning behind the sick slaying of innocent women Rachel had explained that he wanted to see if he could beat the system. He planned to use the law to his advantage to prove how fallible it was. He really was under the impression that he could turn the law on its head to show how it was possible to get away with the worst possible crimes, using the law as an invisible accomplice. When asked her opinion on this, Rachel had stated, matter-of-factly:

He almost did get away with it, didn't he?

"I'm sorry we failed to get you a confession," DI Smyth said.

Professor Wild had stuck to his guns. He'd emphatically denied all involvement in the five murders, and he was still adamant that it was Smith who planted the rope in his microwave, even though there was nothing to prove it.

"Perhaps you should have interviewed him, after all," DI Smyth said.

"It wouldn't have made any difference, boss," Smith said. "I never expected him to own up to what he did. He doesn't have it in him. The man is an arrogant prick with serious delusions of grandeur. Let's see how that works out for him when he's locked up in Full Sutton. The testimonies of the other two are enough. Herman Wild will die in prison. Job done, I reckon."

"There's still the matter of that rope, Smith," DI Smyth said as Smith was getting ready to leave.

"What about it?" Smith said.

"Can I have your word that you will never pull a stunt like that again?"

"Do you really want me to answer that?" Smith said.

"Apparently it wasn't an ulcer," DI Smyth said. "But that doesn't mean it won't happen one day."

"Glad to hear it, boss," Smith said. "I'll see you in the morning. I imagine there's a whole stack of shit to get through before we can finally put this one to bed."

"You're not wrong there. See you tomorrow."

CHAPTER SIXTY ONE

"The professor is planning on challenging the verdict," DI Smyth said. Smith was standing outside the Grand Hotel on Tower Street. When Noddy Holder screamed out *It's Christmas* over the speakers, Smith had seen it as an ideal time to go out for a cigarette. DI Smyth had come outside to join him.

Smith offered him a cigarette. "Verdict? The case hasn't even got to trial yet."

DI Smyth accepted the cigarette. "That's what he's got planned anyway. He claims he has evidence that proves that the rope found in his microwave wasn't used to kill four of the victims."

"He's bluffing," Smith said.

"He could ruin your career, Smith."

"Let him try. He's got nothing."

"According to his lawyer," DI Smyth said. "He's got the actual ropes. We all know that the rope in the microwave was only used in the murder of Belinda James."

"If he produces the other ropes," Smith said. "He'll be damning himself. It'll be tantamount to an admission."

DI Smyth exhaled a cloud of smoke. "He doesn't care - he's going down, regardless. He wants to take you down with him. I had a sinking feeling that your reckless plan was going to come back to bite you eventually."

"It won't."

"How can you be so sure?"

"Because the ropes used to kill the others no longer exist."

"Are you going to explain what you mean by that?"

"I knew there was a possibility of this coming to light," Smith said. "So, I came up with a contingency plan. Let's just say that the interview with the cleaner wasn't exactly kosher."

This was an understatement. Smith recalled every second of it. Towards the end of the third interview, he'd brought up the matter of the ropes with Douglas Gough.

"We appreciate your cooperation so far, Douglas, but there are still a number of loose ends that need tying up. For the record. We know that you were the one who carried out the murders. You've already admitted that. You used a length of rope each time. We were unable to locate that rope. We searched your property and your place of work, and we couldn't find the hemp ropes. Where are they?"

"I've got an allotment over in Newby," Douglas said. "There's a plot of land and a small shed. All four lengths of rope are in the shed."

"Why didn't you get rid of it?" DC King asked.

"The professor told me not to."

"Why would he do that?" DC King said.

"That's not important," Smith said.

He wasn't interested in that. He now knew where the rope was, and he was planning on doing what Douglas Gough should have done immediately after the murders. He was going to destroy it.

"You destroyed evidence," DI Smyth said. "Even though you knew that the location of that evidence was gained during an official police interview. Have you lost your mind?"

"There is nothing in the transcript of that interview relating to the rope, boss."

"I'm struggling to keep up here."

"It was a brainwave that came to me out of nowhere," Smith said. "And with a bit of help from Barry Stone, I put it into practice. Barry set up a tiny remote-control device. When I wanted to ask the cleaner something, and not have it on the tape, all I had to do was press the button on the remote to pause the footage. I listened to the entire interview afterwards and you can't even tell when it was paused."

"What about the cleaner's lawyer?" DI Smyth said. "Surely he will be able to cause problems."

"The man was a duty solicitor who couldn't wait to get the hell out of there," Smith said. "He was hungover as hell, and he probably won't even remember what we discussed. The professor can challenge anything he likes – I'm not worried."

DI Smyth finished his cigarette and stubbed it out in the ashtray.

"I'm concerned about you, Smith."

"Don't be."

"You crossed a number of lines, the likes of which I hope you will never cross again."

"It was necessary," Smith said. "It was the only way. That's my cue to go back inside."

"What?"

Smith didn't elaborate. He turned around and went inside the hotel.

He looked around the hall and found what he was looking for. George Michael was lamenting about *Last Christmas* and Superintendent Smyth was swaying in time with the slow tempo.

"Make sure you get this on camera," Smith said to Bridge.

"What are you doing?" Bridge said.

"Settling a gambling debt. Wish me luck."

Smith picked up his beer and downed it in one go. He put down the empty glass and made his way over to Superintendent Smyth.

"Evening, sir. Would you care to dance?"

Superintendent Smyth's eyes widened. "What did you say?"

"Would you like to dance, sir? This is a great song."

"OK then. You're right – it is a very nice song."

When they reached the dancefloor Smith realised that they'd attracted an audience. Flashes from mobile phone cameras were already going off. Smith grinned and posed for the cameras. He put a hand on Superintendent Smyth's shoulder and began to sway with the music.

"I suggest I lead," Superintendent Smyth said.

Smith was finding it hard not to laugh.

"You're the boss."

Everybody in the room was watching them now. Smith realised that Superintendent Smyth had pulled him closer in and the laughter inside him was in danger of exploding. He caught a glimpse of DCI Chalmers at the edge of the dancefloor. He was shaking his head and grinning widely. Smith smiled back and gave him a thumbs-up.

The song ended and a round of applause sounded. Superintendent Smyth released Smith and wiped the sheen of sweat from his forehead.

"That was most enjoyable."

"Thank you, sir," Smith said. "Chalmers was right – you're a really good dancer."

"I've had lessons. You should consider joining one of my classes."

"I'll give it some serious thought, sir."

He was halfway back to his table and the laughter building up inside him had nowhere else to go. The fit of giggles lasted for some time and when he was sure it was over he realised that people were looking at him. Whitton was standing with Bridge and Billie Jones and all of them were observing him as though he was losing his mind.

"Have you got that out of your system now?" Whitton said.

"I think so," Smith said.

"Did you see the Super's face?" Bridge said. "He looked like the cat that got the cream. I think you made his day."

"Please tell me you got it on camera?"

"The whole thing," Bridge said. "I can't believe you did that."

Smith glanced at Billie Jones and the memory of the kiss they'd shared came back. He turned to Whitton.

"I need to tell you something."

"Sounds serious," she said.

"I'm afraid it is."

Billie was shaking her head. She tried to make eye contact with Smith, but he wasn't paying her any attention.

"Can we talk in private?" he said to Whitton.

"I already know," Whitton said as soon as they got outside.

"You do?" Smith said.

He felt sick, and he was also slightly confused. If Whitton knew about the kiss, she was taking it extremely well.

"My mum phoned earlier," she said. "She told me about Dad's illness."

This wasn't what Smith had expected.

"I'm sorry," he said. "Harold made me promise not to say anything."

"It's fine. We suspected it. I think we already knew, deep down."

"I really am sorry," Smith said.

"We'll deal with whatever we have to deal with when the time comes," Whitton said. "I'd rather not think about it tonight. Was there something else on your mind? I get the feeling that my dad's illness wasn't what you wanted to talk to me about."

"No," Smith lied. "That was it. Let's go back in and get rat-arsed."

"That sounds like a really good idea," Whitton said.

THE END

Printed in Dunstable, United Kingdom